THE · GOLDEN · BIRD
FLIES · AWAY · WITH · THE
· APPLE ·

More Celtic Fairy Tales

Collected by

JOSEPH JACOBS

Illustrated by

JOHN D. BATTEN

Dover Publications, Inc.
New York

To

THE MANY UNKNOWN

L I T T L E F R I E N D S

I HAVE MADE

BY THE FORMER BOOKS

OF THIS SERIES

This Dover edition, first published in 1968, is an unabridged republication of the work originally published by David Nutt in 1894.

International Standard Book Number: 0-486-21827-9

Library of Congress Catalog Card Number: 67-24224

Manufactured in the United States of America
Dover Publications, Inc.
180 Varick Street
New York, N. Y. 10014

Preface

OR the last time, for the present, I give the children of the British Isles a selection of Fairy Tales once or still existing among them. The story store of Great Britain and Ireland is, I hope, now adequately represented in the four volumes which have won me so many little friends, and of which this is the last.

My collections have dealt with the two folk-lore regions of these Isles on different scales. The "English" region, including Lowland Scotland and running up to the Highland line, is, I fancy, as fully represented in "English" and "More English Fairy Tales" as it is ever likely to be. But the Celtic district, including the whole of Ireland and the Gaelic-speaking part of Scotland, still offers a rich harvest to the collector, and will not be exhausted for many a long day. The materials already collected are far richer than those which the "English" region afford, and it has accordingly been my aim in the two volumes devoted to the Celts, rather to offer specimens of the crop than to exhaust the field.

In the present volume I have proceeded on much the same lines as those which I laid down for myself in compiling its predecessor. In making my selection I have attempted to select the tales common both to Erin and Alba. I have included, as specimen of the Irish mediæval hero tales, one of the three sorrowful tales of Erin: "The Tale of the Children of Lir." For the "drolls" or "comic relief" of the volume, I have again drawn upon the inexhaustible Kennedy, while the great J. F. Campbell still stands out as the most prominent figure in the history of the Celtic Fairy Tale.

In my method of telling I have continued the practice which I adopted in the previous volume: where I considered the language too complicated for children, I have simplified; where an incident from another parallel version seemed to add force to the narrative I have inserted it; and in each case mentioned the fact in the corresponding notes. As former statements of mine on this point have somewhat misled my folk-lore friends, I should, perhaps, add that the alterations on this score have been much slighter than they have seemed, and have not affected anything of value to the science of folk-lore.

Preface vii

I fear I am somewhat of a heretic with regard to the evidential value of folk-tales regarded as *capita mortua* of anthropology. The ready transit of a folk-tale from one district to another of the same linguistic area, robs it to my mind of any anthropological or ethnographical value; but on this high topic I have discoursed elsewhere.

This book, like the others of this series, has only been rendered possible by the courtesy and complaisance of the various collectors from whom I have culled my treasures. In particular, I have to thank Mr. Larminie and Mr. Eliot Stock for permission to include that fine tale " Morraha " from the former's "West Irish Folk-tales," the chief addition to the Celtic store since the appearance of my last volume. I have again to thank Dr. Hyde for permission to use another tale from his delightful collection. Mr. Curtin has been good enough to place at my disposal another of the tales collected by him in Connaught, and my colleague, Mr. Duncan, has translated for me a droll from the Erse. Above all, I have to thank Mr. Alfred Nutt for constant supervision over my selection and over my comments upon it. Mr. Nutt, by his own researches, and by the encouragement and aid he has given to the researches of others on Celtic folk-lore, has done much to replace the otherwise irreparable loss of Campbell.

With this volume I part, at any rate for a time, from the

pleasant task which has engaged my attention for the last four years. For the "English" folk-lore district I have attempted to do what the brothers Grimm did for Germany, so far as that was possible at this late day. But for the Celtic area I can claim no such high function; here the materials are so rich that it would tax the resources of a whole clan of Grimms to exhaust the field, and those Celtic Grimms must be Celts themselves, or at any rate fully familiar with the Gaelic. Here then is a task for the newly revived local patriotism of Ireland and the Highlands. I have done little more than spy the land, and bring back some specimen bunches from the Celtic vine. It must be for others, Celts themselves, to enter in and possess the promised land.

JOSEPH JACOBS.

SAY THIS

Three times, with your eyes shut

Ⱥoċuɪʒɪɲ bolaꝺ aɲ Єɪɲeaɲɲaɪʒ bɪɲɲ bɲeuʒaɪʒ
ꝼaoɪ ɱ'ꝼóɪbɪɲ búċaɪʒ

And you will see

What you will see

Contents

x

Contents

PAGE

Full-page Illustrations

The Fate of the Children of Lir

T happened that the five Kings of Ireland met to determine who should have the head kingship over them, and King Lir of the Hill of the White Field expected surely he would be elected. When the nobles went into council together they chose for head king, Dearg, son of Daghda, because his father had been so great a Druid and he was the eldest of his father's sons. But Lir left the Assembly of the Kings and went home to the Hill of the White Field. The other kings would have followed after Lir to give him wounds of spear and wounds of sword for not yielding obedience to the man to whom they had given the over-lordship. But Dearg the

king would not hear of it and said : " Rather let us bind him to us by the bonds of kinship, so that peace may dwell in the land. Send over to him for wife the choice of the three maidens of the fairest form and best repute in Erin, the three daughters of Oilell of Aran, my own three bosom-nurslings."

So the messengers brought word to Lir that Dearg the king would give him a foster-child of his foster-children. Lir thought well of it, and set out next day with fifty chariots from the Hill of the White Field. And he came to the Lake of the Red Eye near Killaloe. And when Lir saw the three daughters of Oilell, Dearg the king said to him : " Take thy choice of the maidens, Lir." " I know not," said Lir, " which is the choicest of them all ; but the eldest of them is the noblest, it is she I had best take." " If so," said Dearg the king, " Ove is the eldest, and she shall be given to thee, if thou willest." So Lir and Ove were married and went back to the Hill of the White Field.

And after this there came to them twins, a son and a daughter, and they gave them for names Fingula and Aod. And two more sons came to them, Fiachra and Conn. When they came Ove died, and Lir mourned bitterly for her, and but for his great love for his children he would have died of his grief. And Dearg the king grieved for Lir and sent to him and said : " We grieve for Ove for thy sake ; but, that our friendship may not be rent asunder, I will give unto thee her sister, Oifa, for a wife." So Lir agreed, and they were united, and he took her with him to his own house. And at first Oifa felt affection and honour for the children of Lir and her sister, and indeed every one who saw the four children could not help giving them the love of his soul. Lir doted upon the children, and they always slept in beds in front of their father, who used to rise at early dawn every morning and lie down among his children. But thereupon the dart of jealousy passed into Oifa on account of this and she came to regard the children with hatred and enmity. One day her chariot was yoked for her and she took with her the four children of Lir in it. Fingula was not willing to go with her on the journey, for she had dreamed a dream in the night warning her against Oifa : but she was not to avoid her fate. And when the chariot came to the Lake of the Oaks, Oifa said to the people : " Kill the four children of Lir and I will give you your own reward of every kind in the world." But they refused and told her it was an evil thought she had. Then she would have raised a sword herself to kill and destroy the children, but her own womanhood and her weakness prevented her ; so she drove the children of Lir into the lake to bathe, and they did as Oifa told them. As soon as they were upon the lake she struck them with a Druid's wand of spells and wizardry and put them into the forms of four beautiful, perfectly white swans, and she sang this song over them :

> " Out with you upon the wild waves, children of the king !
> Henceforth your cries shall be with the flocks of birds."

And Fingula answered :

> " Thou witch ! we know thee by thy right name !
> Thou mayest drive us from wave to wave,
> But sometimes we shall rest on the headlands ;
> We shall receive relief, but thou punishment.
> Though our bodies may be upon the lake,
> Our minds at least shall fly homewards."

And again she spoke: "Assign an end for the ruin and woe which thou hast brought upon us."

Oifa laughed and said: "Never shall ye be free until the woman from the south be united to the man from the north, until Lairgnen of Connaught wed Deoch of Munster; nor shall any have power to bring you out of these forms. Nine hundred years shall you wander over the lakes and streams of Erin. This only I will grant unto you: that you retain your own speech, and there shall be no music in the world equal to yours, the plaintive music you shall sing." This she said because repentance seized her for the evil she had done.

And then she spake this lay:

> "Away from me, ye children of Lir,
>   Henceforth the sport of the wild winds
>   Until Lairgnen and Deoch come together,
>   Until ye are on the north-west of Red Erin.
>
> "A sword of treachery is through the heart of Lir,
>   Of Lir the mighty champion,
>   Yet though I have driven a sword.
>   My victory cuts me to the heart."

Then she turned her steeds and went on to the Hall of Dearg the king. The nobles of the court asked her where were the children of Lir, and Oifa said: "Lir will not trust them to Dearg the king." But Dearg thought in his own mind that the woman had played some treachery upon them, and he accordingly sent messengers to the Hall of the White Field.

Lir asked the messengers: "Wherefore are ye come?"

"To fetch thy children, Lir," said they.

"Have they not reached you with Oifa?" said Lir.

CHILDREN OF LIR

"They have not," said the messengers; "and Oifa said it was you would not let the children go with her."

Then was Lir melancholy and sad at heart, hearing these things, for he knew that Oifa had done wrong upon his children, and he set out towards the Lake of the Red Eye. And when the children of Lir saw him coming Fingula sang the lay:

> "Welcome the cavalcade of steeds
> Approaching the Lake of the Red Eye,
> A company dread and magical
> Surely seek after us.

> "Let us move to the shore, O Aod,
> Fiachra and comely Conn,
> No host under heaven can those horsemen be
> But King Lir with his mighty household."

Now as she said this King Lir had come to the shores of the lake and heard the swans speaking with human voices. And he spake to the swans and asked them who they were. Fingula answered and said : "We are thy own children, ruined by thy wife, sister of our own mother, through her ill mind and her jealousy." "For how long is the spell to be upon you?" said Lir. "None can relieve us till the woman from the south and the man from the north come together, till Lairgnen of Connaught wed Deoch of Munster."

Then Lir and his people raised their shouts of grief, crying, and lamentation, and they stayed by the shore of the lake listening to the wild music of the swans until the swans flew away, and King Lir went on to the Hall of Dearg the king. He told Dearg the king what Oifa had done to his children. And Dearg put his power upon Oifa and bade her say what shape on earth she would think the worst of all. She said it would be in the form of an air-demon. "It is into that form I shall put you," said Dearg the king, and he struck her with a Druid's wand of spells and wizardry and put her into the form of an air-demon. And she flew away at once, and she is still an air-demon, and shall be so for ever.

But the children of Lir continued to delight the Milesian clans with the very sweet fairy music of their songs, so that no delight was ever heard in Erin to compare with their music until the time came appointed for the leaving the Lake of the Red Eye.

Then Fingula sang this parting lay :

> "Farewell to thee, Dearg the king,
> Master of all Druid's lore !
> Farewell to thee, our father dear,
> Lir of the Hill of the White Field !
>
> "We go to pass the appointed time
> Away and apart from the haunts of men
> In the current of the Moyle,
> Our garb shall be bitter and briny,
>
> "Until Deoch come to Lairgnen.
> So come, ye brothers of once ruddy cheeks ;
> Let us depart from this Lake of the Red Eye,
> Let us separate in sorrow from the tribe that has
> loved us."

And after they took to flight, flying highly, lightly, aerially till they reached the Moyle, between Erin and Albain.

The men of Erin were grieved at their leaving, and it was proclaimed throughout Erin that henceforth no swan should be killed. Then they stayed all solitary, all alone, filled with cold and grief and regret, until a thick tempest came upon them and Fingula said : " Brothers, let us appoint a place to meet again if the power of the winds separate us." And they said : " Let us appoint to meet, O sister, at the Rock of the Seals." Then the waves rose up and the thunder roared, the lightnings flashed, the sweeping tempest passed over the sea, so that the children of Lir were scattered from each other over the great sea. There came, however, a placid calm after the great tempest and Fingula found herself alone, and she said this lay :

> " Woe upon me that I am alive !
> My wings are frozen to my sides.
> O beloved three, O beloved three,
> Who hid under the shelter of my feathers,
> Until the dead come back to the living
> I and the three shall never meet again ! "

And she flew to the Lake of the Seals and soon saw Conn coming towards her with heavy step and drenched feathers, and Fiachra also, cold and wet and faint, and no word could they tell, so cold and faint were they : but she nestled them under her wings and said : " If Aod could come to us now our happiness would be complete." But soon they saw Aod coming towards them with dry head and preened feathers : Fingula put him under the feathers of her breast, and Fiachra under her right wing, and Conn under her left : and they made this lay :

> " Bad was our stepmother with us,
> She played her magic on us,
> Sending us north on the sea
> In the shapes of magical swans.
> " Our bath upon the shore's ridge
> Is the foam of the brine-crested tide,
> Our share of the ale feast
> Is the brine of the blue-crested sea."

One day they saw a splendid cavalcade of pure white
steeds coming towards them, and when they came near they
were the two sons of Dearg the king who had been seeking
for them to give them news of Dearg the king and Lir
their father. "They are well," they said, "and live
together happy in all except that ye are not with them, and
for not knowing where ye have gone since the day ye left
the Lake of the Red Eye." "Happy are not we," said
Fingula, and she sang this song :

> " Happy this night the household of Lir,
> Abundant their meat and their wine.
> But the children of Lir—what is their lot ?
> For bed-clothes we have our feathers,
> And as for our food and our wine—
> The white sand and the bitter brine,
> Fiachra's bed and Conn's place
> Under the cover of my wings on the Moyle,
> Aod has the shelter of my breast,
> And so side by side we rest."

So the sons of Dearg the king came to the Hall of Lir
and told the king the condition of his children.

Then the time came for the children of Lir to fulfil their
lot, and they flew in the current of the Moyle to the Bay of
Erris, and remained there till the time of their fate, and
then they flew to the Hill of the White Field and found all
desolate and empty, with nothing but unroofed green raths
and forests of nettles—no house, no fire, no dwelling-place.
The four came close together, and they raised three shouts
of lamentation aloud, and Fingula sang this lay :

> " Uchone ! it is bitterness to my heart
> To see my father's place forlorn—
> No hounds, no packs of dogs,
> No women, and no valiant kings

" No drinking-horns, no cups of wood,
No drinking in its lightsome halls.
Uchone! I see the state of this house
That its lord our father lives no more.

" Much have we suffered in our wandering years,
By winds buffeted, by cold frozen ;
Now has come the greatest of our pain—
There lives no man who knoweth us in the house
     where we were born."

So the children of Lir flew away to the Glory Isle of Brandan the saint, and they settled upon the Lake of the Birds until the holy Patrick came to Erin and the holy Mac Howg came to Glory Isle.

And the first night he came to the island the children of Lir heard the voice of his bell ringing for matins, so that they started and leaped about in terror at hearing it ; and her brothers left Fingula alone. " What is it, beloved brothers ? " said she. " We know not what faint, fearful voice it is we have heard." Then Fingula recited this lay :

" Listen to the Cleric's bell,
Poise your wings and raise
Thanks to God for his coming,
Be grateful that you hear him,

" He shall free you from pain,
And bring you from the rocks and stones.
Ye comely children of Lir
Listen to the bell of the Cleric."

And Mac Howg came down to the brink of the shore and said to them : " Are ye the children of Lir ? " " We are indeed," said they. " Thanks be to God ! " said the saint ; " it is for your sakes I have come to this Isle beyond every other island in Erin. Come ye to land now and put your trust in me." So they came to land, and he made for them chains of bright white silver, and put a chain between Aod and Fingula and a chain between Conn and Fiachra.

It happened at this time that Lairgnen was prince of Connaught and he was to wed Deoch the daughter of the king of Munster.   She had heard the account of the birds and she became filled with love and affection for them, and she said she would not wed till she had the wondrous birds of Glory Isle.   Lairgnen sent for them to the Saint Mac Howg. But the Saint would not give them, and both Lairgnen and Deoch went to Glory Isle.   And Lairgnen went to seize the birds from the altar : but as soon as he had laid hands on them their feathery coats fell off, and the three sons of Lir became three withered bony old men, and Fingula, a lean withered old woman without blood or flesh.   Lairgnen started at this and left the place hastily, but Fingula chanted this lay :

> " Come and baptise us, O Cleric,
> Clear away our stains !
> This day I see our grave—
> Fiachra and Conn on each side,
> And in my lap, between my two arms,
> Place Aod, my beauteous brother."

After this lay, the children of Lir were baptised.   And they died, and were buried as Fingula had said, Fiachra and Conn on either side, and Aod before her face.   A cairn was raised for them, and on it their names were written in runes.   And that is the fate of the children of Lir.

Jack the Cunning Thief

HERE was a poor farmer who had three sons, and on the same day the three boys went to seek their fortune. The eldest two were sensible, industrious young men ; the youngest never did much at home that was any use. He loved to be setting snares for rabbits, and tracing hares in the snow, and inventing all sorts of funny tricks to annoy people at first and then set them laughing.

The three parted at cross-roads, and Jack took the lonesomest. The day turned out rainy, and he was wet and weary, you may depend, at nightfall, when he came to a lonesome house a little off the road.

"What do you want ? " said a blear-eyed old woman, that was sitting at the fire.

" My supper and a bed to be sure," said he.

" You can't get it," said she.

"What's to hinder me ? " said he.

" The owners of the house is," said she, " six honest men that does be out mostly till three or four o'clock in the morning, and if they find you here they'll skin you alive at the very least."

"Well, I think," said Jack, "that their very most couldn't be much worse. Come, give me something out of the cupboard, for here I'll stay. Skinning is not much worse than catching your death of cold in a ditch or under a tree such a night as this."

Begonins she got afraid, and gave him a good supper; and when he was going to bed he said if she let any of the six honest men disturb him when they came home she'd sup sorrow for it. When he awoke in the morning, there were six ugly-looking spalpeens standing round his bed. He leaned on his elbow, and looked at them with great contempt.

"Who are you," said the chief, "and what's your business ? "

"My name," says he, "is Master Thief, and my business just now is to find apprentices and workmen. If I find you any good, maybe I'll give you a few lessons."

Bedad they were a little cowed, and says the head man, "Well, get up, and after breakfast, we'll see who is to be the master, and who the journeyman."

They were just done breakfast, when what should they see but a farmer driving a fine large goat to market. "Will any of you," says Jack, "undertake to steal that goat from the owner before he gets out of the wood, and that without the smallest violence ? "

"I couldn't do it," says one; and "I couldn't do it," says another.

"I'm your master," says Jack, "and I'll do it."

He slipped out, went through the trees to where there was a bend in the road, and laid down his right brogue in the very middle of it. Then he ran on to another bend, and laid down his left brogue and went and hid himself.

When the farmer sees the first brogue, he says to himself, " That would be worth something if it had the fellow, but it is worth nothing by itself."

He goes on till he comes to the second brogue.

"What a fool I was," says he, "not to pick up the other ! I'll go back for it."

So he tied the goat to a sapling in the hedge, and returned for the brogue. But Jack, who was behind a tree had it already on his foot, and when the man was beyond the bend he picked up the other and loosened the goat, and led him off through the wood.

Ochone ! the poor man couldn't find the first brogue, and when he came back he couldn't find the second, nor neither his goat.

" *Mile mollacht!* " says he, " what will I do after promising Johanna to buy her a shawl. I must only go and drive another beast to the market unknownst. I'd never hear the last of it if Joan found out what a fool I made of myself."

The thieves were in great admiration at Jack, and wanted him to tell them how he had done the farmer, but he wouldn't tell them.

By-and-by, they see the poor man driving a fine fat wether the same way.

" Who'll steal that wether," says Jack, "before it's out of the wood, and no roughness used ? "

" I couldn't," says one; and " I couldn't," says another.

" I'll try," says Jack. " Give me a good rope."

The poor farmer was jogging along and thinking of

his misfortune, when he sees a man hanging from the bough of a tree. "Lord save us!" says he, "the corpse wasn't there an hour ago." He went on about half a quarter of a mile, and there was another corpse again hanging over the road. "God between us and harm," said he, "am I in my right senses?" There was another turn about the same distance, and just beyond it the third corpse was hanging. "Oh, murdher!" said he; "I'm beside myself. What would bring three hung men so near one another? I must be mad. I'll go back and see if the others are there still."

He tied the wether to a sapling, and back he went. But when he was round the bend, down came the corpse, and loosened the wether, and drove it home through the wood to the robbers' house. You all may think how the poor farmer felt when he could find no one dead or alive going or coming, nor his wether, nor the rope that fastened him. "Oh, misfortunate day!" cried he, "what'll Joan say to me now? My morning gone, and the goat and wether lost! I must sell something to make the price of the shawl. Well, the fat bullock is in the nearest field. She won't see me taking it."

Well, if the robbers were not surprised when Jack came into the bawn with the wether! "If you do another trick like this," said the captain, "I'll resign the command to you."

They soon saw the farmer going by again, driving a fat bullock this time.

"Who'll bring that fat bullock here," says Jack, "and use no violence?"

"I couldn't," says one; and "I couldn't," says another.

"I'll try," says Jack, and away he went into the wood.

The farmer was about the spot where he saw the first brogue, when he heard the bleating of a goat off at his right in the wood.

He cocked his ears, and the next thing he heard was the maaing of a sheep.

"Blood alive!" says he, "maybe these are my own that I lost." There was more bleating and more maaing. "There they are as sure as a gun," says he, and he tied his bullock to a sapling that grew in the hedge, and away he went into the wood. When he got near the place where the cries came from, he heard them a little before him, and on he followed them. At last, when he was about half a mile from the spot where he tied the beast, the cries stopped altogether. After searching and searching till he was tired, he returned for his bullock; but there wasn't the ghost of a bullock there, nor any where else that he searched.

This time, when the thieves saw Jack and his prize coming into the bawn, they couldn't help shouting out, "Jack must be our chief." So there was nothing but feasting and drinking hand to fist the rest of the day. Before they went to bed, they showed Jack the cave where their money was hid, and all their disguises in another cave, and swore obedience to him.

One morning, when they were at breakfast, about a week after, said they to Jack, "Will you mind the house for us to-day while we are at the fair of Mochurry? We hadn't a spree for ever so long: you must get your turn whenever you like."

"Never say't twice," says Jack, and off they went.

After they were gone says Jack to the wicked housekeeper, "Do these fellows ever make you a present?"

"Ah, catch them at it! indeed, and they don't, purshuin to 'em."

"Well, come along with me, and I'll make you a rich woman."

He took her to the treasure cave; and while she was in raptures, gazing at the heaps of gold and silver, Jack filled his pockets as full as they could hold, put more into a little bag, and walked out, locking the door on the old hag, and leaving the key in the lock. He then put on a rich suit of clothes, took the goat, and the wether, and the bullock, and drove them before him to the farmer's house.

Joan and her husband were at the door ; and when they saw the animals, they clapped their hands and laughed for joy.

" Do you know who owns them bastes, neighbours ? "

" Maybe we don't ! sure they're ours."

" I found them straying in the wood.   Is that bag with ten guineas in it that's hung round the goat's neck yours ? "

" Faith, it isn't."

" Well, you may as well keep it for a Godsend ; I don't want it."

" Heaven be in your road, good gentleman ! "

Jack travelled on till he came to his father's house in the dusk of the evening.   He went in.   " God save all here ! "

" God save you kindly, sir ! "

" Could I have a night's lodging here ? "

" Oh, sir, our place isn't fit for the likes of a gentleman such as yon."

" Oh, *musha*, don't you know your own son ? "

Well, they opened their eyes, and it was only a strife to see who'd have him in their arms first.

" But, Jack asthore, where did you get the fine clothes ? "

" Oh, you may as well ask me where I got all that money ? " said he, emptying his pockets on the table.

Well, they got in a great fright, but when he told them his adventures, they were easier in mind, and all went to bed in great content.

" Father," says Jack, next morning, " go over to the landlord, and tell him I wish to be married to his daughter."

" Faith, I'm afraid he'd only set the dogs at me. If he asks me how you made your money, what'll I say ? "

" Tell him I am a master thief, and that there is no one equal to me in the three kingdoms ; that I am worth a thousand pounds, and all taken from the biggest rogues unhanged. Speak to him when the young lady is by."

" It's a droll message you're sending me on : I'm afraid it won't end well."

The old man came back in two hours.

" Well, what news ? "

" Droll news, enough. The lady didn't seem a bit un-willing : I suppose it's not the first time you spoke to her ; and the squire laughed, and said you would have to steal the goose off o' the spit in his kitchen next Sunday, and he'd see about it."

" O ! that won't be hard, any way."

Next Sunday, after the people came from early Mass, the squire and all his people were in the kitchen, and the goose turning before the fire. The kitchen door opened, and a miserable old beggar man with a big wallet on his back put in his head.

" Would the mistress have anything for me when dinner is over, your honour ? "

" To be sure. We have no room here for you just now ; sit in the porch for a while."

" God bless your honour's family, and yourself ! "

Soon some one that was sitting near the window cried out, " Oh, sir, there's a big hare scampering like the divil round the bawn. Will we run out and pin him ?"

" Pin a hare indeed ! much chance you'd have ; sit where you are."

Jack the Cunning Thief

That hare made his escape into the garden, but Jack
that was in the beggar's clothes soon let another out of the
bag.

"Oh, master, there he is still pegging round. He can't
make his escape : let us have a chase. The hall door is
locked on the inside, and Mr. Jack can't get in."

" Stay quiet, I tell you."

In a few minutes he shouted out again that the hare
was there still, but it was the third that Jack was just after
giving its liberty. Well, by the laws, they couldn't be
kept in any longer. Out pegged every mother's son of
them, and the squire after them.

" Will I turn the spit, your honour, while they're catching
the *hareyeen ?* " says the beggar.

" Do, and don't let any one in for your life."

" Faith, an' I won't, you may depend on it."

The third hare got away after the others, and when they
all came back from the hunt, there was neither beggar nor
goose in the kitchen.

" Purshuin' to you, Jack," says the landlord, " you've
come over me this time."

Well, while they were thinking of making out another
dinner, a messenger came from Jack's father to beg that
the squire, and the mistress, and the young lady would
step across the fields, and take share of what God sent.
There was no dirty mean pride about the family, and they
walked over, and got a dinner with roast turkey, and roast
beef, and their own roast goose ; and the squire had like to
burst his waistcoat with laughing at the trick, and Jack's
good clothes and good manners did not take away any
liking the young lady had for him already.

While they were taking their punch at the old oak table in the nice clean little parlour with the sanded floor, says the squire, "You can't be sure of my daughter, Jack, unless you steal away my six horses from under the six men that will be watching them to-morrow night in the stable."

"I'll do more than that," says Jack, "for a pleasant look from the young lady"; and the young lady's cheeks turned as red as fire.

Monday night the six horses were in their stalls, and a man on every horse, and a good glass of whisky under every man's waistcoat, and the door was left wide open for Jack. They were merry enough for a long time, and joked and sung, and were pitying the poor fellow. But the small hours crept on, and the whisky lost its power, and they began to shiver and wish it was morning. A miserable old colliach, with half a dozen bags round her, and a beard half an inch long on her chin came to the door.

"Ah, then, tendher-hearted Christians," says she, "would you let me in, and allow me a wisp of straw in the corner; the life will be froze out of me, if you don't give me shelter."

Well, they didn't see any harm in that, and she made herself as snug as she could, and they soon saw her pull out a big black bottle, and take a sup. She coughed and smacked her lips, and seemed a little more comfortable, and the men couldn't take their eyes off her.

"Gorsoon," says she, "I'd offer you a drop of this, only you might think it too free-making."

"Oh, hang all impedent pride," says one, "we'll take it, and thankee."

So she gave them the bottle, and they passed it round, and the last man had the manners to leave half a glass in the bottom for the old woman. They all thanked her, and said it was the best drop ever passed their tongue.

"In throth, agras," said she, "it's myself that's glad to show how I value your kindness in giving me shelter; I'm not without another *buideal*, and you may pass it round while myself finishes what the dasent man left me."

Well, what they drank out of the other bottle only gave them a relish for more, and by the time the last man got to the bottom, the first man was dead asleep in the saddle, for the second bottle had a sleepy posset mixed with the whisky. The beggar woman lifted each man down, and laid him in the manger, or under the manger, snug and sausty, drew a stocking over every horse's hoof, and led them away without any noise to one of Jack's father's out-houses. The first thing the squire saw next morning was Jack riding up the avenue, and five horses stepping after the one he rode.

"Confound you, Jack!" says he, "and confound the numskulls that let you outwit them!"

He went out to the stable, and didn't the poor fellows look very lewd o' themselves, when they could be woke up in earnest!

"After all," says the squire, when they were sitting at breakfast, "it was no great thing to outwit such ninny-hammers. I'll be riding out on the common from one to three to-day, and if you can outwit me of the beast I'll be riding, I'll say you deserve to be my son-in-law."

"I'd do more than that," says Jack, "for the honour, if

there was no love at all in the matter," and the young lady held up her saucer before her face.

Well, the squire kept riding about and riding about till he was tired, and no sign of Jack. He was thinking of going home at last, when what should he see but one of his servants running from the house as if he was mad.

" Oh masther, masther," says he, as far as he could be heard, " fly home if you wish to see the poor mistress alive! I'm running for the surgeon. She fell down two flights of stairs, and her neck, or her hips, or both her arms are broke, and she's speechless, and it's a mercy if you find the breath in her. Fly as fast as the baste will carry you."

" But hadn't you better take the horse ?   It's a mile and a half to the surgeon's."

" Oh, anything you like, master. Oh, *Vuya, Vuya!* misthress *alanna*, that I should ever see the day ! and your purty body disfigured as it is !"

" Here, stop your noise, and be off like wildfire ! Oh, my darling, my darling, isn't this a trial ? "

He tore home like a fury, and wondered to see no stir outside, and when he flew into the hall, and from that to the parlour, his wife and daughter that were sewing at the table screeched out at the rush he made, and the wild look that was on his face.

" Oh, my darling !" said he, when he could speak, " how's this ?   Are you hurt ?   Didn't you fall down the stairs ?   What happened at all ?   Tell me !"

" Why, nothing at all happened, thank God, since you rode out ; where did you leave the horse ? "

Well, no one could describe the state he was in for

about a quarter of an hour, between joy for his wife and
anger with Jack, and *sharoose* for being tricked.   He saw
the beast coming up the avenue, and a little gorsoon in the
saddle with his feet in the stirrup leathers.   The servant
didn't make his appearance for a week ; but what did he
care with Jack's ten golden guineas in his pocket.

Jack didn't show his nose till next morning, and it was
a queer reception he met.

"That was all foul play you gave," says the squire.
"I'll never forgive you for the shock you gave me.   But
then I am so happy ever since, that I think I'll give you
only one trial more.   If you will take away the sheet from
under my wife and myself to-night, the marriage may take
place to-morrow."

"We'll try," says Jack, "but if you keep my bride from
me any longer, I'll steal her away if she was minded by
fiery dragons."

When the squire and his wife were in bed, and the moon

shining in through the window, he saw a head rising over the sill to have a peep, and then bobbing down again.

"That's Jack," says the squire; "I'll astonish him a bit," says the squire, pointing a gun at the lower pane.

"Oh Lord, my dear!" says the wife, "sure, you wouldn't shoot the brave fellow?"

"Indeed, an' I wouldn't for a kingdom; there's nothing but powder in it."

Up went the head, bang went the gun, down dropped the body, and a great souse was heard on the gravel walk.

"Oh, Lord," says the lady, "poor Jack is killed or disabled for life."

"I hope not," says the squire, and down the stairs he ran. He never minded to shut the door, but opened the gate and ran into the garden. His wife heard his voice at the room door, before he could be under the window and back, as she thought.

"Wife, wife," says he from the door, "the sheet, the sheet! He is not killed, I hope, but he is bleeding like a pig. I must wipe it away as well as I can, and get some one to carry him in with me." She pulled it off the bed, and threw it to him. Down he ran like lightning, and he had hardly time to be in the garden, when he was back, and this time he came back in his shirt, as he went out.

"High hanging to you, Jack," says he, "for an arrant rogue!"

"Arrant rogue?" says she, "isn't the poor fellow all cut and bruised?"

"I didn't much care if he was. What do you think was

Jack the Cunning Thief   25

bobbing up and down at the window, and sossed down so heavy on the walk ? A man's clothes stuffed with straw, and a couple of stones."

" And what did you want with the sheet just now, to wipe his blood if he was only a man of straw ? "

" Sheet, woman ! I wanted no sheet."

" Well, whether you wanted it or not, I threw it to you, and you standing outside o' the door."

" Oh, Jack, Jack, you terrible tinker ! " says the squire, " there's no use in striving with you. We must do without the sheet for one night. We'll have the marriage to-morrow to get ourselves out of trouble."

So married they were, and Jack turned out a real good husband. And the squire and his lady were never tired of praising their son-in-law, " Jack the Cunning Thief."

Powel, Prince of Dyfed.

 OWEL, Prince of Dyfed, was lord of the seven Cantrevs of Dyfed; and once upon a time Powel was at Narberth, his chief palace, where a feast had been prepared for him, and with him was a great host of men. And after the first meal, Powel arose to walk, and he went to the top of a mound that was above the palace, and was called Gorseth Arberth.

"Lord," said one of the court, "it is peculiar to the mound that whosoever sits upon it cannot go thence without either receiving wounds or blows, or else seeing a wonder."

"I fear not to receive wounds and blows in the midst of such a host as this; but as to the wonder, gladly would I see it. I will go, therefore, and sit upon the mound."

And upon the mound he sat. And while he sat there, they saw a lady, on a pure white horse of large size, with a garment of shining gold around her, coming along the highway that led from the mound; and the horse seemed to move at a slow and even pace, and to be coming up towar he mound.

"My men," said Powel, " is there any among you who knows yonder lady ? "

" There is not, lord," said they.

" Go one of you and meet her, that we may know who she is."

And one of them arose ; and as he came upon the road to meet her she passed by, and he followed as fast as he could, being on foot; and the greater was his speed, the farther was she from him. And when he saw that it profited him nothing to follow her, he returned to Pwyll, and said unto him, "Lord, it is idle for any one in the world to follow her on foot."

" Verily," said Powel, " go unto the palace, and take the fleetest horse that thou seest, and go after her."

And he took a horse and went forward. And he came to an open level plain, and put spurs to his horse ; and the more he urged his horse, the farther was she from him. Yet she held the same pace as at first. And his horse began to fail ; and when his horse's feet failed him, he returned to the place where Powel was.

" Lord," said he, " it will avail nothing for any one to follow yonder lady. I know of no horse in these realms swifter than this, and it availed me not to pursue her."

" Of a truth," said Powel, " there must be some illusion here. Let us go towards the palace." So to the palace they went, and they spent that day. And the next day they arose, and that also they spent until it was time to go to meat. And after the first meal, " Verily," said Powel, " we will go, the same party as yesterday, to the top of the mound. Do thou," said he to one of his young men,

"take the swiftest horse that thou knowest in the field.
And thus did the young man. They went towards the
mound, taking the horse with them. And as they were
sitting down they beheld the lady on the same horse, and
in the same apparel, coming along the same road. "Behold,"
said Powel, "here is the lady of yesterday. Make ready,
youth, to learn who she is."

"My lord," said he "that will I gladly do." And thereupon the lady came opposite to them. So the youth
mounted his horse; and before he had settled himself
in his saddle, she passed by, and there was a clear space
between them. But her speed was no greater than it had
been the day before. Then he put his horse into an amble,
and thought, that, notwithstanding the gentle pace at which
his horse went, he should soon overtake her. But this
availed him not: so he gave his horse the reins. And still
he came no nearer to her than when he went at a foot's
pace. The more he urged his horse, the farther was
she from him. Yet she rode not faster than before. When
he saw that it availed not to follow her, he returned to the
place where Powel was. "Lord," said he, "the horse can
no more than thou hast seen."

"I see indeed that it avails not that any one should
follow her. And by Heaven," said he, "she must needs
have an errand to some one in this plain, if her haste
would allow her to declare it. Let us go back to the
palace." And to the palace they went, and they spent
that night in songs and feasting, as it pleased them.

The next day they amused themselves until it was
time to go to meat. And when meat was ended, Powel
said, "Where are the hosts that went yesterday and the
day before to the top of the mound?"

" Behold, lord, we are here," said they.

" Let us go," said he, " to the mound to sit there. And do thou," said he to the page who tended his horse, " saddle my horse well, and hasten with him to the road, and bring also my spurs with thee." And the youth did thus, They went and sat upon the mound. And ere they had been there but a short time, they beheld the lady coming by the same road, and in the same manner, and at the same pace. " Young man," said Powel, " I see the lady coming ; give me my horse." And no sooner had he mounted his horse than she passed him. And he turned after her, and followed her. And he let his horse go bounding playfully, and thought that at the second step or the third he should come up with her. But he came no nearer to her than at first. Then he urged his horse to his utmost speed, yet he found that it availed nothing to follow her. Then said Powel, " O maiden, " for the sake of him who thou best lovest, stay for me."

" I will stay gladly," said she, " and it were better for thy horse hadst thou asked it long since." So the maiden stopped, and she threw back that part of her head-dress which covered her face. And she fixed her eyes upon him, and began to talk with him.

" Lady," asked he, " whence comest thou, and whereunto dost thou journey ? "

" I journey on mine own errand," said she, " and right glad am I to see thee."

" My greeting be unto thee," said he. Then he thought that the beauty of all the maidens, and all the ladies that he had ever seen, was as nothing compared to her beauty. " Lady," he said, " wilt thou tell me aught concerning thy purpose ? "

" I will tell thee," said she. " My chief quest was to seek thee."

" Behold," said Powel, " this is to me the most pleasing quest on which thou couldst have come. And wilt thou tell me who thou art ? "

· I · JOURNEY ·
· ON · MINE · OWN ·
· ERRAND ·

" I will tell thee, lord," said she. " I am Rhiannon, the daughter of Heveyth Hên, and they sought to give me to a husband against my will. But no husband would I have, and that because of my love for thee, neither will I yet

have one unless thou reject me. And hither have I come
to hear thy answer."

"By Heaven," said Powel, "behold this is my answer.
If I might choose among all the ladies and damsels in the
world, thee would I choose."

"Verily," said she, "if thou art thus minded, make a
pledge to meet me ere I am given to another."

"The sooner I may do so, the more pleasing will it be
unto me," said Powel, "and wheresoever thou wilt, there
will I meet with thee."

"I will that thou meet me this day twelvemonth, at the
palace of Heveyth. And I will cause a feast to be prepared,
so that it be ready against thou come."

"Gladly," said he, "will I keep this tryst."

"Lord," said she, "remain in health, and be mindful
that thou keep thy promise. And now I will go hence."

So they parted, and he went back to his hosts and to
them of his household. And whatsoever questions they
asked him respecting the damsel, he always turned the
discourse upon other matters. And when a year from that
time was gone, he caused a hundred knights to equip themselves, and to go with him to the palace of Heveyth Hên.
And he came to the palace, and there was great joy concerning him, with much concourse of people, and great
rejoicing, and vast preparations for his coming. And the
whole court was placed under his orders.

And the hall was garnished, and they went to meat, and
thus did they sit; Heveyth Hên was on one side of Powel,
and Rhiannon on the other. And all the rest according to
their rank. And they ate and feasted and talked, one with
another; and at the beginning of the carousal after the

meat, there entered a tall auburn-haired youth, of royal bearing, clothed in a garment of satin. And when he came into the hall he saluted Powel and his companions.

"The greeting of Heaven be unto thee, my soul," said Powel. "Come thou and sit down."

"Nay," said he, "a suitor am I; and I will do mine errand."

"Do so willingly," said Powel.

"Lord," said he, "my errand is unto thee; and it is to crave a boon of thee that I come."

"What boon soever thou mayest ask of me, as far as I am able, thou shalt have."

"Ah," said Rhiannon, "wherefore didst thou give that answer?"

"Has he not given it before the presence of these nobles?" asked the youth.

"My soul," said Powel, "what is the boon thou askest?"

"The lady whom best I love is to be thy bride this night; I come to ask her of thee, with the feast and the banquet that are in this place."

And Powel was silent because of the answer which he had given.

"Be silent as long as thou wilt," said Rhiannon. "Never did man make worse use of his wits than thou hast done."

"Lady," said he, "I knew not who he was."

"Behold, this is the man to whom they would have given me against my will," said she. "And he is Gwawl the son of Clud, a man of great power and wealth; and because of the word thou hast spoken, bestow me upon him, lest shame befall thee."

"Lady," said he, "I understand not thine answer. Never can I do as thou sayest."

"Bestow me upon him," said she, "and I will cause that I shall never be his."

"By what means will that be ?" said Powel.

"In thy hand will I give thee a small bag," said she. "See that thou keep it well, and he will ask of thee the banquet and the feast, and the preparations, which are not in thy power. Unto the hosts and the household will I give the feast. And such will be thy answer respecting this. And as concerns myself, I will engage to become his bride this night twelvemonth. And at the end of the year be thou here," said she, "and bring this bag with thee and let thy hundred knights be in the orchard up yonder. And when he is in the midst of joy and feasting, come thou in by thyself, clad in ragged garments, and holding thy bag in thy hand, and ask nothing but a bagful of food : and I will cause that if all the meat and liquor that are in these seven cantrevs were put into it, it would be no fuller than before. And after a great deal has been put therein, he will ask thee whether thy bag will ever be full. Say thou then that it never will, until a man of noble birth and of great wealth arise and press the food in the bag with both his feet, saying, 'Enough has been put therein.' And I will cause him to go and tread down the food in the bag, and when he does so, turn thou the bag, so that he shall be up over his head in it, and then slip a knot upon the thongs of the bag. Let there be also a good bugle-horn about thy neck, and as soon as thou hast bound him in the bag, wind thy horn, and let it be a signal between thee and thy knights. And when they hear the sound of the horn, let them come down upon the palace."

"Lord," said Gwawl, "it is meet that I have an answer to my request."

"As much of that thou hast asked as it is in my power to give, thou shalt have," replied Powel.

"My soul," said Rhiannon unto him, "as for the feast and the banquet that are here, I have bestowed them upon the men of Dyved, and the household, and the warriors that are with us. These can I not suffer to be given to any. In a year from to-night a banquet shall be prepared for thee in this palace, that I may become thy bride."

So Gwawl went forth to his possessions, and Powel went also back to Dyved. And they both spent that year until it was the time for the feast at the palace of Heveyth Hên. Then Gwawl the son of Clud set out to the feast that was prepared for him, and he came to the palace and was received there with rejoicing. Powel also, the chief of Annuvyn, came to the orchard with his hundred knights, as Rhiannon had commanded him, having the bag with him. And Powel was clad in coarse and ragged garments, and wore large clumsy old shoes upon his feet. And when he knew that the carousal after the meat had begun, he went towards the hall, and when he came into the hall, he saluted Gwawl the son of Clud, and his company, both men and women.

"Heaven prosper thee!" said Gwawl, "and the greeting of Heaven be unto thee!"

"Lord," said he, "may Heaven reward thee!" I have an errand unto thee."

"Welcome be thine errand, and, if thou ask of me that which is just, thou shalt have it gladly."

"It is fitting," answered he. "I crave but from want; and the boon that I ask is to have this small bag that thou seest filled with meat."

"A request within reason is this," said he, "and gladly shalt thou have it. Bring him food."

A great number of attendants arose, and began to fill the bag; but for all that they put into it, it was no fuller than at first.

"My soul," said Gwawl, "will thy bag be ever full?"

"It will not, I declare to Heaven," said he, "for all that

may be put into it, unless one possessed of lands and domains and treasure shall arise, and tread down with both his feet the food which is within the bag, and shall say, ' Enough has been put herein.' "

Then said Rhiannon unto Gwawl the son of Clud, " Rise up quickly."

" I will willingly arise," said he. So he rose up, and put his two feet into the bag. And Powel turned up the sides of the bag, so that Gwawl was over his head in it. And he shut it up quickly, and slipped a knot upon the thongs, and blew his horn. And thereupon behold his household came down upon the palace. And they seized all the host that had come with Gwawl, and cast them into his own prison. And Powel threw off his rags, and his old shoes, and his tattered array. And as they came in, every one of Powel's knights struck a blow upon the bag, and asked, " What is here ? "

" A badger," said they. And in this manner they played, each of them striking the bag, either with his foot or with a staff. And thus played they with the bag. Every one as he came in asked, " What game are you playing at thus ? "

" The game of Badger in the Bag," said they. And then was the game of Badger in the Bag first played.

" Lord," said the man in the bag, " if thou wouldest but hear me, I merit not to be slain in a bag."

Said Heveyth Hên, " Lord, he speaks truth. It were fitting that thou listen to him ; for he deserves not this."

" Verily," said Powel, " I will do thy counsel concerning him."

" Behold, this is my counsel then," said Rhiannon. " Thou art now in a position in which it behoves thee to

satisfy suitors and minstrels : let him give unto them in thy
stead, and take a pledge from him that he will never seek
to revenge that which has been done to him. And this will
be punishment enough."

" I will do this gladly," said the man in the bag.

" And gladly will I accept it," said Powel, " since it is the
counsel of Heveyth and Rhiannon."

" Such, then, is our counsel," answered they.

" I accept it," said Powel.

" Seek thyself sureties."

" We will be for him," said Heveyth, " until his men be
free to answer for him." And upon this he was let out of
the bag, and his liege-men were liberated. " Demand now
of Gwawl his sureties," said Heveyth : " we know which
should be taken for him." And Heveyth numbered the
sureties.

Said Gwawl, " Do thou thyself draw up the covenant."

" It will suffice me that it be as Rhiannon said," answered Powel. So unto that covenant were all the sureties
pledged.

" Verily, lord," said Gwawl, " I am greatly hurt, and I
have many bruises. I have need to be anointed ; with
thy leave I will go forth. I will leave nobles in my stead
to answer for me in all that thou shalt require."

" Willingly," said Powel, " mayest thou do thus." So
Gwawl went towards his own possessions.

And the hall was set in order for Powel and the men of
his host, and for them also of the palace, and they went
to the tables and sat down. And as they had sat that time
twelvemonth, so sat they that night. And they ate and
feasted, and spent the night in mirth and tranquillity.

And next morning, at the break of day, "My lord," said Rhiannon, "arise and begin to give thy gifts unto the minstrels. Refuse no one to-day that may claim thy bounty."

"Thus shall it be, gladly," said Powel, "both to-day and every day while the feast shall last." So Powel arose, and he caused silence to be proclaimed, and desired all the suitors and the minstrels to show and to point out what gifts were to their wish and desire. And this being done, the feast went on, and he denied no one while it lasted. And when the feast was ended, Powel said unto Heveyth, "My lord, with thy permission, I will set out for Dyved to-morrow."

"Certainly," said Heveyth. "May Heaven prosper thee! Fix also a time when Rhiannon may follow thee."

Said Powel, "We will go hence together."

"Willest thou this, lord?" said Heveyth.

"Yes," answered Powel.

And the next day they set forward towards Dyved, and journeyed to the palace of Narberth, where a feast was made ready for them. And there came to them great numbers of the chief men and the most noble ladies of the land, and of these there was none to whom Rhiannon did not give some rich gift, either a bracelet, or a ring, or a precious stone. And they ruled the land prosperously both that year and the next.

And in the fourth year a son was born to them, and women were brought to watch the babe at night. And the women slept, as did also Rhiannon. And when they awoke they looked where they had put the boy, and behold he was not there. And the women were frightened; and, having

plotted together, they accused Rhiannon of having murdered
her child before their eyes.

"For pity's sake," said Rhiannon, "the Lord God knows
all things. Charge me not falsely. If you tell me this from
fear, I assert before Heaven that I will defend you."

"Truly," said they, "we would not bring evil on ourselves
for any one in the world."

"For pity's sake," said Rhiannon, "you will receive no
evil by telling the truth." But for all her words, whether fair
or harsh, she received but the same answer from the women.

And Powel the chief of Annuvyn arose, and his household
and his hosts. And this occurrence could not be concealed;
but the story went forth throughout the land, and all the
nobles heard it. Then the nobles came to Powel, and
besought him to put away his wife because of the great
crime which she had done. But Powel answered them that
they had no cause wherefore they might ask him to put
away his wife.

So Rhiannon sent for the teachers and the wise men, and
as she preferred doing penance to contending with the
women, she took upon her a penance. And the penance
that was imposed upon her was that she should remain in
that palace of Narberth until the end of seven years, and that
she should sit every day near unto a horse-block that was
without the gate; and that she should relate the story to
all who should come there whom she might suppose not to
know it already; and that she should offer the guests and
strangers, if they would permit her, to carry them upon her
back into the palace. But it rarely happened that any
would permit. And thus did she spend part of the year.

Now at that time Teirnyon Twryv Vliant was lord of

Gwent Is Coed, and he was the best man in the world. And unto his house there belonged a mare than which neither mare nor horse in the kingdom was more beautiful. And on the night of every first of May she foaled, and no one ever knew what became of the colt. And one night Teirnyon talked with his wife: "Wife," said he, "it is very simple of us that our mare should foal every year, and that we should have none of her colts."

"What can be done in the matter?" said she.

"This is the night of the first of May," said he. "The vengeance of Heaven be upon me, if I learn not what it is that takes away the colts." So he armed himself, and began to watch that night. Teirnyon heard a great tumult, and after the tumult behold a claw came through the window into the house, and it seized the colt by the mane. Then Teirnyon drew his sword, and struck off the arm at the elbow: so that portion of the arm, together with the colt, was in the house with him. And then did he hear a tumult and wailing both at once. And he opened the door, and rushed out in the direction of the noise, and he could not see the cause of the tumult because of the darkness of the night; but he rushed after it and followed it. Then he remembered that he had left the door open, and he returned. And at the door behold there was an infant-boy in swaddling clothes, wrapped around in a mantle of satin. And he took up the boy, and behold he was very strong for the age that he was of.

Then he shut the door, and went into the chamber where his wife was. "Lady," said he, "art thou sleeping?"

"No, lord," said she: "I was asleep, but as thou camest in I did awake."

"Behold, here is a boy for thee, if thou wilt," said he, "since thou hast never had one."

"My lord," said she, "what adventure is this?"

"It was thus," said Teirnyon. And he told her how it all befell.

"Verily, lord," said she, "what sort of garments are there upon the boy?"

"A mantle of satin," said he.

"He is then a boy of gentle lineage," she replied.

And they caused the boy to be baptised, and the ceremony was performed there. And the name which they gave unto him was Goldenlocks, because what hair was upon his head was as yellow as gold. And they had the boy nursed in the court until he was a year old. And before the year was over he could walk stoutly; and he was larger than a boy of three years old, even one of great growth and

size. And the boy was nursed the second year, and then
he was as large as a child six years old. And before the
end of the fourth year, he would bribe the grooms to allow
him to take the horses to water.

"My lord," said his wife unto Tiernyon, "where is the
colt which thou didst save on the night that thou didst find
the boy?"

"I have commanded the grooms of the horses," said he,
"that they take care of him."

"Would it not be well, lord," said she, "if thou wert to
cause him to be broken in, and given to the boy, seeing
that on the same night that thou didst find the boy, the colt
was foaled, and thou didst save him?"

"I will not oppose thee in this matter," said Tiernyon.
"I will allow thee to give him the colt."

"Lord," said she, "may Heaven reward thee! I will
give it him." So the horse was given to the boy. Then
she went to the grooms and those who tended the horses,
and commanded them to be careful of the horse, so that he
might be broken in by the time that the boy could ride him.

And while these things were going forward, they heard
tidings of Rhiannon and her punishment. And Teirnyon
Twryv Vliant, by reason of the pity that he felt on hearing
this story of Rhiannon and her punishment, inquired closely
concerning it, until he had heard from many of those who
came to his court. Then did Teirnyon, often lamenting the
sad history, ponder with himself; and he looked steadfastly
on the boy, and as he looked upon him, it seemed to him
that he had never beheld so great a likeness between father
and son as between the boy and Powel the chief of Annuvyn.
Now the semblance of Powel was well known to him, for he

had of yore been one of his followers. And thereupon he became grieved for the wrong that he did in keeping with him a boy whom he knew to be the son of another man. And the first time that he was alone with his wife he told her that it was not right that they should keep the boy with them, and suffer so excellent a lady as Rhiannon to be punished so greatly on his account, whereas the boy was the son of Powel the chief of Annuvyn. And Teirnyon's wife agreed with him that they should send the boy to Powel. "And three things, lord," said she, "shall we gain thereby—thanks and gifts for releasing Rhiannon from her punishment, and thanks from Powel for nursing his son and restoring him unto him ; and, thirdly, if the boy is of gentle nature, he will be our foster-son, and he will do for us all the good in his power." So it was settled according to this counsel.

And no later than the next day was Teirnyon equipped and two other knights with him. And the boy, as a fourth in their company, went with them upon the horse which Teirnyon had given him. And they journeyed towards Narberth, and it was not long before they reached that place. And as they drew near to the palace, they beheld Rhiannon sitting beside the horse-block. And when they were opposite to her, "Chieftain," said she, "go not farther thus : "I will bear every one of you into the palace. And this is my penance for slaying my own son, and devouring him."

"Oh, fair lady," said Teirnyon, "think not that I will be one to be carried upon thy back."

"Neither will I," said the boy.

"Truly, my soul," said Teirnyon, "we will not go." So they went forward to the palace, and there was great joy at

their coming. And at the palace a feast was prepared
because Powel was come back from the confines of Dyfed
And they went into the hall and washed, and Powel rejoiced
to see Teirnyon. And in this order they sat : Teirnyon
between Powel and Rhiannon, and Teirnyon's two companions on the other side of Powel, with the boy between
them. And after meat they began to carouse and discourse.
And Teirnyon's discourse was concerning the adventure of
the mare and the boy, and how he and his wife had nursed
and reared the child as their own. "Behold here is
thy son, lady," said Teirnyon. "And whosoever told that
lie concerning thee has done wrong. When I heard of
thy sorrow, I was troubled and grieved. And I believe that
there is none of this host who will not perceive that the boy
is the son of Powel," said Teirnyon.

"There is none," said they all, "who is not certain
thereof."

"I declare to Heaven," said Rhiannon, "that if this be
true, there is indeed an end to my trouble."

"Lady," said Pendaran Dyfed, "well hast thou named
thy son Pryderi (end of trouble), and well becomes him the
name of Pryderi son of Powel chief of Annuvyn."

"Look you," said Rhiannon : "will not his own name
become him better ? "

"What name has he ? " asked Pendaran Dyfed.

"Goldenlocks is the name that we gave him."

"Pryderi," said Pendaran, "shall his name be."

"It were more proper," said Powel, "that the boy should
take his name from the word his mother spoke when she
received the joyful tidings of him." And thus was it
arranged.

"Teirnyon," said Powel, "Heaven reward thee that thou hast reared the boy up to this time, and, being of gentle lineage, it were fitting that he repay thee for it."

"My lord," said Teirnyon, "it was my wife who nursed him, and there is no one in the world so afflicted as she at parting with him. It were well that he should bear in mind what I and my wife have done for him."

"I call Heaven to witness," said Powel, "that while I live I will support thee and thy possessions as long as I am able to preserve my own. And when he shall have power, he will more fitly maintain them than I. And if this counsel be pleasing unto thee and to my nobles, it shall be, that, as thou hast reared him up to the present time, I will give him to be brought up by Pendaran Dyfed from henceforth. And you shall be companions, and shall both be foster-fathers unto him."

"This is good counsel," said they all. So the boy was given to Pendaran Dyfed, and the nobles of the land were sent with him. And Teirnyon Twryv Vliant and his companions set out for his country and his possessions, with love and gladness. And he went not without being offered the fairest jewels, and the fairest horses, and the choicest dogs ; but he would take none of them.

Thereupon they all remained in their own dominions. And Pryderi the son of Powel the chief of Annuvyn was brought up carefully, as was fit, so that he became the fairest youth, and the most comely, and the best skilled in all good games, of any in the kingdom. And thus passed years and years until the end of Powel the chief of Annuvyn's life came, and he died.

Paddy O'Kelly and the Weasel

LONG time ago there was once a man of the name of Paddy O'Kelly, living near Tuam, in the county Galway. He rose up one morning early, and he did not know what time of day it was, for there was fine light coming from the moon. He wanted to go to the fair of Cauher-na-mart to sell a *sturk* of an ass that he had.

He had not gone more than three miles of the road when a great darkness came on, and a shower began falling. He saw a large house among trees about five hundred yards in from the road, and he said to himself that he would go to that house till the shower would be over. When he got to the house he found the door open before him, and in with him. He saw a large room to his left, and a fine fire in the grate. He sat down on a stool that was beside the wall, and began falling asleep, when he saw a big weasel coming to the fire with something yellow in his mouth, which it dropped on the hearth-stone, and then it went away. She soon came back again with the same thing in her mouth, and he saw that it was a guinea she had. She dropped it on the hearth-stone, and went away again. She was coming and going, until there was a great heap of guineas on the hearth. But at last, when she got her gone, Paddy rose up, thrust all the gold she had gathered into his pockets, and out with him.

He had not gone far till he heard the weasel coming after him, and she screeching as loud as a bag-pipes. She went before Paddy and got on the road, and she was twisting herself back and forwards, and trying to get a hold of his throat. Paddy had a good oak stick, and he kept her from him, until two men came up who were going to the same fair, and one of them had a good dog, and it routed the weasel into a hole in the wall.

Paddy went to the fair, and instead of coming home with the money he got for his old ass, as he thought would be the way with him in the morning, he went and bought a horse with some of the money he took from the weasel, and he came home riding. When he came to the place where the dog had routed the weasel into the hole in the wall, she came out before him, gave a leap, and caught the horse by the throat. The horse made off, and Paddy could not stop him, till at last he gave a leap into a big drain that was full up of water and black mud, and he was drowning and choking as fast as he could, until men who were coming from Galway came up and drove away the weasel.

Paddy brought the horse home with him, and put him into the cow's byre and fell asleep.

Next morning, the day on the morrow, Paddy rose up early, and went out to give his horse hay and oats. When he got to the door he saw the weasel coming out of the byre and she covered with blood.

"My seven thousand curses on you," said Paddy, "but I'm afraid you've done harm."

He went in and found the horse, a pair of milch cows, and two calves dead.

He came out and set a dog he had after the weasel. The dog got a hold of her, and she got a hold of the dog. The dog was a good one, but he was forced to loose his hold of her before Paddy could come up. He kept his eye on her, however, all through, until he saw her creeping into a little hovel that was on the brink of a lake. Paddy came running, and when he got to the little hut he gave the dog a shake to rouse him up and put anger on him, and then he sent him in. When the dog went in he began barking. Paddy went in after him, and saw an old hag in the corner. He asked her if she saw a weasel coming in there.

"I did not," said she; "I'm all destroyed with a plague of sickness, and if you don't go out quick, you'll catch it from me."

While Paddy and the hag were talking, the dog kept moving in all the time, till at last he gave a leap and caught the hag by the throat. She screeched and said :

" Paddy Kelly, take off your dog, and I'll make you a rich man."

Paddy made the dog loose his hold, and said :

" Tell me who you are, or why did you kill my horse and my cows ? "

" And why did you bring away my gold that I was gathering for five hundred years throughout the hills and hollows of the world ? "

" I thought you were a weasel," said Paddy, " or I wouldn't touch your gold ; and another thing," says he, " if you're for five hundred years in this world, it's time for you to go to rest now."

" I committed a great crime in my youth," said the hag, " and now I am to be released from my sufferings if you can pay twenty pounds for a hundred and three-score masses for me."

" Where's the money ? " said Paddy.

" Go and dig under a bush that's over a little well in the corner of that field there without, and you'll get a pot filled with gold. Pay the twenty pounds for the masses, and yourself shall have the rest. When you'll lift the flag off the pot, you'll see a big black dog coming out ; but don't be afraid before him ; he is a son of mine. When you get the gold, buy the house in which you saw me at first. You'll get it cheap, for it has the name of there being a ghost in it. My son will be down in the cellar. He'll do you no harm, but he'll be a good friend to you. I shall be dead a month from this day, and when you get me

dead, put a coal under this little hut and burn it. Don't tell a
living soul anything about me—and the luck will be on you."

"What is your name ? " said Paddy.

"Mary Kerwan," said the hag.

Paddy went home, and when the darkness of the night
came on, he took with him a spade and went to the bush
that was in the corner of the field, and began digging.
It was not long till he found the pot, and when he took the
flag off of it a big black dog leaped out, and off and away
with him, and Paddy's dog after him.

Paddy brought home the gold, and hid it in the cow-
house. About a month after that he went to the fair of
Galway, and bought a pair of cows, a horse, and a dozen
sheep. The neighbours did not know where he had got
all the money ; they said that he had a share with the
good people.

One day Paddy dressed himself, and went to the gentleman who owned the large house where he first saw the
weasel, and asked to buy the house of him, and the land
that was round about.

"You can have the house without paying any rent at all ;
but there is a ghost in it, and I wouldn't like you to go to
live in it without my telling you, but I couldn't part with
the land without getting a hundred pounds more than you
have to offer me."

"Perhaps I have as much as you have yourself," said
Paddy. "I'll be here to-morrow with the money, if you're
ready to give me possession."

"I'll be ready," said the gentleman.

Paddy went home and told his wife that he had bought
a large house and a holding of land.

" Where did you get the money ? " says the wife.

" Isn't it all one to you where I got it ? " says Paddy.

The day on the morrow Paddy went to the gentleman, gave him the money, and got possession of the house and land ; and the gentleman left him the furniture and everything that was in the house, into the bargain.

Paddy remained in the house that night, and when darkness came he went down to the cellar, and he saw a little man with his two legs spread on a barrel.

" God save you, honest man," says he to Paddy.

" The same to you," says Paddy.

" Don't be afraid of me, at all," says the little man. " I'll be a friend to you, if you are able to keep a secret."

" I am able, indeed ; I kept your mother's secret, and I'll keep yours as well."

" Maybe you're thirsty ? " said the little man.

" I'm not free from it," said Paddy.

The little man put a hand in his bosom and drew out a gold goblet. He gave it to Paddy, and said : " Draw wine out of that barrel under me."

Paddy drew the full up of the goblet, and handed it to the little man.

" Drink yourself first," says he.

Paddy drank, drew another goblet, and handed it to the little man, and he drank it.

" Fill up and drink again," said the little man. " I have a mind to be merry to-night."

The pair of them sat there drinking until they were half drunk. Then the little man gave a leap down to the floor, and said to Paddy :

" Don't you like music ? "

" I do, surely," said Paddy, " and I'm a good dancer, too."

" Lift up the big flag over there in the corner, and you'll get my pipes under it."

Paddy lifted the flag, got the pipes, and gave them to the little man. He squeezed the pipes on him, and began playing melodious music. Paddy began dancing till he was tired. Then they had another drink, and the little man said :

" Do as my mother told you, and I'll show you great riches. You can bring your wife in here, but don't tell her that I'm there, and she won't see me. Any time at all that ale or wine are wanting, come here and draw. Farewell, now ; go to sleep, and come again to me to-morrow night."

Paddy went to bed, and it wasn't long till he fell asleep.

On the morning of the day on the morrow, Paddy went home, and brought his wife and children to the big house, and they were very comfortable. That night Paddy went down to the cellar ; the little man welcomed him and asked him did he wish to dance ?

" Not till I get a drink," said Paddy.

" Drink your fill," said the little man ; " that barrel will never be empty as long as you live."

Paddy drank the full of the goblet, and gave a drink to the little man. Then the little man said to him :

" I am going to the Fortress of the Fairies to-night, to play music for the good people, and if you come with me you'll see fine fun. I'll give you a horse that you never saw the like of him before."

" I'll go with you, and welcome," said Paddy ; "but what excuse will I make to my wife ? "

" I'll bring you away from her side without her knowing it, when you are both asleep together, and I'll bring you back to her the same way," said the little man.

" I'm obedient," says Paddy ; " we'll have another drink before I leave you."

He drank drink after drink, till he was half drunk, and he went to bed with his wife.

When he awoke he found himself riding on a broom near Doon-na-shee, and the little man riding on another besom by his side. When they came as far as the green hill of the Doon, the little man said a couple of words that Paddy did not understand. The green hill opened, and the pair went into a fine chamber.

Paddy never saw before a gathering like that which was in the Doon. The whole place was full up of little people, men and women, young and old. They all welcomed little Donal—that was the name of the piper—and Paddy O'Kelly. The king and queen of the fairies came up to them, and said :

" We are all going on a visit to-night to Cnoc Matha, to the high king and queen of our people."

They all rose up then and went out. There were horses ready for each one of them, and the *coash-t'ya bower* for the king and queen. The king and queen got into the coach, each man leaped on his own horse, and be certain that Paddy was not behind. The piper went out before them, and began playing them music, and then off and away with them. It was not long till they came to Cnoc Matha. The hill opened, and the king of the fairy host passed in.

Finvara and Nuala were there, the arch-king and queen of the fairy host of Connacht, and thousands of little persons. Finvara came up and said:

` "We are going to play a hurling match to-night against

the fairy host of Munster, and unless we beat them our fame is gone for ever. The match is to be fought out on Moytura, under Slieve Belgadaun."

The Connacht host cried out: "We are all ready, and we have no doubt but we'll beat them."

"Out with ye all," cried the high king; "the men of the hill of Nephin will be on the ground before us."

They all went out, and little Donal and twelve pipers more before them, playing melodious music. When they came to Moytura, the fairy host of Munster and the fairy men of the hill of Nephin were there before them.

Now it is necessary for the fairy host to have two live men beside them when they are fighting or at a hurling match, and that was the reason that little Donal took Paddy O'Kelly with him. There was a man they called the " *Yellow Stongirya,*" with the fairy host of Munster, from Ennis, in the County Clare.

It was not long till the two hosts took sides; the ball was thrown up between them, and the fun began in earnest.

They were hurling away, and the pipers playing music, until Paddy O'Kelly saw the host of Munster getting the

strong hand, and he began helping the fairy host of Con-nacht.

The *Stongirya* came up and he made at Paddy O'Kelly, but Paddy turned him head over heels. From hurling the two hosts began at fighting, but it was not long until the host of Connacht beat the other host. Then the host of Munster made flying beetles of themselves, and they began eating every green thing that they came up to. They were destroying the country before them until they came as far as Cong. Then there rose up thousands of doves out of the hole, and they swallowed down the beetles.

That hole has no other name until this day but Pull-na-gullam, the dove's hole.

When the fairy host of Connacht won their battle, they came back to Cnoc Matha joyous enough, and the king Finvara gave Paddy O'Kelly a purse of gold, and the little piper brought him home, and put him into bed beside his wife, and left him sleeping there.

A month went by after that without anything worth mentioning, until one night Paddy went down to the cellar, and the little man said to him : " My mother is dead ; burn the house over her."

" It is true for you," said Paddy. " She told me that she hadn't but a month to be in the world, and the month was up yesterday."

On the next morning of the next day Paddy went to the hut and he found the hag dead. He put a coal under the hut and burned it. He came home and told the little man that the hag was burnt. The little man gave him a purse and said to him : " This purse will never be empty as long as you are alive. Now, you will never see me more ; but have a loving remembrance of the weasel. She was the beginning and the prime cause of your riches." Then he went away and Paddy never saw him again.

Paddy O'Kelly and his wife lived for years after this in the large house, and when he died he left great wealth behind him, and a large family to spend it.

There now is the story for you, from the first word to the last, as I heard it from my grandmother.

The Black Horse

NCE there was a king and he had three sons, and when the king died, they did not give a shade of anything to the youngest son, but an old white limping garron.

"If I get but this," quoth he, "it seems that I had best go with this same."

He was going with it right before him, sometimes walking, sometimes riding. When he had been riding a good while he thought that the garron would need a while of eating, so he came down to earth, and what should he see coming out of the heart of the western airt towards him but a rider riding high, well, and right well.

"All hail, my lad," said he.

"Hail, king's son," said the other.

"What's your news?" said the king's son.

"I have got that," said the lad who came. "I am after breaking my heart riding this ass of a horse; but will you give me the limping white garron for him?"

"No," said the prince; "it would be a bad business for me."

"You need not fear," said the man that came, "there is no saying but that you might make better use of him than I. He has one value, there is no single place that you can think of in the four parts of the wheel of the world that the black horse will not take you there."

So the king's son got the black horse, and he gave the limping white garron.

Where should he think of being when he mounted but in the Realm Underwaves. He went, and before sunrise on the morrow he was there. What should he find when he got there but the son of the King Underwaves holding a Court, and the people of the realm gathered to see if there was any one who would undertake to go to seek the daughter of the King of the Greeks to be the prince's wife. No one came forward, when who should come up but the rider of the black horse.

"You, rider of the black horse," said the prince, "I lay you under crosses and under spells to have the daughter of the King of the Greeks here before the sun rises to-morrow."

He went out and he reached the black horse and leaned his elbow on his mane, and he heaved a sigh.

"Sigh of a king's son under spells!" said the horse; "but have no care; we shall do the thing that was set before you." And so off they went.

"Now," said the horse, "when we get near the great town of the Greeks, you will notice that the four feet of a horse never went to the town before. The king's daughter will see me from the top of the castle looking out of a window, and she will not be content without a turn of a ride upon me. Say that she may have that, but the horse

will suffer no man but you to ride before a woman on
him."

They came near the big town, and he fell to horsemanship; and the princess was looking out of the windows, and
noticed the horse. The horsemanship pleased her, and she
came out just as the horse had come.

"Give me a ride on the horse," said she.

"You shall have that," said he, "but the horse will let
no man ride him before a woman but me."

"I have a horseman of my own," said she.

"If so, set him in front," said he.

Before the horseman mounted at all, when he tried to get
up, the horse lifted his legs and kicked him off.

"Come then yourself and mount before me," said she; "I won't leave the matter so."

He mounted the horse and she behind him, and before she glanced from her she was nearer sky than earth. He was in Realm Underwaves with her before sunrise.

"You are come," said Prince Underwaves.

"I am come," said he.

"There you are, my hero," said the prince. "You are the son of a king, but I am a son of success. Anyhow, we shall have no delay or neglect now, but a wedding."

"Just gently," said the princess; "your wedding is not so short a way off as you suppose. Till I get the silver cup that my grandmother had at her wedding, and that my mother had as well, I will not marry, for I need to have it at my own wedding."

"You, rider of the black horse," said the Prince Underwaves, "I set you under spells and under crosses unless the silver cup is here before dawn to-morrow."

Out he went and reached the horse and leaned his elbow on his mane, and he heaved a sigh.

"Sigh of a king's son under spells!" said the horse; "mount and you shall get the silver cup. The people of the realm are gathered about the king to-night, for he has missed his daughter, and when you get to the palace go in and leave me without; they will have the cup there going round the company. Go in and sit in their midst. Say nothing, and seem to be as one of the people of the place. But when the cup comes round to you, take it under your oxter, and come out to me with it, and we'll go."

Away they went and they got to Greece, and he went in to the palace and did as the black horse bade. He took the cup and came out and mounted, and before sunrise he was in the Realm Underwaves.

" You are come," said Prince Underwaves.

" I am come," said he.

" We had better get married now," said the prince to the Greek princess.

" Slowly and softly," said she. " I will not marry till I get the silver ring that my grandmother and my mother wore when they were wedded."

" You, rider of the black horse," said the Prince Underwaves, " do that. Let's have that ring here to-morrow at sunrise."

The lad went to the black horse and put his elbow on his crest and told him how it was.

" There never was a matter set before me harder than this matter which has now been set in front of me," said the horse, " but there is no help for it at any rate. Mount me. There is a snow mountain and an ice mountain and a mountain of fire between us and the winning of that ring. It is right hard for us to pass them."

Thus they went as they were, and about a mile from the snow mountain they were in a bad case with cold. As they came near it he struck the horse, and with the bound he gave the black horse was on the top of the snow mountain ; at the next bound he was on the top of the ice mountain ; at the third bound he went through the mountain of fire. When he had passed the mountains he was dragging at the horse's neck, as though he were about to lose himself. He went on before him down to a town below.

" Go down," said the black horse, " to a smithy ; make an iron spike for every bone end in me."

Down he went as the horse desired, and he got the
spikes made, and back he came with them.

" Stick them into me," said the horse, " every spike of
them in every bone end that I have."

That he did ; he stuck the spikes into the horse.

" There is a loch here," said the horse, " four miles long
and four miles wide, and when I go out into it the loch
will take fire and blaze. If you see the Loch of Fire
going out before the sun rises, expect me, and if not, go
your way."

Out went the black horse into the lake, and the lake
became flame. Long was he stretched about the lake,
beating his palms and roaring. Day came, and the loch
did not go out.

But at the hour when the sun was rising out of the
water the lake went out.

And the black horse rose in the middle of the water
with one single spike in him, and the ring upon its
end.

He came on shore, and down he fell beside the loch.

Then down went the rider. He got the ring, and he
dragged the horse down to the side of a hill. He fell to
sheltering him with his arms about him, and as the sun
was rising he got better and better, till about midday,
when he rose on his feet.

" Mount," said the horse, " and let us begone."

He mounted on the black horse, and away they went.

He reached the mountains, and he leaped the horse at the
fire mountain and was on the top. From the mountain of
fire he leaped to the mountain of ice, and from the mountain of ice to the mountain of snow. He put the mountains

· THE · BLACK · HORSE ·

past him, and by morning he was in realm under the waves.

"You are come," said the prince.

"I am," said he.

"That's true," said Prince Underwaves. "A king's son are you, but a son of success am I. We shall have no more mistakes and delays, but a wedding this time."

"Go easy," said the Princess of the Greeks. "Your wedding is not so near as you think yet. Till you make a castle, I won't marry you. Not to your father's castle nor to your mother's will I go to dwell; but make me a castle for which your father's castle will not make washing water."

"You, rider of the black horse, make that," said Prince Underwaves, "before the morrow's sun rises."

The lad went out to the horse and leaned his elbow on his neck and sighed, thinking that this castle never could be made for ever.

"There never came a turn in my road yet that is easier for me to pass than this," said the black horse.

Glance that the lad gave from him he saw all that there were, and ever so many wrights and stone masons at work, and the castle was ready before the sun rose.

He shouted at the Prince Underwaves, and he saw the castle. He tried to pluck out his eye, thinking that it was a false sight.

"Son of King Underwaves," said the rider of the black horse, "don't think that you have a false sight; this is a true sight."

"That's true," said the prince. "You are a son of success, but I am a son of success too. There will be no more mistakes and delays, but a wedding now."

"No," said she. " The time is come. Should we not go to look at the castle ?   There's time enough to get married before the night comes."

They went to the castle and the castle was without a " but "———

" I see one," said the prince.   " One want at least to be made good.   A well to be made inside, so that water may not be far to fetch when there is a feast or a wedding in the castle."

" That won't be long undone," said the rider of the black horse.

The well was made, and it was seven fathoms deep and two or three fathoms wide, and they looked at the well on the way to the wedding.

" It is very well made," said she, " but for one little fault yonder."

" Where is it ? " said Prince Underwaves.

" There," said she.

He bent him down to look. She came out, and she put her two hands at his back, and cast him in.

" Be thou there," said she. " If I go to be married, thou art not the man ; but the man who did each exploit that has been done, and, if he chooses, him will I have."

Away she went with the rider of the little black horse to the wedding.

And at the end of three years after that so it was that he first remembered the black horse or where he left him.

He got up and went out, and he was very sorry for his neglect of the black horse. He found him just where he left him.

"Good luck to you, gentleman," said the horse. "You seem as if you had got something that you like better than me."

"I have not got that, and I won't; but it came over me to forget you," said he.

"I don't mind," said the horse, "it will make no difference. Raise your sword and smite off my head."

"Fortune will now allow that I should do that," said he.

"Do it instantly, or I will do it to you," said the horse.

So the lad drew his sword and smote off the horse's head; then he lifted his two palms and uttered a doleful cry.

What should he hear behind him but "All hail, my brother-in-law."

He looked behind him, and there was the finest man he ever set eyes upon.

"What set you weeping for the black horse?" said he.

"This," said the lad, "that there never was born of man or beast a creature in this world that I was fonder of."

"Would you take me for him?" said the stranger.

"If I could think you the horse, I would; but if not, I would rather the horse," said the rider.

"I am the black horse," said the lad, "and if I were not, how should you have all these things that you went to seek in my father's house. Since I went under spells, many a man have I ran at before you met me. They had but one word amongst them: they could not keep me, nor manage me, and they never kept me a couple of days. But when I fell in with you, you kept me till the time ran out that was to come from the spells. And now you shall gc home with me, and we will make a wedding in my father's house."

The Vision of MacConglinney

ATHAL, King of Munster, was a good king and a great warrior. But there came to dwell within him a lawless evil beast, that afflicted him with hunger that ceased not, and might not be satisfied, so that he would devour a pig, a cow, and a bull calf and three-score cakes of pure wheat, and a vat of new ale, for his breakfast, whilst as for his great feast, what he ate there passes account or reckoning. He was like this for three half-years, and during that time it was the ruin of Munster he was, and it is likely he would have ruined all Ireland in another half-year.

Now there lived in Armagh a famous young scholar and his name was Anier MacConglinney. He heard of the strange disease of King Cathal, and of the abundance of food and drink, of whitemeats, ale and mead, there were always to be found at the king's court. Thither then was he minded to go to try his own fortune, and to see of what help he could be to the king.

He arose early in the morning and tucked up his shirt

and wrapped him in the folds of his white cloak. In his right hand he grasped his even-poised knotty staff, and going right-hand-wise round his home, he bade farewell to his tutors and started off.

He journeyed across all Ireland till he came to the house of Pichan. And there he stayed and told tales, and made all merry. But Pichan said :

"Though great thy mirth, son of learning, it does not make me glad."

"And why ? " asked MacConglinney.

"Knowest thou not, scholar, that Cathal is coming here to-night with all his host. And if the great host is troublesome, the king's first meal is more troublesome still ; and troublesome though the first be, most troublesome of all is the great feast. Three things are wanted for this last: a bushel of oats, and a bushel of wild apples, and a bushel of flour cakes."

"What reward would you give me if I shield you from the king from this hour to the same hour to-morrow ? "

"A white sheep from every fold between Carn and Cork."

"I will take that," said MacConglinney.

Cathal, the king, came with the companies, and a host of horse of the Munster men. But Cathal did not let the thong of his shoe be half loosed before he began supplying his mouth with both hands from the apples round about him. Pichan and all the men of Munster looked on sadly and sorrowfully. Then rose MacConglinney, hastily and impatiently, and seized a stone, against which swords were used to be sharpened ; this he thrust into his mouth and began grinding his teeth against the stone.

"What makes thee mad, son of learning?" asked Cathal.

"I grieve to see you eating alone," said the scholar.

Then the king was ashamed and flung him the apples, and it is said that for three half-years he had not performed such an act of humanity.

"Grant me a further boon," said MacConglinney.

"It is granted, on my troth," said the king.

"Fast with me the whole night," said the scholar.

And grievous though it was to the king, he did so, for he had passed his princely troth, and no King of Munster might transgress that.

In the morning MacConglinney called for juicy old bacon, and tender corned beef, honey in the comb, and English salt on a beautiful polished dish of white silver. A fire he lighted of oak wood without smoke, without fumes, without sparks.

And sticking spits into the portion of meat, he set to work to roast them. Then he shouted, "Ropes and cords here."

Ropes and cords were given to him, and the strongest of the warriors.

And they seized the king and bound him securely, and made him fast with knots and hooks and staples. When the king was thus fastened, MacConglinney sat himself down before him, and taking his knife out of his girdle, he carved the portion of meat that was on the spits, and every morsel he dipped in the honey, and, passing it in front of the king's mouth, put it in his own.

When the king saw that he was getting nothing, and he had been fasting for twenty-four hours, he roared and bellowed, and commanded the killing of the scholar. But that was not done for him.

"Listen, King of Munster," said MacConglinney, "a vision appeared to me last night, and I will relate it to you."

He then began his vision, and as he related it he put morsel after morsel past Cathal's mouth into his own.

> "A lake of new milk I beheld
> In the midst of a fair plain,
> Therein a well-appointed house,
> Thatched with butter.
> Puddings fresh boiled,
> Such were its thatch-rods,
> Its two soft door posts of custard,
> Its beds of glorious bacon.
> Cheeses were the palisades,
> Sausages the rafters.
> Truly 'twas a rich filled house,
> In which was great store of good feed.

Such was the vision I beheld, and a voice sounded into my ears. ' Go now, thither, MacConglinney, for you have no power of eating in you.' ' What must I do,' said I, for the sight of that had made me greedy. Then the voice bade me go to the hermitage of the Wizard Doctor, and there I should find appetite for all kinds of savoury tender sweet food, acceptable to the body.

"There in the harbour of the lake before me I saw a juicy little coracle of beef; its thwarts were of curds, its prow of lard; its stern of butter; its oars were flitches of venison. Then I rowed across the wide expanse of the New Milk Lake, through seas of broth, past river mouths of meat, over swelling boisterous waves of butter milk, by perpetual pools of savoury lard, by islands of cheese, by headlands of old curds, until I reached the firm level land between Butter Mount and Milk Lake, in the land of O'Early-eating, in front of the hermitage of the Wizard Doctor.

" Marvellous, indeed, was the hermitage. Around it were seven-score hundred smooth stakes of old bacon, and instead of thorns above the top of every stake was fixed juicy lard. There was a gate of cream, whereon was a bolt of sausage. And there I saw the doorkeeper, Bacon Lad, son of Butterkins, son of Lardipole, with his smooth sandals of old bacon, his legging of pot-meat round his shins, his tunic of corned beef, his girdle of salmon skin round him, his hood of flummery about him, his steed of bacon under him, with its four legs of custard, its four hoofs of oaten bread, its ears of curds, its two eyes of honey in its head ; in his hand a whip, the cords whereof were four-and-twenty fair white puddings, and every juicy drop that fell from each of these puddings would have made a meal for an ordinary man.

" On going in I beheld the Wizard Doctor with his two gloves of rump steak on his hands, setting in order the house, which was hung all round with tripe, from roof to floor.

" I went into the kitchen, and there I saw the Wizard Doctor's son, with his fishing hook of lard in his hand, and the line was made of marrow, and he was angling in a lake of whey. Now he would bring up a flitch of ham, and now a fillet of corned beef. And as he was angling, he fell in, and was drowned.

" As I set my foot across the threshold into the house, I saw a pure white bed of butter, on which I sat down, but

I sank down into it up to the tips of my hair.   Hard work
had the eight strongest men in the house to pull me out
by the top of the crown of my head.

"Then I was taken in to the Wizard Doctor.   'What
aileth thee ?' said he.

"My wish would be, that all the many wonderful viands
of the world were before me, that I might eat my fill and
satisfy my greed.   But alas! great is the misfortune to
me, who cannot obtain any of these.

" 'On my word,' said the Doctor, 'the disease is
grievous.   But thou shall take home with thee a medicine
to cure thy disease, and shalt be for ever healed there-
from.'

" 'What is that ?' asked I.

" 'When thou goest home to-night, warm thyself before a
glowing red fire of oak, made up on a dry hearth, so that
its embers may warm thee, its blaze may not burn thee, its
smoke may not touch thee.   And make for thyself thrice
nine morsels, and every morsel as big as an heath fowl's
egg, and in each morsel eight kinds of grain, wheat and
barley, oats and rye, and therewith eight condiments, and
to every condiment eight sauces.   And when thou hast
prepared thy food, take a drop of drink, a tiny drop, only
as much as twenty men will drink, and let it be of thick
milk, of yellow bubbling milk, of milk that will gurgle as
it rushes down thy throat.'

" 'And when thou hast done this, whatever disease thou
hast, shall be removed.   Go now,' said he, 'in the name
of cheese, and may the smooth juicy bacon protect thee,
may yellow curdy cream protect, may the cauldron full of
pottage protect thee.' "

Now, as MacConglinney recited his vision, what with the pleasure of the recital and the recounting of these many pleasant viands, and the sweet savour of the honeyed morsels roasting on the spits, the lawless beast that dwelt

within the king, came forth until it was licking its lips outside its head.

Then MacConglinney bent his hand with the two spits of food, and put them to the lips of the king, who longed to swallow them, wood, food, and all. So he took them an arm's length away from the king, and the lawless beast

jumped from the throat of Cathal on to the spit. MacConglinney put the spit into the embers, and upset the cauldron
of the royal house over the spit. The house was emptied,
so that not the value of a cockchafer's leg was left in it, and
four huge fires were kindled here and there in it. When
the house was a tower of red flame and a huge blaze, the
lawless beast sprang to the rooftree of the palace, and from
thence he vanished, and was seen no more.

As for the king, a bed was prepared for him on a downy
quilt, and musicians and singers entertained him going from
noon till twilight. And when he awoke, this is what he
bestowed upon the scholar—a cow from every farm, and a
sheep from every house in Munster. Moreover, that so
long as he lived, he should carve the king's food, and sit
at his right hand.

Thus was Cathal, King of Munster, cured of his craving,
and MacConglinney honoured.

Dream of Owen O'Mulready

HERE was a man long ago living near Ballaghadereen named Owen O'Mulready, who was a workman for the gentleman of the place, and was a prosperous, quiet, contented man. There was no one but himself and his wife Margaret, and they had a nice little house and enough potatoes in the year, in addition to their share of wages, from their master. There wasn't a want or anxiety on Owen, except one desire, and that was to have a dream—for he had never had one.

One day when he was digging potatoes, his master— James Taafe—came out to his ridge, and they began talking, as was the custom with them. The talk fell on dreams, and said Owen that he would like better than anything if he could only have one.

"You'll have one to-night," says his master, "if you do as I tell you."

"Musha, I'll do it, and welcome," says Owen.

"Now," says his master, "when you go home to-night, draw the fire from the hearth, put it out, make your bed in its place and sleep there to-night, and you'll get your enough of dreaming before the morning."

Owen promised to do this. When, however, he began to draw the fire out, Margaret thought that he had lost his senses, so he explained everything James Taafe had said to him, had his own way, and they went to lie down together on the hearth.

Not long was Owen asleep when there came a knock at the door.

"Get up, Owen O'Mulready, and go with a letter from the master to America."

Owen got up, and put his feet into his boots, saying to himself, "It's late you come, messenger."

He took the letter, and he went forward and never tarried till he came to the foot of Sliabh Charn, where he met a cow-boy, and he herding cows.

"The blessing of God be with you, Owen O'Mulready," says the boy.

"The blessing of God and Mary be with you, my boy," says Owen. "Every one knows me, and I don't know any one at all."

"Where are you going this time of night?" says the boy.

"I'm going to America, with a letter from the master; is this the right road?" says Owen.

"It is; keep straight to the west; but how are you going to get over the water?" says the boy.

"Time enough to think of that when I get to it," replied Owen.

He went on the road again, till he came to the brink of the sea; there he saw a crane standing on one foot on the shore.

" The blessing of God be with you, Owen O'Mulready,"
says the crane.

" The blessing of God and Mary be with you, Mrs.
Crane," says Owen. " Everybody knows me, and I don't
know any one."

" What are you doing here ? "

Owen told her his business, and that he didn't know
how he'd get over the water.

" Leave your two feet on my two wings, and sit on my
back, and I'll take you to the other side," says the
crane.

" What would I do if tiredness should come on you
before we got over ? " says Owen.

" Don't be afraid, I won't be tired or wearied till I fly
over."

Then Owen went on the back of the crane, and she
arose over the sea and went forward, but she hadn't flown
more than half-way, when she cried out :

" Owen O'Mulready get off me ; I'm tired."

" That you may be seven times worse this day twelve-
months, you rogue of a crane," says Owen ; " I can't get
off you now, so don't ask me."

" I don't care," replied the crane, " if you'll rise off me a
while till I'll take a rest."

With that they saw threshers over their heads, and
Owen shouted :

" Och ! thresher, thresher, leave down your flail at me,
that I may give the crane a rest ! "

The thresher left down the flail, but when Owen took a
hold with his two hands, the crane went from him laughing
and mocking.

"My share of misfortunes go with you!" said Owen, "It's you've left me in a fix hanging between the heavens and the water in the middle of the great sea."

It wasn't long till the thresher shouted to him to leave go the flail.

"I won't let it go," said Owen; "shan't I be drowned?"

"If you don't let it go, I'll cut the whang."

"I don't care," says Owen; "I have the flail;" and

with that he looked away from him, and what should he see but a boat a long way off.

" O sailor dear, sailor, come, come ; perhaps you'll take my lot of bones," said Owen.

" Are we under you now ? " says the sailor.

" Not yet, not yet," says Owen.

" Fling down one of your shoes, till we see the way it falls," says the captain.

Owen shook one foot, and down fell the shoe.

" Uill, uill, puil, uil liu—who is killing me ? " came a scream from Margaret in the bed. " Where are you, Owen ? "

" I didn't know whether 'twas you were in it, Margaret."

" Indeed, then it is," says she, " who else would it be ? "

She got up and lit the candle. She found Owen half-way up the chimney, climbing by the hands on the crook, and he black with soot ! He had one shoe on, but the point of the other struck Margaret, and 'twas that which awoke her.

Owen came down off the crook and washed himself, and from that out there was no envy on him ever to have a dream again.

Morraha

ORRAHA rose in the morning and washed his hands and face, and said his prayers, and ate his food; and he asked God to prosper the day for him. So he went down to the brink of the sea, and he saw a currach, short and green, coming towards him; and in it there was but one youthful champion, and he was playing hurly from prow to stern of the currach. He had a hurl of gold and a ball of silver; and he stopped not till the currach was in on the shore; and he drew her up on the green grass, and put fastenings on her for a year and a day, whether he should be there all that time or should only be on land for an hour by the clock. And Morraha saluted the young man courteously; and the other saluted him in the same fashion, and asked him would he play a game of cards with him; and Morraha said that he had not the wherewithal; and the other answered that he was never without a candle or the making of it; and he put his hand in his pocket and drew out a table and two chairs and a pack of cards, and they sat down on the chairs and went to card-playing. The first game Morraha won, and the Slender Red Champion bade him make his claim; and he asked that the land above him should be filled with stock of sheep in the morning. It was well; and he played no second game, but home he went.

The next day Morraha went to the brink of the sea, and the young man came in the currach and asked him would he play cards; they played, and Morraha won. The young man bade him make his claim; and he asked that the land above should be filled with cattle in the morning. It was well; and he played no other game, but went home.

On the third morning Morraha went to the brink of the sea, and he saw the young man coming. He drew up his boat on the shore and asked him would he play cards. They played, and Morraha won the game; and the young man bade him give his claim. And he said he would have a castle and a wife, the finest and fairest in the world; and they were his. It was well; and the Red Champion went away.

On the fourth day his wife asked him how he had found her. And he told her. "And I am going out," said he, "to play again to-day."

"I forbid you to go again to him. If you have won so much, you will lose more; have no more to do with him."

But he went against her will, and he saw the currach coming; and the Red Champion was driving his balls from end to end of the currach; he had balls of silver and a hurl of gold, and he stopped not till he drew his boat on the shore, and made her fast for a year and a day. Morraha

and he saluted each other ; and he asked Morraha if he
would play a game of cards, and they played, and he won.
Morraha said to him, " Give your claim now."

Said he, " You will hear it too soon. I lay on you bonds
of the art of the Druid, not to sleep two nights in one house,
nor finish a second meal at the one table, till you bring
me the sword of light and news of the death of Anshgayliacht."

He went home to his wife and sat down in a chair, and
gave a groan, and the chair broke in pieces.

" That is the groan of the son of a king under spells," said
his wife ; "and you had better have taken my counsel than
that the spells should be on you."

He told her he had to bring news of the death of
Anshgayliacht and the sword of light to the Slender Red
Champion.

" Go out," said she, " in the morning of the morrow, and
take the bridle in the window. and shake it ; and whatever
beast, handsome or ugly, puts its head in it, take that one
with you.   Do not speak a word to her till she speaks to
you ; and take with you three pint bottles of ale and three
sixpenny loaves, and do the thing she tells you ; and when
she runs to my father's land, on a height above the castle,
she will shake herself, and the bells will ring, and my father
will say, ' Brown Allree is in the land. And if the son of
a king or queen is there, bring him to me on your shoulders ;
but if it is the son of a poor man, let him come no
further.' "

He rose in the morning, and took the bridle that was in
the window, and went out and shook it ; and Brown Allree
came and put her head in it. He took the three loaves and

three bottles of ale, and went riding; and when he was riding she bent her head down to take hold of her feet with her mouth, in hopes he would speak in ignorance; but he spoke not a word during the time, and the mare at last spoke to him, and told him to dismount and give her her dinner. He gave her the sixpenny loaf toasted, and a bottle of ale to drink.

"Sit up now riding, and take good heed of yourself: there are three miles of fire I have to clear at a leap."

She cleared the three miles of fire at a leap, and asked if he were still riding, and he said he was. Then they went on, and she told him to dismount and give her a meal; and he did so, and gave her a sixpenny loaf and a bottle; she consumed them and said to him there were before them three miles of hill covered with steel thistles, and that she must clear it. She cleared the hill with a leap, and she asked him if he were still riding, and he said he was. They went on, and she went not far before she told him to give her a meal, and he gave her the bread and the bottleful. She went over three miles of sea with a leap, and she came then to the land of the King of France; she went up on a height above the castle, and she shook herself and neighed, and the bells rang; and the king said that it was Brown Allree was in the land.

"Go out," said he; "and if it is the son of a king or queen, carry him in on your shoulders; if it is not, leave him there."

They went out; and the stars of the son of a king were on his breast; they lifted him high on their shoulders and bore him in to the king. They passed the night cheerfully, playing and drinking, with sport and with diversion, till the whiteness of the day came upon the morrow morning.

Then the young king told the cause of his journey, and he asked the queen to give him counsel and good luck, and she told him everything he was to do.

"Go now," said she, "and take with you the best mare in the stable, and go to the door of Rough Niall of the Speckled Rock, and knock, and call on him to give you news of the death of Anshgayliacht and the sword of light: and let the horse's back be to the door, and apply the spurs, and away with you."

In the morning he did so, and he took the best horse from the stable and rode to the door of Niall, and turned the horse's back to the door, and demanded news of the death of Anshgayliacht and the sword of light; then he applied the spurs, and away with him. Niall followed him hard, and, as he was passing the gate, cut the horse in two. His wife was there with a dish of puddings and flesh, and she threw it in his eyes and blinded him, and said, "Fool! whatever kind of man it is that's mocking you, isn't that a fine condition you have got your father's horse into?"

On the morning of the next day Morraha rose, and took another horse from the stable, and went again to the door of Niall, and knocked and demanded news of the death of Anshgayliacht and the sword of light, and applied the spurs to the horse and away with him. Niall followed, and as Morraha was passing, the gate cut the horse in two and took half the saddle with him; but his wife met him and threw flesh in his eyes and blinded him.

On the third day, Morraha went again to the door of

Niall; and Niall followed him, and as he was passing the gate, cut away the saddle from under him and the clothes from his back. Then his wife said to Niall:

"The fool that's mocking you, is out yonder in the little currach, going home; and take good heed to yourself, and don't sleep one wink for three days."

For three days the little currach kept in sight, but then Niall's wife came to him and said:

"Sleep as much as you want now. He is gone."

He went to sleep, and there was heavy sleep on him, and Morraha went in and took hold of the sword that was on the bed at his head. And the sword thought to draw itself out of the hand of Morraha; but it failed. Then it gave a cry, and it wakened Niall, and Niall said it was a rude and rough thing to come into his house like that; and said Morraha to him:

"Leave your much talking, or I will cut the head off you. Tell me the news of the death of Anshgayliacht."

"Oh, you can have my head."

"But your head is no good to me; tell me the story."

"Oh," said Niall's wife, "you must get the story."

"Well," said Niall, "let us sit down together till I tell the story. I thought no one would ever get it; but now it will be heard by all."

THE STORY.

When I was growing up, my mother taught me the language of the birds; and when I got married, I used to be listening to their conversation; and I would be laughing; and my wife would be asking me what was the reason of my laughing, but I did not like to tell her, as women are always asking questions. We went out walking one fine morning, and the birds were arguing with one another. One of them said to another :

" Why should you be comparing yourself with me, when there is not a king nor knight that does not come to look at my tree ? "

" What advantage has your tree over mine, on which there are three rods of magic mastery growing ? "

When I heard them arguing, and knew that the rods were there, I began to laugh.

" Oh," asked my wife, " why are you always laughing ? I believe it is at myself you are jesting, and I'll walk with you no more."

" Oh, it is not about you I am laughing. It is because I understand the language of the birds."

Then I had to tell her what the birds were saying to one another ; and she was greatly delighted, and she asked me to go home, and she gave orders to the cook to have breakfast ready at six o'clock in the morning. I did not know why she was going out early, and breakfast was ready in the morning at the hour she appointed. She asked me to go out walking. I went with her. She went to the tree, and asked me to cut a rod for her.

" Oh, I will not cut it. Are we not better without it ? "

" I will not leave this until I get the rod, to see if there is any good in it."

I cut the rod and gave it to her. She turned from me and struck a blow on a stone, and changed it ; and she struck a second blow on me, and made of me a black raven, and she went home and left me after her. I thought she would come back ; she did not come, and I had to go into

a tree till morning. In the morning, at six o'clock, there
was a bellman out, proclaiming that every one who killed a
raven would get a fourpenny-bit. At last you could not
find man or boy without a gun, nor, if you were to walk
three miles, a raven that was not killed. I had to make

a nest in the top of the parlour chimney, and hide myself
all day till night came, and go out to pick up a bit to
support me, till I spent a month. Here she is herself to
say if it is a lie I am telling.

"It is not," said she.

Then I saw her out walking. I went up to her, and I

thought she would turn me back to my own shape, and she struck me with the rod and made of me an old white horse, and she ordered me to be put to a cart with a man, to draw stones from morning till night. I was worse off then. She spread abroad a report that I had died suddenly in my bed, and prepared a coffin, and waked and buried me. Then she had no trouble. But when I got tired I began to kill every one who came near me, and I used to go intc the haggard every night and destroy the stacks of corn ; and when a man came near me in the morning I would follow him till I broke his bones. Every one got afraid of me. When she saw I was doing mischief she came to meet me, and I thought she would change me. And she did change me, and made a fox of me. When I saw she was doing me every sort of damage I went away from her. I knew there was a badger's hole in the garden, and I went there till night came, and I made great slaughter among the geese and ducks. There she is herself to say if I am telling a lie.

" Oh ! you are telling nothing but the truth, only less than the truth."

When she had enough of my killing the fowl she came out into the garden, for she knew I was in the badger's hole. She came to me and made me a wolf. I had to be off, and go to an island, where no one at all would see me, and now and then I used to be killing sheep, for there were not many of them, and I was afraid of being seen and hunted; and so I passed a year, till a shepherd saw me among the sheep and a pursuit was made after me. And when the dogs came near me there was no place for me to escape to from them ; but I recognised the sign of the king among the men, and I made for him, and the king cried out to stop the hounds. I took a leap upon the front of the king's saddle, and the woman behind cried out, " My king and my lord, kill him, or he will kill you ! "

" Oh ! he will not kill me. He knew me ; he must be pardoned."

The king took me home with him, and gave orders I should be well cared for. I was so wise, when I got food, I would not eat one morsel until I got a knife and fork. The man told the king, and the king came to see if it was true, and I got a knife and fork, and I took the knife in one paw and the fork in the other, and I bowed to the king. The king gave orders to bring him drink, and it came ; and the king filled a glass of wine and gave it to me.

I took hold of it in my paw and drank it, and thanked the king.

" On my honour," said he, " it is some king or other has lost him, when he came on the island ; and I will keep him, as he is trained ; and perhaps he will serve us yet."

And this is the sort of king he was,—a king who had not a child living. Eight sons were born to him and three daughters, and they were stolen the same night they were born. No matter what guard was placed over them, the child would be gone in the morning. A twelfth child now came to the queen, and the king took me with him to watch the baby. The women were not satisfied with me.

" Oh," said the king, " what was all your watching ever good for ? One that was born to me I have not ; I will leave this one in the dog's care, and he will not let it go."

A coupling was put between me and the cradle, and when every one went to sleep I was watching till the person woke who attended in the daytime ; but I was there only two nights ; when it was near the day, I saw a hand coming down through the chimney, and the hand was so big that it took round the child altogether, and thought to take him away. I caught hold of the hand above the wrist, and as I was fastened to the cradle, I did not let go my hold till I cut the hand from the wrist, and there was a howl from the person without. I laid the hand in the cradle with the child, and as I was tired I fell asleep ; and when I awoke, I had neither child nor hand ; and I began to howl, and the king heard me, and he cried out that something was wrong with me, and he sent servants to see what was the matter with me, and when the messenger came he saw me covered with blood, and he could not see the child ; and he went to the king and told him the child was not to be got. The king came and saw the cradle coloured with the blood, and he cried out " where was the child gone ? " and every one said it was the dog had eaten it.

The king said : " It is not : loose him, and he will get the pursuit himself."

When I was loosed, I found the scent of the blood till I came to a door of the room in which the child was. I went back to the king and took hold of him, and went back again and began to tear at the door. The king followed me and asked for the key. The servant said it was in the room of the stranger woman. The king caused search to be made for her, and she was not to be found. " I will break the door," said the king, " as I can't get the key." The king

MORRAHA

broke the door, and I went in, and went to the trunk, and the king asked for a key to unlock it. He got no key, and he broke the lock. When he opened the trunk, the child and the hand were stretched side by side, and the child was asleep. The king took the hand and ordered a woman to come for the child, and he showed the hand to every one in the house. But the stranger woman was gone, and she did not see the king ;—and here she is herself to say if I am telling lies of her.

"Oh, it's nothing but the truth you have!"

The king did not allow me to be tied any more. He said there was nothing so much to wonder at as that I cut the hand off, as I was tied.

The child was growing till he was a year old. He was beginning to walk, and no one cared for him more than I did. He was growing till he was three, and he was running out every minute ; so the king ordered a silver chain to be put between me and the child, that he might not go away from me. I was out with him in the garden every day, and the king was as proud as the world of the child. He would be watching him everywhere we went, till the child grew so wise that he would loose the chain and get off. But one day that he loosed it I failed to find him ; and I ran into the house and searched the house, but there was no getting him for me. The king cried to go out and find the child, that had got loose from the dog. They went searching for him, but could not find him. When they failed altogether to find him, there remained no more favour with the king towards me, and every one disliked me, and I grew weak, for I did not get a morsel to eat half the time. When summer came, I said I would try and go home to my own country. I went away one fine morning, and I went swimming, and God helped me till I came home. I went into the garden, for I knew there was a place in the garden where I could hide myself, for fear my wife should see me. In the morning I saw her out walking, and the child with her, held by the hand. I pushed out to see the

child, and as he was looking about him everywhere, he saw me and called out, " I see my shaggy papa. Oh ! " said he ; " oh, my heart's love, my shaggy papa, come here till I see you ! "

I was afraid the woman would see me, as she was asking the child where he saw me, and he said I was up in a tree ; and the more the child called me, the more I hid myself.

The woman took the child home with her, but I knew he would be up early in the morning.

I went to the parlour-window, and the child was within, and he playing. When he saw me he cried out, "Oh! my heart's love, come here till I see you, shaggy papa." I broke the window and went in, and he began to kiss me. I saw the rod in front of the chimney, and I jumped up at the rod and knocked it down. "Oh! my heart's love, no one would give me the pretty rod," said he. I hoped he would strike me with the rod, but he did not. When I saw the time was short I raised my paw, and I gave him a scratch below the knee. "Oh! you naughty, dirty, shaggy papa, you have hurt me so much, I'll give you a blow of the rod." He struck me a light blow, and so I came back to my own shape again. When he saw a man standing before him he gave a cry, and I took him up in my arms. The servants heard the child. A maid came in to see what was the matter with him. When she saw me she gave a cry out of her, and she said, "Oh, if the master isn't come to life again!"

Another came in, and said it was he really. When the mistress heard of it, she came to see with her own eyes, for she would not believe I was there; and when she saw me she said she'd drown herself. But I said to her, "If you yourself will keep the secret, no living man will ever get the story from me until I lose my head." Here she is herself to say if I am telling the truth. "Oh, it's nothing but truth you are telling."

When I saw I was in a man's shape, I said I would take the child back to his father and mother, as I knew the grief they were in after him. I got a ship, and took the child with me; and as I journeyed I came to land on an island, and I saw not a living soul on it, only a castle dark and gloomy.   I went in to see was there any one in it.   There was no one but an old hag, tall and frightful, and she asked me, "What sort of person are you?"   I heard some one groaning in another room, and I said I was a doctor, and I asked her what ailed the person who was groaning.

"Oh," said she, "it is my son, whose hand has been bitten from his wrist by a dog."

I knew then that it was he who had taken the child from me, and I said I would cure him if I got a good reward.

"I have nothing; but there are eight young lads and three young women, as handsome as any one ever laid eyes on, and if you cure him I will give you them."

"Tell me first in what place his hand was cut from him?"

"Oh, it was out in another country, twelve years ago."

"Show me the way, that I may see him."

She brought me into a room, so that I saw him, and his arm was swelled up to the shoulder.   He asked me if I would cure him; and I said I would cure him if he would give me the reward his mother promised.

"Oh, I will give it; but cure me."

"Well, bring them out to me."

The hag brought them out of the room.   I said I should burn the flesh that was on his arm.   When I looked on him he was howling with pain.   I said that I would not leave him in pain long.   The wretch had only one eye in his forehead.   I took a bar of iron, and put it in the fire till it was red, and I said to the hag, "He will be howling at first, but will fall asleep presently, and do not wake him till he has slept as much as he wants. I will close the door when I am going out." I took the bar with me, and I stood over him, and I turned it across through his eye as far as I could. He began to bellow, and tried to catch me, but I was out and away, having closed the door. The hag asked me, " Why is he bellowing ? "

" Oh, he will be quiet presently, and will sleep for a good while, and I'll come again to have a look at him ; but bring me out the young men and the young women."

I took them with me, and I said to her, " Tell me where you got them."

" My son brought them with him, and they are all the children of one king."

I was well satisfied, and I had no wish for delay to get myself free from the hag, so I took them on board the ship, and the child I had myself. I thought the king might leave me the child I nursed myself ; but when I came to land, and all those young people with me, the king and queen were out walking. The king was very aged, and the queen aged likewise. When I came to converse with them, and the twelve with me, the king and queen began to cry. I asked, " Why are you crying ? "

" It is for good cause I am crying. As many children as these I should have, and now I am withered, grey, at the end of my life, and I have not one at all."

I told him all I went through, and I gave him the child in his hand, and " These are your other children who were stolen from you, whom I am giving to you safe. They are gently reared."

When the king heard who they were he smothered them

with kisses and drowned them with tears, and dried them with fine cloths silken and the hair of his own head, and so also did their mother, and great was his welcome for me, as it was I who found them all. The king said to me, " I will give you the last child, as it is you who have earned him best ; but you must come to my court every year, and the child with you, and I will share with you my possessions.

" I have enough of my own, and after my death I will leave it to the child."

I spent a time, till my visit was over, and I told the king all the troubles I went through, only I said nothing about my wife. And now you have the story.

And now when you go home, and the Slender Red Champion asks you for news of the death of Anshgayliacht and for the sword of light, tell him the way in which his brother was killed, and say you have the sword ; and he will ask the sword from you. Say you to him, " If I promised to bring it to you, I did not promise to bring it for you ; " and then throw the sword into the air and it will come back to me.

He went home, and he told the story of the death of Anshgayliacht to the Slender Red Champion, " And here," said he, " is the sword." The Slender Red Champion asked for the sword ; but he said : " If I promised to bring it to you, I did not promise to bring it for you ; " and he threw it into the air and it returned to Blue Niall.

The Story of the McAndrew Family

LONG time ago, in the County Mayo, there lived a rich man of the name of McAndrew. He owned cows and horses without number, not to mention ducks and geese and pigs; and his land extended as far as the eye could reach on the four sides of you.

McAndrew was a lucky man, the neighbours all said; but as for himself, when he looked on his seven big sons growing up like weeds and with scarcely any more sense, he felt sore enough, for of all the stupid omadhauns the seven McAndrew brothers were the stupidest.

When the youngest grew to be a man, the father built a house for each of them, and gave every one a piece of land and a few cows, hoping to make men of them before he died, for, as the old man said :

" While God spares my life, I'll be able to have an eye to them, and maybe they will learn from experience."

The seven young McAndrews were happy enough. Their fields were green, their cows were fat and sleek, and they thought they would never see a poor day.

All went well for a time, and the day of the Fair of Killalla was as fine a day as ever shone in Ireland, when the whole seven got ready to be off, bright and early, in the morning.

Each one of them drove before him three fine cows, and a finer herd, when they were all together, was never seen in the country far or near.

Now, there was a smart farmer, named O'Toole, whose fields were nearing on the McAndrews', and he had many a time set his heart on the fine cattle belonging to his easy-going neighbours; so when he saw them passing with their twenty-one cows he went out and hailed them.

"Where are ye going to, this fine morning ? "

" It's to the Fair of Killalla we're going, to sell these fine cows our father gave us," they all answered together.

" And are ye going to sell cows that the Evil Eye has long been set on ?   Oh, Con and Shamus, I would never belave it of ye, even if that spalpeen of a Pat would do such a thing; any one would think that the spirit of the good mother that bore ye would stretch out a hand and kape ye from committing such a mortal sin."

This O'Toole said to the three eldest, who stood trembling, while the four younger ones stuck their knuckles into their eyes and began to cry.

" Oh, indade, Mr. O'Toole, we never knew that the cows were under the Evil Eye.   How did ye find it out ?   Oh, sorra the day when such a fine lot of cattle should go to the bad," answered Con.

"Indade ye may well ask it, whin it's meself that was always a good neighbour and kept watch on auld Judy, the witch, when she used to stand over there laughing at the ravens flying over the cows. Do ye mind the time yer father spoke ugly to her down by the cross-roads? She never forgot it, and now yer twenty-one fine cows will never be worth the hides on their backs."

"Worra, worra, worra," roared the seven McAndrews, so loud that pretty Katie O'Toole bobbed her head out of the window, and the hindermost cows began to caper like mad.

"The spell has come upon them!" cried Shamus. "Oh! what'll we do? What'll we do?"

"Hould yer whist, man alive," said O'Toole. "I'm a good neighbour, as I said before, so to give ye a lift in the world I'll take the risk on meself and buy the cows from ye for the price of their hides. Sure no harm can be done to the hides for making leather, so I'll give ye a shilling apiece, and that's better than nothing. Twenty-one bright shillings going to the fair may make yer fortune."

It seemed neck or nothing with the McAndrews, and they accepted the offer, thanking O'Toole for his generosity, and helped him drive the cows into his field. Then they set off for the fair.

They had never been in a fair before, and when they saw the fine sights they forgot all about the cows, and only remembered that they had each a shilling to spend.

Every one knew the McAndrews, and soon a crowd gathered round them, praising their fine looks and telling them what a fine father they had to give them so much money, so that the seven omadhauns lost their heads entirely, and treated right and left until there wasn't a farthing left of the twenty-one shillings. Then they staggered home a little the worse for the fine whisky they drank with the boys.

It was a sorry day for old McAndrew when his seven sons came home without a penny of the price of their twenty-one fine cows, and he vowed he'd never give them any more.

So one day passed with another, and the seven young McAndrews were as happy as could be until the fine old father fell sick and died.

The eldest son came in for all the father had, so he felt like a lord. To see him strut and swagger was a sight to make a grum growdy laugh.

One day, to show how fine he could be, he dressed in his best, and with a purse filled with gold pieces started off for the market town.

When he got there, in he walked to a public-house, and called for the best of everything, and to make a fine fellow of himself he tripled the price of everything to the land-lord. As soon as he got through his eye suddenly caught sight of a little keg, all gilded over to look like gold, that hung outside the door for a sign. Con had never heeded it before, and he asked the landlord what it was.

Now the landlord, like many another, had it in mind that he might as well get all he could out of a McAndrew, and he answered quickly :

"You stupid omadhaun, don't you know what that is ? It's a mare's egg."

"And will a foal come out of it ? "

"Of course ; what a question to ask a dacent man ! "

" I niver saw one before," said the amazed McAndrew.

"Well, ye see one now, Con, and take a good look at it."

" Will ye sell it ? "

" Och, Con McAndrew, do ye think I want to sell that fine egg afther kaping it so long hung up there before the sun—when it is ready to hatch out a foal that will be worth twenty good guineas to me ? "

" I'll give ye twenty guineas for it," answered Con.

" Thin it's a bargain," said the landlord ; and he took down the keg and handed it to Con, who handed out the twenty guineas, all the money he had.

"Be careful of it, and carry it as aisy as ye can, and when ye get home hang it up in the sun."

Con promised, and set off home with his prize.

Near the rise of a hill he met his brothers.

"What have ye, Con ? "

" The most wonderful thing in the world—a mare's egg."

"Faith, what is it like ? " asked Pat, taking it from Con.

" Go aisy, can't ye ?   It's very careful ye have to be "

But the brothers took no heed to Con, and before one could say, " whist," away rolled the keg down the hill, while all seven ran after it ; but before any one could catch it, it rolled into a clump of bushes, and in an instant out hopped a hare.

"Bedad, there's the foal," cried Con, and all seven gave chase; but there was no use trying to catch a hare.

"That's the foinest foal that ever was, if he was five year old the devil himself could not catch him," Con said; and with that the seven omadhauns gave up the chase and went quietly home.

As I said before, every one had it in mind to get all he could out of the McAndrews. Every one said, "One man might as well have it as another, for they're bound to spend every penny they have."

So their money dwindled away; then a fine horse would go for a few bits of glass they took for precious stones, and by-and-by a couple of pigs or a pair of fine geese for a bit of ribbon to tie on a hat; and at last their land began to go.

One day Shamus was sitting by his fire-place warming himself, and to make a good fire he threw on a big heap of turf so that by-and-by it got roaring hot, and instead of feeling chilly as he had before, Shamus got as hot as a spare-rib on a spit. Just then in came his youngest brother.

"That's a great fire ye have here, Shamus."

"It is, indade, and too near it is to me ; run like a good boy to Giblin, the mason, and see if he can't move the chimney to the other side of the room."

The youngest McAndrew did as he was bid, and soon in came Giblin, the mason.

"Ye're in a sad plight, Shamus, roasting alive ; what can I do for ye ? "

"Can ye move the chimney over beyant ? "

"Faith, I can, but ye will have to move a bit; just go out for a walk with yer brother, and the job will be done when ye come back."

Shamus did as he was bid, and Giblin took the chair the omadhaun was sitting on and moved it away from the fire, and then sat down for a quiet laugh for himself and to consider on the price he'd charge for the job.

When Shamus came back, Giblin led him to the chair, saying :

"Now, isn't that a great deal better ? "

"Ye're a fine man, Giblin, and ye did it without making a bit of dirt ; what'll I give ye for so fine a job ? "

"If ye wouldn't mind, I'd like the meadow field nearing on mine. It's little enough for a job like that."

"It's yours and welcome, Giblin ; " and without another word the deed was drawn.

That was the finest of the McAndrew fields, and the only pasture land left to Shamus.

It was not long before it came about that first one and

then another lost the house he lived in, until all had to live together in the father's old place.

O'Toole and Giblin had encroached field by field, and there was nothing left but the old house and a strip of garden that none of them knew how to till.

It was hard times for the seven McAndrews, but they were happy and contented as long as they had enough to eat, and that they had surely, for the wives of the men who got away all their fine lands and cattle, had sore hearts when they saw their men enriched at the expense of the omadhauns, and every day, unbeknown to their husbands, they carried them meat and drink.

O'Toole and Giblin now had their avaricious eyes set on the house and garden, and they were on the watch for a chance to clutch them, when luck, or something worse, threw the chance in the way of O'Toole.

He was returning from town one day just in the cool of the afternoon, when he spied the seven brothers by the roadside, sitting in a circle facing each other.

"What may ye be doing here instead of earning yer salt, ye seven big sturks?"

"We're in a bad fix, Mr. O'Toole," answered Pat. "We can't get up."

"What's to hinder ye from getting up? I'd like to know."

"Don't ye see our feet are all here together in the middle, and not for the life of us can we each tell our own. You see if one of us gets up he don't know what pair of feet to take with him.'

O'Toole was never so ready to laugh before in his life, but he thought:

" Now's me chance to get the house and garden before Giblin, the mason, comes round ; " so he looked very grave and said : " I suppose it is hard to tell one man's feet from another's when they're all there in a heap, but I think I can help you as I have many a time before. It would be a sorry day for ye if ye did not have me for a neighbour. What will ye give me if I help you find yer feet ? "

" Anything, anything we have, so that we can get up from here," answered the whole seven together.

" Will ye give me the house and garden ? "

" Indade we will ; what good is a house and garden, if we have to sit here all the rest of our lives ? "

" Then it's a bargain," said O'Toole ; and with that he went over to the side of the road and pulled a good stout rod. Then he commenced to belabour the poor McAndrews over the heads, feet, shoulders, and any place he could get in a stroke, until with screeches of pain they all jumped up, every one finding his own feet, and away they ran.

So O'Toole got the last of the property of the McAndrews, and there was nothing left for them but to go and beg.

The Farmer of Liddesdale

HERE was in Liddesdale (in Morven) a Farmer who suffered great loss within the space of one year. In the first place, his wife and children died, and shortly after their death the Ploughman left him. The hiring-markets were then over, and there was no way of getting another ploughman in place of the one that left. When spring came his neighbours began ploughing ; but he had not a man to hold the plough, and he knew not what he should do. The time was passing, and he was therefore losing patience. At last he said to himself, in a fit of passion, that he would engage the first man that came his way, whoever he should be.

Shortly after that a man came to the house. The Farmer met him at the door, and asked him whither was he going, or what was he seeking ? He answered that he was a ploughman, and that he wanted an engagement. "I want a ploughman, and if we agree about the wages, I will engage thee. What dost thou ask from this day to the day when the crop will be gathered in ? " "Only as much of the corn when it shall be dry as I can carry with me in one burden-withe." "Thou shalt get that," said the Farmer, and they agreed.

Next morning the Farmer went out with the Ploughman, and showed him the fields which he had to plough. Before they returned, the Ploughman went to the wood, and having cut three stakes, came back with them, and placed one of them at the head of each one of the fields. After he had done that he said to the Farmer, "I will do the work now alone, and the ploughing need no longer give thee anxiety."

Having said this, he went home and remained idle all that day. The next day came, but he remained idle as on the day before. After he had spent a good while in that manner, the Farmer said to him that it was time for him to begin work now, because the spring was passing away, and the neighbours had half their work finished. He replied, " Oh, our land is not ready yet." " How dost thou think that ? " " Oh, I know it by the stakes."

If the delay of the Ploughman made the Farmer wonder, this answer made him wonder more. He resolved that he would keep his eye on him, and see what he was doing.

The Farmer rose early next morning, and saw the Ploughman going to the first field. When he reached the field, he pulled the stake at its end out of the ground, and put it to his nose. He shook his head and put the stake back in the ground. He then left the first field and went to the rest. He tried the stakes, shook his head, and returned home. In the dusk he went out the second time to the fields, tried the stakes, shook his head, and after putting them again in the ground, went home. Next morning he went out to the fields the third time. When he reached the first stake he pulled it out of the ground and put it to his nose as he did on the foregoing days. But no sooner had he done that than he threw the stake from him, and stretched away for the houses with all his might.

He got the horses, the withes, and the plough, and when he reached the end of the first field with them, he thrust the plough into the ground, and cried :

"My horses and my leather-traces, and mettlesome lads,
    The earth is coming up!"

He then began ploughing, kept at it all day at a terrible rate, and before the sun went down that night there was not a palm-breadth of the three fields which he had not ploughed, sowed, and harrowed. When the Farmer saw this he was exceedingly well pleased, for he had his work finished as soon as his neighbours.

The Ploughman was quick and ready to do everything that he was told, and so he and the Farmer agreed well until the harvest came. But on a certain day when the reaping was over, the Farmer said to him that he thought the corn was dry enough for putting in. The Ploughman tried a sheaf or two, and answered that it was not dry yet. But shortly after that day he said that it was now ready. " If it is," said the Farmer, " we better begin putting it in." " We will not until I get my share out of it first," said the Ploughman. He then went off to the wood, and in a short time returned, having in his hand a withe scraped and twisted. He stretched the withe on the field, and began to put the corn in it. He continued putting sheaf after sheaf in the withe until he had taken almost all the sheaves that were on the field. The Farmer asked of him what he meant? " Thou didst promise me as wages as much corn as I could carry with me in one burden-withe, and here I have it now," said the Ploughman, as he was shutting the withe.

The Farmer saw that he would be ruined by the Ploughman, and therefore said :

> " 'Twas in the Màrt I sowed,
> 'Twas in the Màrt I baked,
> 'Twas in the Màrt I harrowed.
> Thou Who hast ordained the three Màrts,
> Let not my share go in one burden-withe."

Instantly the withe broke, and it made a loud report, which echo answered from every rock far and near. Then the corn spread over the field, and the Ploughman went away in a white mist in the skies, and was seen no more.

The Greek Princess and the Young Gardener

HERE was once a king, but I didn't hear what country he was over, and he had one very beautiful daughter. Well, he was getting old and sickly, and the doctors found out that the finest medicine in the world for him was the apples of a tree that grew in the orchard just under his window. So you may be sure he had the tree well minded, and used to get the apples counted from the time they were the size of small marbles. One harvest, just as they were beginning to turn ripe, the king was awakened one night by the flapping of wings outside in the orchard ; and when he looked out, what did he see but a bird among the branches of his tree. Its feathers were so bright that they made a light all round them, and the minute it saw the king in his night-cap and night-shirt it picked off an apple, and flew away. "Oh, botheration to that thief of a gardener!" says the king, "this is a nice way he's watching my precious fruit."

He didn't sleep a wink the rest of the night ; and as soon as any one was stirring in the palace, he sent for the gardener, and abused him for his neglect.

"Please your Majesty !" says he, "not another apple you shall lose. My three sons are the best shots at the bow and arrow in the kingdom, and they and myself will watch in turn every night."

When the night came, the gardener's eldest son took his post in the garden, with his bow strung and his arrow between his fingers, and watched, and watched. But at the dead hour, the king, that was wide awake, heard the flapping of wings, and ran to the window. There was the bright bird in the tree, and the boy fast asleep, sitting with his back to the wall, and his bow on his lap.

"Rise, you lazy thief !" says the king, "there's the bird again, botheration to her !"

Up jumped the poor fellow ; but while he was fumbling with the arrow and the string, away was the bird with the nicest apple on the tree. Well, to be sure, how the king fumed and fretted, and how he abused the gardener and the boy, and what a twenty-four hours he spent till midnight came again !

He had his eye this time on the second son of the gardener ; but though he was up and lively enough when the clock began to strike twelve, it wasn't done with the last bang when he saw him stretched like one dead on the long grass, and saw the bright bird again, and heard the flap of her wings, and saw her carry away the third apple. The poor fellow woke with the roar the king let at him, and even was in time enough to let fly an arrow after the bird. He did not hit her, you may depend ; and though the king

was mad enough, he saw the poor fellows were under
pishtrogues, and could not help it.

Well, he had some hopes out of the youngest, for he
was a brave, active young fellow, that had everybody's good
word. There he was ready, and there was the king watching him, and talking to him at the first stroke of twelve.
At the last clang, the brightness coming before the bird
lighted up the wall and the trees, and the rushing of the
wings was heard as it flew into the branches ; but at the
same instant the crack of the arrow on her side might be
heard a quarter of a mile off. Down came the arrow and
a large bright feather along with it, and away was the bird,
with a screech that was enough to break the drum of your
ear. She hadn't time to carry off an apple ; and bedad,
when the feather was thrown up into the king's room it
was heavier than lead, and turned out to be the finest
beaten gold.

Well, there was great *cooramuch* made about the youngest
boy next day, and he watched night after night for a week,
but not a mite of a bird or bird's feather was to be seen,
and then the king told him to go home and sleep. Every
one admired the beauty of the gold feather beyond anything,
but the king was fairly bewitched. He was turning it
round and round, and rubbing it against his forehead and
his nose the live-long day ; and at last he proclaimed that
he'd give his daughter and half his kingdom to whoever
would bring him the bird with the gold feathers, dead or
alive.

The gardener's eldest son had great conceit of himself, and away he went to look for the bird. In the afternoon he sat down under a tree to rest himself, and eat a

bit of bread and cold meat that he had in his wallet, when up comes as fine a looking fox as you'd see in the burrow of Munfin. " Musha, sir," says he, " would you spare a bit of that meat to a poor body that's hungry ? "

" Well," says the other, " you must have the divil's own assurance, you common robber, to ask me such a question. Here's the answer," and he let fly at the *moddhereen rua.*

The arrow scraped from his side up over his back, as if he was made of hammered iron, and stuck in a tree a couple of perches off.

" Foul play," says the fox ; " but I respect your young brother, and will give a bit of advice. At nightfall you'll come into a village. One side of the street you'll see a large room lighted up, and filled with young men and women, dancing and drinking. The other side you'll see a house with no light, only from the fire in the front room, and no one near it but a man and his wife, and their child. Take a fool's advice, and get lodging there." With that he curled his tail over his crupper, and trotted off.

The boy found things as the fox said, but *begonies* he chose the dancing and drinking, and there we'll leave him. In a week's time, when they got tired at home waiting for him, the second son said he'd try his fortune, and off he set. He was just as ill-natured and foolish as his brother, and the same thing happened to him. Well, when a week was over, away went the youngest of all, and as sure as the hearth-money, he sat under the same tree, and pulled out his bread and meat, and the same fox came up and saluted him. Well, the young fellow shared his dinner with the *moddhereen,* and he wasn't long beating about the bush, but told the other he knew all about his business.

" I'll help you," says he, " if I find you're biddable.   So just at nightfall you'll come into a village. . . . . Good-bye till to-morrow."

It was just as the fox said, but the boy took care not to go near dancer, drinker, fiddler, or piper.   He got welcome in the quiet house to supper and bed, and was on his journey next morning before the sun was the height of the trees.

He wasn't gone a quarter of a mile when he saw the fox coming out of a wood that was by the roadside.

" Good-morrow, fox," says one.

" Good-morrow, sir," says the other.

" Have you any notion how far you have to travel till you find the golden bird ? "

" Dickens a notion have I ;—how could I ? "

" Well, I have.   She's in the King of Spain's palace, and that's a good two hundred miles off."

" Oh, dear ! we'll be a week going."

" No, we won't.   Sit down on my tail, and we'll soon make the road short."

" Tail, indeed ! that 'ud be the droll saddle, my poor *moddhereen*."

" Do as I tell you, or I'll leave you to yourself."

Well, rather than vex him he sat down on the tail that was spread out level like a wing, and away they went like thought.   They overtook the wind that was before them, and the wind that came after didn't overtake them.   In the afternoon, they stopped in a wood near the King of Spain's palace, and there they stayed till nightfall.

" Now," says the fox, " I'll go before you to make the minds of the guards easy, and you'll have nothing to do but go from lighted hall to another lighted hall till you find the golden bird in the last. If you have a head on you, you'll bring himself and his cage outside the door, and no one then can lay hands on him or you. If you haven't a head I can't help you, nor no one else." So he went over to the gates.

In a quarter of an hour the boy followed, and in the first hall he passed he saw a score of armed guards standing upright, but all dead asleep. In the next he saw a dozen, and in the next half a dozen, and in the next three, and in the room beyond that there was no guard at all, nor lamp, nor candle, but it was as bright as day ; for there was the golden bird in a common wood and wire cage, and on the table were the three apples turned into solid gold.

On the same table was the most lovely golden cage eye ever beheld, and it entered the boy's head that it would be a thousand pities not to put the precious bird into it, the common cage was so unfit for her. Maybe he thought of the money it was worth ; anyhow he made the exchange, and he had soon good reason to be sorry for it. The instant the shoulder of the bird's wing touched the golden wires, he let such a *squawk* out of him as was enough to break all the panes of glass in the windows, and at the same minute the three men, and the half-dozen, and the dozen, and the score men, woke up and clattered their swords and spears, and surrounded the poor boy, and jibed, and cursed, and swore at home, till he didn't know whether it's his foot or head he was standing on. They called the king, and told him what happened, and he put on a very grim face. " It's on a gibbet you ought to be this moment," says he, " but I'll give you a chance of your life, and of the golden bird, too. I lay you under prohibitions, and restrictions, and death, and destruction, to go and bring me the King of *Morōco's* bay filly that outruns the wind, and leaps over the walls of castle-bawns. When you fetch

her into the bawn of this palace, you must get the golden bird, and liberty to go where you please."

Out passed the boy, very down-hearted, but as he went along, who should come out of a brake but the fox again.

"Ah, my friend," says he, "I was right when I suspected you hadn't a head on you; but I won't rub your hair again' the grain. Get on my tail again, and when we come to the King of Morōco's palace, we'll see what we can do."

So away they went like thought. The wind that was before them they would overtake; the wind that was behind them would not overtake them.

Well, the nightfall came on them in a wood near the palace, and says the fox, " I'll go and make things easy for you at the stables, and when you are leading out the filly, don't let her touch the door, nor doorposts, nor anything but the ground, and that with her hoofs; and if you haven't a head on you once you are in the stable, you'll be worse off than before."

So the boy delayed for a quarter of an hour, and then he went into the big bawn of the palace. There were two rows of armed men reaching from the gate to the stable, and every man was in the depth of deep sleep, and through them went the boy till he got into the stable. There was the filly, as handsome a beast as ever stretched leg, and there was one stable-boy with a currycomb in his hand, and another with a bridle, and another with a sieve of oats, and another with an armful of hay, and all as if they were cut out of stone. The filly was the only live thing in the place except himself. She had a common wood and leather saddle on her back, but a golden saddle with the nicest work on it was hung from the post, and he thought it the greatest pity not to put it in place of the other. Well, I believe there was some *pishrogues* over it for a saddle; anyhow, he took off the other, and put the gold one in its place.

Out came a squeal from the filly's throat when she felt the strange article, that might be heard from Tombrick to

Bunclody, and all as ready were the armed men and the stable-boys to run and surround the *omadhan* of a boy, and the King of Moroco was soon there along with the rest, with a face on him as black as the sole of your foot. After he stood enjoying the abuse the poor boy got from everybody for some time, he says to him, " You deserve high hanging for your impudence, but I'll give you a chance for your life and the filly, too. I lay on you all sorts of prohibitions, and restrictions, and death, and destruction to go bring me Princess Golden Locks, the King of Greek's daughter. When you deliver her into my hand, you may have the ' daughter of the wind,' and welcome. Come in and take your supper and your rest, and be off at the flight of night."

The poor boy was down in the mouth, you may suppose, as he was walking away next morning, and very much ashamed when the fox looked up in his face after coming out of the wood.

" What a thing it is," says he, " not to have a head when a body wants it worst ; and here we have a fine long journey before us to the King of Greek's palace. The worse luck now, the same always. Here, get on my tail, and we'll be making the road shorter."

So he sat on the fox's tail, and swift as thought they went. The wind that was before them they would overtake it, the wind that was behind them would not overtake them, and in the evening they were eating their bread and cold meat in the wood near the castle.

" Now," says the fox, when they were done, " I'll go before you to make things easy. Follow me in a quarter of an hour. Don't let Princess Golden Locks touch the

jambs of the doors with her hands, or hair, or clothes, and
if you're asked any favour, mind how you answer. Once
she's outside the door, no one can take her from you."

Into the palace walked the boy at the proper time, and
there were the score, and the dozen, and the half-dozen,
and the three guards all standing up or leaning on their
arms, and all dead asleep, and in the farthest room of all
was the Princess Golden Locks, as lovely as Venus herself.
She was asleep in one chair, and her father, the King of
Greek, in another. He stood before her for ever so long
with the love sinking deeper into his heart every minute,
till at last he went down on one knee, and took her darling
white hand in his hand, and kissed it.

When she opened her eyes, she was a little frightened,
but I believe not very angry, for the boy, as I call him, was
a fine handsome young fellow, and all the respect and love
that ever you could think of was in his face. She asked
him what he wanted, and he stammered, and blushed, and
began his story six times, before she understood it.

"And would you give me up to that ugly black King of
Moroco ? " says she.

" I am obliged to do so," says he, " by prohibitions, and
restrictions, and death, and destruction, but I'll have his life
and free you, or lose my own. If I can't get you for my
wife, my days on the earth will be short."

" Well," says she, " let me take leave of my father at
any rate."

" Ah, I can't do that," says he, " or they'd all waken,
and myself would be put to death, or sent to some task
worse than any I got yet."

But she asked leave at any rate to kiss the old man ;

that wouldn't waken him, and then she'd go.   How could
he refuse her, and his heart tied up in every curl of her
hair ?   But, bedad, the moment her lips touched her father's,
he let a cry, and every one of the score, the dozen guards
woke up, and clashed their arms, and were going to make
gibbets of the foolish boy.

But the king ordered them to hold their hands, till he'd
be *insensed* of what it was all about, and when he heard the
boy's story he gave him a chance for his life.

"There is," says he, "a great heap of clay in front of
the palace, that won't let the sun shine on the walls in the
middle of summer.   Every one that ever worked at it found
two shovelfuls added to it for every one they threw away.
Remove it, and I'll let my daugher go with you.   If you're
the man I suspect you to be, I think she'll be in no danger
of being wife to that yellow *Molott*."

Early next morning was the boy tackled to his work,
and for every shovelful he flung away two came back on
him, and at last he could hardly get out of the heap that
gathered round him.   Well, the poor fellow scrambled out
some way, and sat down on a sod, and he'd have cried
only for the shame of it.   He began at it in ever so many
places, and one was still worse than the other, and in the
heel of the evening, when he was sitting with his head
between his hands, who should be standing before him but
the fox.

"Well, my poor fellow," says he, "you're low enough.
Go in : I won't say anything to add to your trouble.   Take
your supper and your rest : to-morrow will be a new
day."

"How is the work going off ? " says the king, when they
were at supper.

THE GREEK PRINCESS

The Greek Princess

" Faith, your Majesty," says the poor boy, " it's not going off, but coming on it is. I suppose you'll have the trouble of digging me out at sunset to-morrow, and waking me."

" I hope not," says the princess, with a smile on her kind face ; and the boy was as happy as anything the rest of the evening.

He was wakened up next morning with voices shouting, and bugles blowing, and drums beating, and such a hulli-bulloo he never heard in his life before. He ran out to see what was the matter, and there, where the heap of clay was the evening before, were soldiers, and servants, and lords, and ladies, dancing like mad for joy that it was gone.

" Ah, my poor fox ! " says he to himself, "this is your work."

Well, there was little delay about his return. The king was going to send a great retinue with the princess and himself, but he wouldn't let him take the trouble.

" I have a friend," says he, "that will bring us both to the King of Morōco's palace in a day, d—— fly away with him ! "

There was great crying when she was parting from her father.

" Ah ! " says he, " what a lonesome life I'll have now ! Your poor brother in the power of that wicked witch, and kept away from us, and now you taken from me in my old age ! "

Well, they both were walking on through the wood, and he telling her how much he loved her ; out walked the fox from behind a brake, and in a short time he and she were sitting on the brush, and holding one another fast for fear of slipping off, and away they went like thought. The wind that was before them they would overtake it, and in the evening he and she were in the big bawn of the King of Morōco's castle.

"Well," says he to the boy, "you've done your duty well; bring out the bay filly. I'd give the full of the bawn of such fillies, if I had them, for this handsome princess. Get on your steed, and here is a good purse of guineas for the road."

"Thank you," says he. "I suppose you'll let me shake hands with the princess before I start."

"Yes, indeed, and welcome."

Well, he was some little time about the hand-shaking, and before it was over he had her fixed snug behind him; and while you could count three, he, and she, and the filly were through all the guards, and a hundred perches away. On they went, and next morning they were in the wood near the King of Spain's palace, and there was the fox before them.

"Leave your princess here with me," says he, "and go get the golden bird and the three apples. If you don't bring us back the filly along with the bird, I must carry you both home myself."

Well, when the King of Spain saw the boy and the filly in the bawn, he made the golden bird, and the golden cage, and the golden apples be brought out and handed to him, and was very thankful and very glad of his prize. But the boy could not part with the nice beast without petting it and rubbing it; and while no one was expecting such a thing, he was up on its back, and through the guards, and a hundred perches away, and he wasn't long till he came to where he left his princess and the fox.

They hurried away till they were safe out of the King of Spain's land, and then they went on easier; and if I was to tell you all the loving things they said to one another, the story wouldn't be over till morning. When they were passing the village of the dance house, they found his two brothers begging, and they brought them along. When they came to where the fox appeared first, he begged the young man to cut off his head and his tail. He would not do it for him ; he shivered at the very thought, but the eldest brother was ready enough. The head and tail vanished with the blows, and the body changed into the finest young man you could see, and who was he but the princess's brother that was bewitched. Whatever joy they had before, they had twice as much now, and when they arrived at the palace bonfires were set blazing, oxes roasting, and puncheons of wine put out in the lawn.

The young Prince of Greece was married to the king's daughter, and the prince's sister to the gardener's son. He and she went a shorter way back to her father's house, with many attendants, and the king was so glad of the golden bird and the golden apples, that he had sent a waggon full of gold and a waggon full of silver along with them.

The Russet Dog

H, he's a rare clever fellow, is the Russet Dog, the Fox, I suppose you call him. Have you ever heard the way he gets rid of his fleas? He hunts about and he hunts about till he finds a lock of wool: then he takes it in his mouth, and down he goes to the river and turns his tail to the stream, and goes in backwards. And as the water comes up to his haunches the little fleas come forward, and the more he dips into the river the more they come forward, till at last he has got nothing but his snout and the lock of wool above water; then the little fleas rush into his snout and into the lock of wool. Down he dips his nose, and as soon as he feels his nose free of them, he lets go the lock of wool, and so he is free of his fleas. Ah, but that is nothing to the way in which he catches ducks for his dinner. He will gather some heather, and put his head in the midst of it, and then will slip down stream to the place where the ducks are swimming, for all the world like a piece of floating heather. Then he lets go, and—gobble, gobble, gobble, till not a duck is left alive. And he is as brave as he is clever. It is said that once he found the bagpipes lying all alone, and being very hungry began to gnaw at them : but as soon as he made a hole in the bag, out came a squeal. Was the Russet Dog afraid ? Never a bit : all he said was : " Here's music with my dinner."

Now a Russet Dog had noticed for some days a family of wrens, off which he wished to dine. He might have been satisfied with one, but he was determined to have the whole lot—father and eighteen sons—but all so like that he could not tell one from the other, or the father from the children.

" It is no use to kill one son," he said to himself, " because the old cock will take warning and fly away with the seventeen. I wish I knew which is the old gentleman."

He set his wits to work to find out, and one day seeing them all threshing in a barn, he sat down to watch them ; still he could not be sure.

" Now I have it," he said ; " well done the old man's stroke ! He hits true," he cried.

" Oh ! " replied the one he suspected of being the head of the family, " if you had seen my grandfather's strokes, you might have said that."

The sly fox pounced on the cock, ate him up in a trice, and then soon caught and disposed of the eighteen sons, all flying in terror about the barn.

For a long time a Tod-hunter had been very anxious to catch our friend the fox, and had stopped all the earths

in cold weather. One evening he fell asleep in his hut ;
and when he opened his eyes he saw the fox sitting very
demurely at the side of the fire. It had entered by the
hole under the door provided for the convenience of the
dog, the cat, the pig, and the hen.

"Oh! ho!" said the Tod-hunter, "now I have you."
And he went and sat down at the hole to prevent Reynard's escape.

"Oh! ho!" said the fox, "I will soon make that stupid

fellow get up." So he found the man's shoes, and putting
them into the fire, wondered if that would make the
enemy move.

"I shan't get up for that, my fine gentleman," cried the
Tod-hunter.

Stockings followed the shoes, coat and trousers shared
the same fate, but still the man sat over the hole. At
last the fox having set the bed and bedding on fire, put
a light to the straw on which his jailer lay, and it blazed
up to the ceiling.

"No! that I cannot stand," shouted the man, jumping up; and the fox, taking advantage of the smoke and confusion, made good his exit.

But Master Rory did not always have it his own way. One day he met a cock, and they began talking.

"How many tricks canst thou do?" said the fox.

"Well," said the cock, "I could do three; how many canst thou do thyself?"

"I could do three score and thirteen," said the fox.

"What tricks canst thou do?" said the cock.

"Well," said the fox, "my grandfather used to shut one eye and give a great shout."

" I could do that myself," said the cock.

" Do it," said the fox. And the cock shut one eye and crowed as loud as ever he could, but he shut the eye that was next the fox, and the fox gripped him by the neck and ran away with him. But the wife to whom the cock belonged saw him and cried out, "Let go the cock ; he's mine."

" Say, 'Oh sweet-tongued singer, it is my own cock,' wilt thou not ?" said the cock to the fox.

Then the fox opened his mouth to say as the cock did, and he dropped the cock, and he sprung up on the top of a house, and shut one eye and gave a loud crow.

But it was through that very fox that Master Wolf lost his tail. Have you never heard about that ?

One day the wolf and the fox were out together, and they stole a dish of crowdie. Now in those days the wolf was the biggest beast of the two, and he had a long tail like a greyhound and great teeth.

The fox was afraid of him, and did not dare to say a word when the wolf ate the most of the crowdie, and left only a little at the bottom of the dish for him, but he determined to punish him for it ; so the next night when they were out together the fox pointed to the image of the moon in a pool left in the ice, and said :

" I smell a very nice cheese, and there it is, too."

" And how will you get it ?" said the wolf.

" Well, stop you here till I see if the farmer is asleep, and if you keep your tail on it, nobody will see you or know that it is there. Keep it steady. I may be some time coming back."

So the wolf lay down and laid his tail on the moonshine

in the ice, and kept it for an hour till it was fast.   Then
the fox, who had been watching, ran in to the farmer and
said : " The wolf is there ; he will eat up the children—
the wolf ! the wolf ! "

Then the farmer and his wife came out with sticks to
kill the wolf, but the wolf ran off leaving his tail behind
him, and that's why the wolf is stumpy-tailed to this day,
though the fox has a long brush.

One day shortly after this Master Rory chanced to see
a fine cock and fat hen, off which he wished to dine, but at
his approach they both jumped up into a tree.   He did
not lose heart, but soon began to make talk with them,
inviting them at last to go a little way with him.

" There was no danger," he said, " nor fear of his hurting
them, for there was peace between men and beasts, and
among all animals."

At last after much parleying the cock said to the hen,
" My dear, do you not see a couple of hounds coming across
the field ? "

" Yes," said the hen, " and they will soon be here."

" If that is the case, it is time I should be off," said the
sly fox, " for I am afraid these stupid hounds may not
have heard of the peace."

And with that he took to his heels and never drew
breath till he reached his den.

Now Master Rory had not finished with his friend the
wolf.   So he went round to see him when his stump got
better.

" It is lucky you are," he said to the wolf.   " How much
better you will be able to run now you haven't got all
that to carry behind you."

"Away from me, traitor!" said the wolf.

But Master Rory said : "Is it a traitor I am, when all I have come to see you for is to tell you about a keg of butter I have found ? "

After much grumbling the wolf agreed to go with Master Rory.

So the Russet Dog and the wild dog, the fox and the wolf, were going together ; and they went round about the sea-shore, and they found the keg of butter, and they buried it.

On the morrow the fox went out, and when he returned in he said that a man had come to ask him to a baptism. He arrayed himself in excellent attire, and he went away, and where should he go but to the butter keg; and when he came home the wolf asked him what the child's name was ; and he said it was HEAD OFF.

On the morrow he said that a man had sent to ask him to a baptism, and he reached the keg and he took out about half.   The wolf asked when he came home what the child's name was.

"Well," said he, "it is a queer name that I myself would not give to my child, if I had him; it is HALF AND HALF."

On the morrow he said that there was a man there came to ask him to a baptism again ; off he went and he reached the keg, and he ate it all up.   When he came home the wolf asked him what the child's name was, and he said it was ALL GONE.

On the morrow he said to the wolf that they ought to bring the keg home.   They went, and when they reached the keg there was not a shadow of the butter in it.

"Well, thou wert surely coming here to watch this, though I was not," quoth the fox.

The other one swore that he had not come near it.

"Thou needst not be swearing that thou didst not come here; I know that thou didst come, and that it was thou that took it out; but I will know it from thee when thou goest home, if it was thou that ate the butter," said the fox.

Off they went, and when they got home he hung the wolf by his hind legs, with his head dangling below him, and he had a dab of the butter and he put it under the wolf's mouth, as if it was out of the wolf's belly that it came.

"Thou red thief!" said he, "I said before that it was thou that ate the butter."

They slept that night, and on the morrow when they rose the fox said :

"Well, then, it is silly for ourselves to be starving to death in this way merely for laziness; we will go to a town-land, and we will take a piece of land in it."

They reached the town-land, and the man to whom it belonged gave them a piece of land the worth of seven Saxon pounds.

It was oats that they set that year, and they reaped it and they began to divide it.

"Well, then," said the fox, "wouldst thou rather have the root or the tip? thou shalt have thy choice."

"I'd rather the root," said the wolf.

Then the fox had fine oaten bread all the year, and the other one had fodder.

On the next year they set a crop; and it was potatoes that they set, and they grew well.

"Which wouldst thou like best, the root or the crop this year?" said the fox.

"Indeed, thou shalt not take the twist out of me any more; I will have the top this year," quoth the wolf.

"Good enough, my hero," said the fox.

Thus the wolf had the potato tops, and the fox the potatoes. But the wolf used to keep stealing the potatoes from the fox.

"Thou hadst best go yonder, and read the name that I have in the hoofs of the grey mare," quoth the fox.

Away went the wolf, and he begun to read the name; and on a time of these times the white mare drew up her leg, and she broke the wolf's head.

"Oh!" said the fox, "it is long since I heard my name. Better to catch geese than to read books."

He went home, and the wolf was not troubling him any more.

But the Russet Dog found his match at last, as I shall tell you.

One day the fox was once going over a loch, and there met him a little bonnach, and the fox asked him where he was going. The little bonnach told him he was going to such a place.

"And whence camest thou?" said the fox.

"I came from Geeogan, and I came from Cooaigean, and I came from the slab of the bonnach stone, and I came from the eye of the quern, and I will come from thee if I may," quoth the little bonnach.

"Well, I myself will take thee over on my back," said the fox.

"Thou'lt eat me, thou'lt eat me," quoth the little bonnach.

"Come then on the tip of my tail," said the fox.

"Oh no! I will not; thou wilt eat me," said the little bonnach.

"Come into my ear," said the fox.

"I will not go; thou wilt eat me," said the little bonnach.

"Come into my mouth," said the fox.

"Thou wilt eat me that way at all events," said the little bonnach.

"Oh no, I will not eat thee," said the fox. "When I am swimming I cannot eat anything at all."

He went into the fox's mouth.

"Oh! ho!" said the fox, "I may do my own pleasure on thee now. It was long ago said that a hard morsel is no good in the mouth."

The fox ate the little bonnach. Then he went to a loch, and he caught hold of a duck that was in it, and he ate that.

He went up to a hillside, and he began to stroke his sides on the hill.

"Oh, king! how finely a bullet would spank upon my rib just now."

Who was listening but a hunter.

"Ill try that upon thee directly," said the hunter.

"Bad luck to this place," quoth the fox, "in which a creature dares not say a word in fun that is not taken in earnest."

The hunter put a bullet in his gun, and he fired at him and killed him, and that was the end of the Russet Dog.

Smallhead and the King's Sons

ONG ago there lived in Erin a woman who married a man of high degree and had one daughter. Soon after the birth of the daughter the husband died.

The woman was not long a widow when she married a second time, and had two daughters. These two daughters hated their half-sister, thought she was not so wise as another, and nicknamed her Smallhead. When the elder of the two sisters was fourteen years old their father died. The mother was in great grief then, and began to pine away. She used to sit at home in the corner and never left the house. Smallhead was kind to her mother, and the mother was fonder of her eldest daughter than of the other two, who were ashamed of her.

At last the two sisters made up in their minds to kill their mother. One day, while their half-sister was gone, they put the mother in a pot, boiled her, and threw the bones outside. When Smallhead came home there was no sign of the mother.

"Where is my mother?" asked she of the other two.

"She went out somewhere. How should we know where she is?"

"Oh, wicked girls! you have killed my mother," said Smallhead.

Smallhead wouldn't leave the house now at all, and the sisters were very angry.

"No man will marry either one of us," said they, "if he sees our fool of a sister."

Since they could not drive Smallhead from the house they made up their minds to go away themselves. One fine morning they left home unknown to their half-sister and travelled on many miles. When Smallhead discovered that her sisters were gone she hurried after them and never stopped till she came up with the two. They had to go home with her that day, but they scolded her bitterly.

The two settled then to kill Smallhead, so one day they took twenty needles and scattered them outside in a pile of straw. "We are going to that hill beyond," said they, "to stay till evening, and if you have not all the needles that are in that straw outside gathered and on the tables before us, we'll have your life."

Away they went to the hill. Smallhead sat down, and was crying bitterly when a short grey cat walked in and spoke to her.

"Why do you cry and lament so?" asked the cat.

"My sisters abuse me and beat me," answered Smallhead. " This morning they said they would kill me in the evening unless I had all the needles in the straw outside gathered before them."

" Sit down here," said the cat, " and dry your tears."

The cat soon found the twenty needles and brought them to Smallhead. " Stop there now," said the cat, "and listen to what I tell you. I am your mother ; your sisters killed me and destroyed my body, but don't harm them ; do them good, do the best you can for them, save them : obey my words and it will be better for you in the end."

The cat went away for herself, and the sisters came home in the evening. The needles were on the table before them. Oh, but they were vexed and angry when they saw the twenty needles, and they said some one was helping their sister !

One night when Smallhead was in bed and asleep they started away again, resolved this time never to return. Smallhead slept till morning. When she saw that the sisters were gone she followed, traced them from place to place, inquired here and there day after day, till one evening some person told her that they were in the house of an old hag, a terrible enchantress, who had one son and three daughters : that the house was a bad place to be in, for the old hag had more power of witchcraft than any one and was very wicked.

Smallhead hurried away to save her sisters, and facing the house knocked at the door, and asked lodgings for God's sake.

" Oh, then," said the hag, " it is hard to refuse any one lodgings, and besides on such a wild, stormy night.

I wonder if you are anything to the young ladies who
came the way this evening ? "

The two sisters heard this and were angry enough
that Smallhead was in it, but they said nothing, not
wishing the old hag to know their relationship. After
supper the hag told the three strangers to sleep in a room
on the right side of the house.   When her own daughters
were going to bed Smallhead saw her tie a ribbon around
the neck of each one of them, and heard her say : " Do
you sleep in the left-hand bed."   Smallhead hurried and
said to her sisters : " Come quickly, or I'll tell the woman
who you are."

They took the bed in the left-hand room and were in it
before the hag's daughters came.

" Oh," said the daughers, " the other bed is as good.'
So they took the bed in the right-hand room.   When
Smallhead knew that the hag's daughters were asleep she
rose, took the ribbons off their necks, and put them on
her sister's necks and on her own.   She lay awake and
watched them.   After a while she heard the hag say to her
son :

" Go, now, and kill the three girls ; they have the
clothes and money."

" You have killed enough in your life and so let these
go," said the son.

But the old woman would not listen.   The boy rose up,
fearing his mother, and taking a long knife, went to the
right-hand room and cut the throats of the three girls without ribbons.   He went to bed then for himself, and when
Smallhead found that the old hag was asleep she roused
her sisters, told what had happened, made them dress

THE BRIDGE OF BLOOD

quickly and follow her. Believe me, they were willing and glad to follow her this time.

The three travelled briskly and came soon to a bridge, called at that time "The Bridge of Blood." Whoever had killed a person could not cross the bridge. When the three girls came to the bridge the two sisters stopped : they could not go a step further. Smallhead ran across and went back again.

"If I did not know that you killed our mother," said she, "I might know it now, for this is the Bridge of Blood."

She carried one sister over the bridge on her back and then the other. Hardly was this done when the hag was at the bridge.

"Bad luck to you, Smallhead!" said she, "I did not know that it was you that was in it last evening. You have killed my three daughters."

"It wasn't I that killed them, but yourself," said Smallhead.

The old hag could not cross the bridge, so she began to curse, and she put every curse · on Smallhead that she could remember. The sisters travelled on till they came to a King's castle. They heard that two servants were needed in the castle.

"Go now," said Smallhead to the two sisters, "and ask for service. Be faithful and do well. You can never go back by the road you came."

The two found employment at the King's castle. Smallhead took lodgings in the house of a blacksmith near by.

"I should be glad to find a place as kitchen-maid in the castle," said Smallhead to the blacksmith's wife.

"I will go to the castle and find a place for you if I can," said the woman.

The blacksmith's wife found a place for Smallhead as kitchen-maid in the castle, and she went there next day.

"I must be careful," thought Smallhead, "and do my best. I am in a strange place. My two sisters are here in the King's castle. Who knows, we may have great fortune yet."

She dressed neatly and was cheerful. Every one liked her, liked her better than her sisters, though they were beautiful. The King had two sons, one at home and the other abroad. Smallhead thought to herself one day: "It is time for the son who is here in the castle to marry. I will speak to him the first time I can." One day she saw him alone in the garden, went up to him, and said:

"Why are you not getting married, it is high time for you?"

He only laughed and thought she was too bold, but then thinking that she was a simple-minded girl who wished to be pleasant, he said:

"I will tell you the reason: My grandfather bound my father by an oath never to let his oldest son marry until he could get the Sword of Light, and I am afraid that I shall be long without marrying."

"Do you know where the Sword of Light is, or who has it?" asked Smallhead.

"I do," said the King's son, "an old hag who has great power and enchantment, and she lives a long distance from this, beyond the Bridge of Blood. I cannot go there myself, I cannot cross the bridge, for I have killed men in battle. Even if I could cross the bridge I would not go, for many is the King's son that hag has destroyed or enchanted."

"Suppose some person were to bring the Sword of Light, and that person a woman, would you marry her?"

"I would, indeed," said the King's son.

"If you promise to marry my elder sister I will strive to bring the Sword of Light."

"I will promise most willingly," said the King's son.

Next morning early, Smallhead set out on her journey. Calling at the first shop she bought a stone weight of salt, and went on her way, never stopping or resting till she reached the hag's house at nightfall. She climbed to the gable, looked down, and saw the son making a great pot of stirabout for his mother, and she hurrying him. "I am as hungry as a hawk!" cried she.

Whenever the boy looked away, Smallhead dropped salt down, dropped it when he was not looking, dropped it till she had the whole stone of salt in the stirabout. The old hag waited and waited till at last she cried out: "Bring the stirabout. I am starving! Bring the pot. I will eat from the pot. Give the milk here as well."

The boy brought the stirabout and the milk, the old woman began to eat, but the first taste she got she spat out and screamed: "You put salt in the pot in place of meal!"

"I did not, mother."

"You did, and it's a mean trick that you played on me. Throw this stirabout to the pig outside and go for water to the well in the field."

"I cannot go," said the boy, "the night is too dark; I might fall into the well."

"You must go and bring the water; I cannot live till morning without eating."

"I am as hungry as yourself," said the boy, "but how can I go to the well without a light? I will not go unless you give me a light."

"If I give you the Sword of Light there is no knowing who may follow you; maybe that devil öf a Smallhead is outside."

But sooner than fast till morning the old hag gave the Sword of Light to her son, warning him to take good care of it. He took the Sword of Light and went out. As he saw no one when he came to the well he left the sword on the top of the steps going down to the water, so as to have good light. He had not gone down many steps when Smallhead had the sword, and away she ran over hills, dales, and valleys towards the Bridge of Blood.

The boy shouted and screamed with all his might. Out ran the hag. "Where is the sword?" cried she.

"Some one took it from the step."

Off rushed the hag, following the light, but she didn't come near Smallhead till she was over the bridge.

"Give me the Sword of Light, or bad luck to you," cried the hag.

"Indeed, then, I will not; I will keep it, and bad luck to yourself," answered Smallhead.

On the following morning she walked up to the King's son and said:

"I have the Sword of Light; now will you marry my sister?"

"I will," said he.

The King's son married Smallhead's sister and got the

Sword of Light. Smallhead stayed no longer in the kitchen
—the sister didn't care to have her in kitchen or parlour.

The King's second son came home. He was not long
in the castle when Smallhead said to herself, " Maybe he
will marry my second sister."

She saw him one day in the garden, went toward him ;
he said something, she answered, then asked : " Is it not
time for you to be getting married like your brother ? "

" When my grandfather was dying," said the young
man, " he bound my father not to let his second son marry
till he had the Black Book. This book used to shine and
give brighter light than ever the Sword of Light did, and I
suppose it does yet. The old hag beyond the Bridge ot
Blood has the book, and no one dares to go near her,
for many is the King's son killed or enchanted by that
woman."

" Would you marry my second sister if you were to get
the Black Book ? "

" I would, indeed ; I would marry any woman if I got
the Black Book with her. The Sword of Light and the
Black Book were in our family till my grandfather's time,
then they were stolen by that cursed old hag."

" I will have the book," said Smallhead, " or die in the
trial to get it."

Knowing that stirabout was the main food of the hag,
Smallhead settled in her mind to play another trick. Taking
a bag she scraped the chimney, gathered about a stone of
soot, and took it with her. The night was dark and rainy.
When she reached the hag's house, she climbed up the
gable to the chimney and found that the son was making
stirabout for his mother. She dropped the soot down by

degrees till at last the whole stone of soot was in the pot; then she scraped around the top of the chimney till a lump of soot fell on the boy's hand.

"Oh, mother," said he, "the night is wet and soft, the soot is falling."

"Cover the pot," said the hag. "Be quick with that stirabout, I am starving."

The boy took the pot to his mother.

"Bad luck to you," cried the hag the moment she tasted the stirabout, "this is full of soot; throw it out to the pig."

"If I throw it out there is no water inside to make more, and I'll not go in the dark and rain to the well."

"You must go!" screamed she.

"I'll not stir a foot out of this unless I get a light," said the boy.

"Is it the book you are thinking of, you fool, to take it and lose it as you did the sword? Smallhead is watching you."

"How could Smallhead, the creature, be outside all the time? If you have no use for the water you can do without it."

Sooner than stop fasting till morning, the hag gave her son the book, saying: "Do not put this down or let it from your hand till you come in, or I'll have your life."

The boy took the book and went to the well. Smallhead followed him carefully. He took the book down into the well with him, and when he was stooping to dip water she snatched the book and pushed him into the well, where he came very near drowning.

Smallhead was far away when the boy recovered, and

began to scream and shout to his mother. She came in a hurry, and finding that the book was gone, fell into such a rage that she thrust a knife into her son's heart and ran after Smallhead, who had crossed the bridge before the hag could come up with her.

When the old woman saw Smallhead on the other side of the bridge facing her and dancing with delight, she screamed :

" You took the Sword of Light and the Black Book, and your two sisters are married. Oh, then, bad luck to you. I will put my curse on you wherever you go. You have all my children killed, and I a poor, feeble, old woman."

" Bad luck to yourself," said Smallhead. " I am not afraid of a curse from the like of you. If you had lived an honest life you wouldn't be as you are to-day."

" Now, Smallhead," said the old hag, " you have me robbed of everything, and my children destroyed. Your two sisters are well married. Your fortune began with my ruin. Come, now, and take care of me in my old age. I'll take my curse from you, and you will have good luck. I bind myself never to harm a hair of your head."

Smallhead thought awhile, promised to do this, and said : " If you harm me, or try to harm me, it will be the worse for yourself."

The old hag was satisfied and went home. Smallhead went to the castle and was received with great joy. Next morning she found the King's son in the garden, and said : " If you marry my sister to-morrow, you will have the Black Book."

" I will marry her gladly," said the King's son.

Next day the marriage was celebrated and the King's

son got the book.   Smallhead remained in the castle about
a week, then she left good health with her sisters and went
to the hag's house.   The old woman was glad to see her
and showed the girl her work.   All Smallhead had to do
was to wait on the hag and feed a large pig that she had.

" I am fatting that pig," said the hag ; "he is seven
years old now, and the longer you keep a pig the harder
his meat is : we'll keep this pig a while longer, and then
we'll kill and eat him."

Smallhead did her work ; the old hag taught her some
things, and Smallhead learned herself far more than the
hag dreamt of.   The girl fed the pig three times a day,
never thinking that he could be anything but a pig.   The
hag had sent word to a sister that she had in the Eastern
World, bidding her come and they would kill the pig
and have a great feast.   The sister came, and one day
when the hag was going to walk with her sister she
said to Smallhead :

" Give the pig plenty of meal to-day ; this is the last
food he'll have ; give him his fill."

The pig had his own mind and knew what was coming.
He put his nose under the pot and threw it on Smallhead's
toes, and she barefoot.   With that she ran into the house
for a stick, and seeing a rod on the edge of the loft,
snatched it and hit the pig.

That moment the pig was a splendid young man.

Smallhead was amazed.

" Never fear," said the young man, "I am the son of a
King that the old hag hated, the King of Munster.   She
stole me from my father seven years ago and enchanted
me—made a pig of me."

Smallhead told the King's son, then, how the hag had treated her. "I must make a pig of you again," said she,

"for the hag is coming. Be patient and I'll save you, if you promise to marry me."

"I promise you," said the King's son.

With that she struck him, and he was a pig again. She put the switch in its place and was at her work when the two sisters came. The pig ate his meal now with a good heart, for he felt sure of rescue.

"Who is that girl you have in the house, and where did you find her?" asked the sister.

"All my children died of the plague, and I took this girl to help me. She is a very good servant."

At night the hag slept in one room, her sister in another, and Smallhead in a third. When the two sisters were sleeping soundly Smallhead rose, stole the hag's magic book, and then took the rod. She went next to where the pig was, and with one blow of the rod made a man of him.

With the help of the magic book Smallhead made two doves of herself and the King's son, and they took flight through the air and flew on without stopping. Next morning the hag called Smallhead, but she did not come. She hurried out to see the pig. The pig was gone. She ran to her book. Not a sign of it.

"Oh!" cried she, "that villain of a Smallhead has robbed me. She has stolen my book, made a man of the pig, and taken him away with her."

What could she do but tell her whole story to the sister. "Go you," said she, " and follow them. You have more enchantment than Smallhead has."

"How am I to know them?" asked the sister.

"Bring the first two strange things that you find; they will turn themselves into something wonderful."

The sister then made a hawk of herself and flew away as swiftly as any March wind.

"Look behind," said Smallhead to the King's son some hours later ; "see what is coming."

"I see nothing," said he, "but a hawk coming swiftly."

"That is the hag's sister. She has three times more enchantment than the hag herself. But fly down on the ditch and be picking yourself as doves do in rainy weather, and maybe she'll pass without seeing us."

The hawk saw the doves, but thinking them nothing wonderful, flew on till evening, and then went back to her sister.

"Did you see anything wonderful ? "

"I did not ; I saw only two doves, and they picking themselves."

"You fool, those doves were Smallhead and the King's son. Off with you in the morning and don't let me see you again without the two with you."

Away went the hawk a second time, and swiftly as Smallhead and the King's son flew, the hawk was gaining on them. Seeing this Smallhead and the King's son dropped down into a large village, and, it being market-day, they made two heather brooms of themselves. The two brooms began to sweep the road without any one holding them, and swept toward each other. This was a great wonder. Crowds gathered at once around the two brooms.

The old hag flying over in the form of a hawk saw this and thinking that it must be Smallhead and the King's son were in it, came down, turned into a woman, and said to herself :

"I'll have those two brooms."

She pushed forward so quickly through the crowd that

she came near knocking down a man standing before her. The man was vexed.

"You cursed old hag!" cried he, "do you want to knock us down?" With that he gave her a blow and drove her against another man, that man gave her a push that sent her spinning against a third man, and so on till between them all they came near putting the life out of her, and pushed her away from the brooms. A woman in the crowd called out then:

"It would be nothing but right to knock the head off that old hag, and she trying to push us away from the mercy of God, for it was God who sent the brooms to sweep the road for us."

"True for you," said another woman. With that the people were as angry as angry could be, and were ready to kill the hag. They were going to take the head off the hag when she made a hawk of herself and flew away, vowing never to do another stroke of work for her sister. She might do her own work or let it alone.

When the hawk disappeared the two heather brooms rose and turned into doves. The people felt sure when they saw the doves that the brooms were a blessing from heaven, and it was the old hag that drove them away.

On the following day Smallhead and the King's son saw his father's castle, and the two came down not too far from it in their own forms. Smallhead was a very beautiful woman now, and why not? She had the magic and didn't spare it. She made herself as beautiful as ever she could: the like of her was not to be seen in that kingdom or the next one.

The King's son was in love with her that minute, and

did not wish to part with her, but she would not go with him.

" When you are at your father's castle," said Smallhead, " all will be overjoyed to see you, and the king will give a great feast in your honour. If you kiss any one or let any living thing kiss you, you'll forget me for ever."

" I will not let even my own mother kiss me," said he.

The King's son went to the castle. All were overjoyed ; they had thought him dead, had not seen him for seven years. He would let no one come near to kiss him. " I am bound by oath to kiss no one," said he to his mother. At that moment an old grey hound came in, and with one spring was on his shoulder licking his face : all that the King's son had gone through in seven years was forgotten in one moment.

Smallhead went toward a forge near the castle. The smith had a wife far younger than himself, and a stepdaughter. They were no beauties. In the rear of the forge was a well and a tree growing over it. " I will go up in that tree," thought Smallhead. " and spend the night in it." She went up and sat just over the well. She was not long in the tree when the moon came out high above the hill tops and shone on the well. The blacksmith's stepdaughter, coming for water, looked down in the well, saw the face of the woman above in the tree, thought it her own face, and cried :

" Oh, then, to have me bringing water to a smith, and I such a beauty. I'll never bring another drop to him." With that she cast the pail in the ditch and ran off to find a king's son to marry.

When she was not coming with the water, and the

blacksmith waiting to wash after his day's work in the forge, he sent the mother. The mother had nothing but a pot to get the water in, so off she went with that, and coming to the well saw the beautiful face in the water.

"Oh, you black, swarthy villain of a smith," cried she, "bad luck to the hour that I met you, and I such a beauty. I'll never draw another drop of water for the life of you!"

She threw the pot down, broke it, and hurried away to find some king's son.

When neither mother nor daughter came back with water the smith himself went to see what was keeping them. He saw the pail in the ditch, and, catching it, went to the well; looking down, he saw the beautiful face of a woman in the water. Being a man, he knew that it was not his own face that was in it, so he looked up, and there in the tree saw a woman. He spoke to her and said:

"I know now why my wife and her daughter did not bring water. They saw your face in the well, and, thinking themselves too good for me, ran away. You must come now and keep the house till I find them."

"I will help you," said Smallhead. She came down, went to the smith's house, and showed the road that the women took. The smith hurried after them, and found the two in a village ten miles away. He explained their own folly to them, and they came home.

The mother and daughter washed fine linen for the castle. Smallhead saw them ironing one day, and said:

"Sit down: I will iron for you."

She caught the iron, and in an hour had the work of the day done.

The women were delighted. In the evening the daughter took the linen to the housekeeper at the castle.

" Who ironed this linen ?" asked the housekeeper.

" My mother and I."

" Indeed, then, you did not. You can't do the like of that work, and tell me who did it."

The girl was in dread now and answered :

" It is a woman who is stopping with us who did the ironing."

The housekeeper went to the Queen and showed her the linen.

" Send that woman to the castle," said the Queen.

Smallhead went : the Queen welcomed her, wondered at her beauty ; put her over all the maids in the castle. Smallhead could do anything ; everybody was fond of her. The King's son never knew that he had seen her before, and she lived in the castle a year ; what the Queen told her she did.

The King had made a match for his son with the daughter of the King of Ulster. There was a great feast in the castle in honour of the young couple, the marriage, was to be a week later. The bride's father brought many of his people who were versed in all kinds of tricks and en-chantment.

The King knew that Smallhead could do many things, for neither the Queen nor himself had asked her to do a thing that she did not do in a twinkle.

" Now," said the King to the Queen, " I think she can do something that his people cannot do." He summoned Smallhead and asked :

"Can you amuse the strangers ? "

" I can if you wish me to do so."

When the time came and the Ulster men had shown their best tricks, Smallhead came forward and raised the window, which was forty feet from the ground. She had a small ball of thread in her hand ; she tied one end of the thread to the window, threw the ball out and over a wall near the castle ; then she passed out the window, walked on the thread and kept time to music from players that no man could see. She came in ; all cheered her and were greatly delighted.

"I can do that," said the King of Ulster's daughter, and sprang out on the string ; but if she did she fell and broke her neck on the stones below. There were cries, there was lamentation, and, in place of a marriage, a funeral.

The King's son was angry and grieved and wanted to drive Smallhead from the castle in some way.

"She is not to blame," said the King of Munster, who did nothing but praise her.

Another year passed : the King got the daughter of the King of Connacht for his son. There was a great feast before the wedding day, and as the Connacht people are full of enchantment and witchcraft, the King of Munster called Smallhead and said :

" Now show the best trick of any."

" I will," said Smallhead.

When the feast was over and the Connacht men had shown their tricks the King of Munster called Smallhead.

She stood before the company, threw two grains of wheat on the floor, and spoke some magic words. There was a hen and a cock there before her of beautiful plumage ; she threw a grain of wheat between them ; the hen sprang to eat the wheat, the cock gave her a blow of his bill, the hen drew back, looked at him, and said :

" Bad luck to you, you wouldn t do the like of that when I was serving the old hag and you her pig, and I made a man of you and gave you back your own form.

The King's son looked at her and thought, " There must be something in this."

Smallhead threw a second grain. The cock pecked the hen again. " Oh," said the hen, " you would not do that the day the hag's sister was hunting us, and we two doves."

The King's son was still more astonished.

She threw a third grain. The cock struck the hen, and she said, " You would not do that to me the day I made two heather brooms out of you and myself." She threw a fourth grain. The cock pecked the hen a fourth time. " You would not do that the day you promised not to let any living thing kiss you or kiss any one yourself but me—you let the hound kiss you and you forgot me."

The King's son made one bound forward, embraced and kissed Smallhead, and told the King his whole story from beginning to end.

" This is my wife," said he ; " I'll marry no other woman."

" Whose wife will my daughter be ? " asked the King of Connacht.

" Oh, she will be the wife of the man who will marry her," said the King of Munster, " my son gave his word to this woman before he saw your daughter, and he must keep it."

So Smallhead married the King of Munster's son.

The Legend of Knockgrafton.

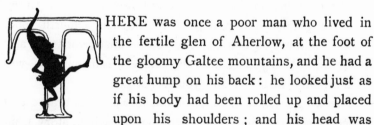

HERE was once a poor man who lived in the fertile glen of Aherlow, at the foot of the gloomy Galtee mountains, and he had a great hump on his back: he looked just as if his body had been rolled up and placed upon his shoulders; and his head was pressed down with the weight so much that his chin, when he was sitting, used to rest upon his knees for support. The country people were rather shy of meeting him in any lonesome place, for though, poor creature, he was as harmless and as inoffensive as a new-born infant, yet his deformity was so great that he scarcely appeared to be a human creature, and some ill-minded persons had set strange stories about him afloat. He was said to have a great knowledge of herbs and charms; but certain it was that he had a mighty skilful hand in plaiting straw and rushes into hats and baskets, which was the way he made his livelihood.

Lusmore, for that was the nickname put upon him by reason of his always wearing a sprig of the fairy cap, or lusmore (the foxglove), in his little straw hat, would ever get a higher penny for his plaited work than any one else, and perhaps that was the reason why some one, out of envy, had circulated the strange stories about him. Be that as it may, it happened that he was returning one evening from the pretty town of Cahir towards Cappagh, and as little Lusmore walked very slowly, on account of the great hump upon his back, it was quite dark when he came to the old moat of Knockgrafton, which stood on the right-hand side of his road. Tired and weary was he, and noways comfortable in his own mind at thinking how much farther he had to travel, and that he should be walking all the night; so he sat down under the moat to rest himself, and began looking mournfully enough upon the moon.

Presently there rose a wild strain of unearthly melody upon the ear of little Lusmore; he listened, and he thought that he had never heard such ravishing music before. It was like the sound of many voices, each mingling and blending with the other so strangely that they seemed to be one, though all singing different strains, and the words of the song were these—

Da Luan, Da Mort, Da Luan, Da Mort, Da Luan, Da Mort;

when there would be a moment's pause, and then the round of melody went on again.

Lusmore listened attentively, scarcely drawing his breath lest he might lose the slightest note. He now plainly

perceived that the singing was within the moat; and
though at first it had charmed him so much, he began to
get tired of hearing the same round sung over and over
so often without any change; so availing himself of the

pause when the *Da Luan, Da Mort,* had been sung three
times, he took up the tune, and raised it with the words
augus Da Cadine, and then went on singing with the voices
inside of the moat, *Da Luan, Da Mort,* finishing the melody,
when the pause again came, with *augus Da Cadine.*

The fairies within Knockgrafton, for the song was a fairy
melody, when they heard this addition to the tune, were so
much delighted that, with instant resolve, it was determined

to bring the mortal among them, whose musical skill so far exceeded theirs, and little Lusmore was conveyed into their company with the eddying speed of a whirlwind.

Glorious to behold was the sight that burst upon him as he came down through the moat, twirling round and round, with the lightness of a straw, to the sweetest music that kept time to his motion. The greatest honour was then paid him, for he was put above all the musicians, and he had servants tending upon him, and everything to his heart's content, and a hearty welcome to all ; and, in short, he was made as much of as if he had been the first man in the land.

Presently Lusmore saw a great consultation going forward among the fairies, and, notwithstanding all their civility, he felt very much frightened, until one stepping out from the rest came up to him and said,—

> " Lusmore ! Lusmore !
> Doubt not, nor deplore,
> For the hump which you bore
> On your back is no more ;
> Look down on the floor,
> And view it, Lusmore ! "

When these words were said, poor little Lusmore felt himself so light, and so happy, that he thought he could have bounded at one jump over the moon, like the cow in the history of the cat and the fiddle ; and he saw, with inexpressible pleasure, his hump tumble down upon the ground from his shoulders. He then tried to lift up his head, and he did so with becoming caution, fearing that he might knock it against the ceiling of the grand hall, where he was ; he looked round and round again with greatest wonder and delight upon everything, which appeared more

and more beautiful ; and, overpowered at beholding such a
resplendent scene, his head grew dizzy, and his eyesight
became dim.   At last he fell into a sound sleep, and when
he awoke he found that it was broad daylight, the sun shining
brightly, and the birds singing sweetly ; and that he was
lying just at the foot of the moat of Knockgrafton, with the
cows and sheep grazing peacefully round about him.   The
first thing Lusmore did, after saying his prayers, was to
put his hand behind to feel for his hump, but no sign of
one was there on his back, and he looked at himself with
great pride, for he had now become a well-shaped dapper
little fellow, and more than that, found himself in a full suit
of new clothes, which he concluded the fairies had made
for him.

Towards Cappagh he went, stepping out as lightly, and
springing up at every step as if he had been all his life
a dancing-master.   Not a creature who met Lusmore
knew him without his hump, and he had a great work to
persuade every one that he was the same man—in truth
he was not, so far as outward appearance went.

Of course it was not long before the story of Lusmore's
hump got about, and a great wonder was made of it.
Through the country, for miles round, it was the talk of
every one, high and low.

One morning, as Lusmore was sitting contented enough,
at his cabin door, up came an old woman to him, and asked
him if he could direct her to Cappagh.

" I need give you no directions, my good woman," said
Lusmore, " for this is Cappagh ; and whom may you want
here ? "

" I have come," said the woman, " out of Decie's country,

in the county of Waterford looking after one Lusmore, who, I have heard tell, had his hump taken off by the fairies; for there is a son of a gossip of mine who has got a hump on him that will be his death; and maybe if he could use the same charm as Lusmore, the hump may be taken off him. And now I have told you the reason of my coming so far: 'tis to find out about this charm, if I can."

Lusmore, who was ever a good-natured little fellow, told the woman all the particulars, how he had raised the tune for the fairies at Knockgrafton, how his hump had been removed from his shoulders, and how he had got a new suit of clothes into the bargain.

The woman thanked him very much, and then went away quite happy and easy in her own mind. When she came back to her gossip's house, in the county of Waterford, she told her everything that Lusmore had said, and they put the little hump-backed man, who was a peevish and cunning creature from his birth, upon a car, and took him all the way across the country. It was a long journey, but they did not care for that, so the hump was taken from off him; and they brought him, just at nightfall, and left him under the old moat of Knockgrafton.

Jack Madden, for that was the humpy man's name, had not been sitting there long when he heard the tune going on within the moat much sweeter than before; for the fairies were singing it the way Lusmore had settled their music for them, and the song was going on; *Da Luan, Da Mort, Da Luan, Da Mort, Da Luan, Da Mort, augus Da Cadine*, without ever stopping. Jack Madden, who was in a great hurry to get quit of his hump, never thought of

waiting until the fairies had done, or watching for a fit
opportunity to raise the tune higher again than Lusmore
had ; so having heard them sing it over seven times without
stopping, out he bawls, never minding the time or the
humour of the tune, or how he could bring his words in
properly, *augus Da Cadine, augus Da Hena*, thinking that if
one day was good, two were better ; and that if Lusmore
had one new suit of clothes given him, he should have two.

No sooner had the words passed his lips than he was
taken up and whisked into the moat with prodigious force ;
and the fairies came crowding round about him with great
anger, screeching, and screaming, and roaring out, " Who
spoiled our tune? who spoiled our tune ? " and one stepped
up to him, above all the rest and said :

> "Jack Madden ! Jack Madden !
> Your words came so bad in
> The tune we felt glad in ;—
> This castle you're had in,
> That your life we may sadden ;
> Here's two humps for Jack Madden ! "

And twenty of the strongest fairies brought Lusmore's hump
and put it down upon poor Jack's back, over his own,
where it became fixed as firmly as if it was nailed on
with twelve-penny nails, by the best carpenter that ever
drove one.   Out of their castle they then kicked him ; and,
in the morning, when Jack Madden's mother and her gossip
came to look after their little man, they found him half dead,
lying at the foot of the moat, with the other hump upon his
back.   Well to be sure, how they did look at each other !
but they were afraid to say anything, lest a hump might be
put upon their own shoulders.   Home they brought the

unlucky Jack Madden with them, as downcast in their hearts
and their looks as ever two gossips were ; and what through
the weight of his other hump, and the long journey, he died
soon after, leaving they say his heavy curse to any one who
would go to listen to fairy tunes again.

Elidore.

THE days of Henry Beauclerc of England there was a little lad named Elidore, who was being brought up to be a cleric. Day after day he would trudge from his mother's house, and she was a widow, up to the monks' Scriptorium. There he would learn his A B C, to read it and to write it. But he was a lazy little rogue was this Elidore, and as fast as he learned to write one letter, he forgot another; so it was very little progress he was making. Now when the good monks saw this they remembered the saying of the Book : " Spare the rod and spoil the child," and whenever Elidore forgot a letter they tried to make him remember it with the rod. At first they used it seldom and lightly, but Elidore was not a boy to be driven, and the more they thwacked him the less he learned : so the thwackings became more frequent and more severe, till Elidore could not stand them any longer. So one day when he was twelve years old he upped with him and offed with him into the great forest near St. David's. There for two long days and

two long nights he wandered about eating nothing but
hips and haws. At last he found himself at the mouth of
a cave, at the side of a river, and there he sank down, all
tired and exhausted. Suddenly two little pigmies appeared
to him and said : " Come with us, and we will lead you

into a land full of games and sports : " so Elidore raised
himself and went with these two; at first through an
underground passage all in the dark, but soon they came
out into a most beautiful country, with rivers and meadows,
woods and plains, as pleasant as can be ; only this there
was curious about it, that the sun never shone and clouds

were always over the sky, so that neither sun was seen by day, nor moon and stars at night.

The two little men led Elidore before their king, who asked why and whence he came. Elidore told him, and the king said : "Thou shalt attend on my son," and waved him away. So for a long time Elidore waited on the king's son, and joined in all the games and sports of the little men.

They were little, but they were not dwarfs, for all their limbs were of suitable size one with another. Their hair was fair, and hung upon their shoulders like that of women. They had little horses, about the size of greyhounds ; and did not eat flesh, fowl, or fish, but lived on milk flavoured with saffron. And as they had such curious ways, so they had strange thoughts. No oath took they, but never a lie they spoke. They would jeer and scoff at men for their struggles, lying, and treachery. Yet though they were so good they worshipped none, unless you might say they were worshippers of Truth.

After a time Elidore began to long to see boys and men of his own size, and he begged permission to go and visit his mother. So the King gave him permission : so the little men led him along the passage, and guided him through the forest, till he came near his mother's cottage, and when he entered, was not she rejoiced to see her dear son again ? "Where have you been ? What have you done ? " she cried ; and he had to tell her all that had happened to him. She begged of him to stay with her, but he had promised the King to go back. And soon he returned, after making his mother promise not to tell where he was, or with whom. Henceforth Elidore lived, partly with the little men, and partly with his mother. Now one day, when he was with his mother, he told her of the yellow balls they used in their play, and which she felt sure must be of gold. So she begged of him that the next time he came back to her he would bring with him one of these balls. When the time came for him to go back to his mother again, he did not wait for the little men to guide him back, as he now knew the road. But seizing one of the yellow balls with which he used to play, he rushed home through the passage. Now as he got near his mother's house he seemed to hear tiny footsteps behind him, and he rushed up to the door as quickly as he could. Just as he reached it his foot slipped, and he fell down, and the ball rolled out of his hand, just to the feet of his mother. At that moment two little men rushed forward, seized the ball and ran away, making faces, and spitting at the boy as they passed him. Elidore remained with his mother for a time; but he missed the play and games of the little men, and determined to go back to them. But when he came to where the cave had been, near the river where the underground passage commenced, he could not find it again, and though he searched again and again in the years to come, he could not get back to that fair country. So after a time he went back to the monastery, and became in due course a monk. And men used to come and seek him out, and ask him what had happened to him when he was in the Land of the Little Men. Nor could he ever speak of that happy time without shedding tears.

Now it happened once, when this Elidore was old, that David, Bishop of St. David's, came to visit his monastery and ask him about the manners and customs of the little

men, and above all, he was curious to know what language
they spoke ; and Elidore told him some of their words.
When they asked for water, they would say : *Udor udorum* ;
and when they wanted salt, they would say : *Hapru udorum.*
And from this, the Bishop, who was a learned man, discovered that they spoke some sort of Greek.   For *Udor* is
Greek for *Water*, and *Hap* for *Salt.*

Hence we know that the Britons came from Troy, being
descendants from Brito, son of Priam, King of Troy.

The Leeching of Kayn's Leg.

HERE were five hundred blind men, and five hundred deaf men, and five hundred limping men, and five hundred dumb men, and five hundred cripple men. The five hundred deaf men had five hundred wives, and the five hundred limping men had five hundred wives, and the five hundred dumb men had five hundred wives, and the five hundred cripple men had five hundred wives. Each five hundred of these had five hundred children and five hundred dogs. They were in the habit of going about in one band, and were called the Sturdy Strolling Beggarly Brotherhood. There was a knight in Erin called O'Cronicert, with whom they spent a day and a year; and they ate up all that he had, and made a poor man of him, till he had nothing left but an old tumble-down black house, and an old lame white horse. There was a king in Erin called Brian Boru; and O'Cronicert went to him for help. He cut a cudgel of grey oak on the outskirts of the wood, mounted the old lame white horse, and set off at speed through wood and over moss and rugged ground, till he reached the king's house. When he arrived he went on his knees to the king ; and the king said to him, " What is your news, O'Cronicert ? "

" I have but poor news for you, king."

" What poor news have you ? " said the king.

" That I have had the Sturdy Strolling Beggarly Brotherhood for a day and a year, and they have eaten all that I had, and made a poor man of me," said he.

" Well ! " said the king, " I am sorry for you ; what do you want ? "

" I want help," said O'Cronicert ; " anything that you may be willing to give me."

The king promised him a hundred cows. He went to the queen, and made his complaint to her, and she gave him another hundred. He went to the king's son, Murdoch Mac Brian, and he got another hundred from him. He got food and drink at the king's ; and when he was going away he said, " Now I am very much obliged to you. This will set me very well on my feet. After all that I have got there is another thing that I want."

" What is it ? " said the king.

" It is the lap-dog that is in and out after the queen that I wish for."

" Ha ! " said the king, " it is your mightiness and pride that has caused the loss of your means ; but if you become a good man you shall get this along with the rest."

O'Cronicert bade the king good-bye, took the lap-dog, leapt on the back of the old lame white horse, and went off at speed through wood, and over moss and rugged ground. After he had gone some distance through the wood a roebuck leapt up and the lap-dog went after it. In a moment the deer started up as a woman behind O'Cronicert, the handsomest that eye had ever seen from the beginning of the universe till the end of eternity.   She said to him, " Call your dog off me."

" I will do so if you promise to marry me," said O'Cronicert.

" If you keep three vows that I shall lay upon you I will marry you," said she.

" What vows are they ? " said he.

"The first is that you do not go to ask your worldly king to a feast or a dinner without first letting me know," said she.

" Hoch ! " said O'Cronicert, " do you think that I cannot keep that vow ?   I would never go to invite my worldly king without informing you that I was going to do so.   It is easy to keep that vow."

" You are likely to keep it ! " said she.

" The second vow is," said she, " that you do not cast up to me in any company or meeting in which we shall be together, that you found me in the form of a deer."

" Hoo ! " said O'Cronicert, " you need not to lay that vow upon me.   I would keep it at any rate."

" You are likely to keep it ! " said she.

" The third vow is," said she, " that you do not leave me in the company of only one man while you go out."   It was agreed between them that she should marry him.

They reached the old tumble-down black house.   Grass they cut in the clefts and ledges of the rocks ; a bed they made and laid down.   O'Cronicert's wakening from sleep was the lowing of cattle and the bleating of sheep and the neighing of mares, while he himself was in a bed of gold on

wheels of silver, going from end to end of the Tower of
Castle Town.

"I am sure that you are surprised," said she.

"I am indeed," said he.

"You are in your own room," said she.

"In my own room," said he. "I never had such a
room."

"I know well that you never had," said she ; "but you
have it now. So long as you keep me you shall keep the
room."

He then rose, and put on his clothes, and went out. He
took a look at the house when he went out ; and it was a
palace, the like of which he had never seen, and the king
himself did not possess. He then took a walk round the
farm ; and he never saw so many cattle, sheep, and horses
as were on it. He returned to the house, and said to his
wife that the farm was being ruined by other people's cattle
and sheep. "It is not," said she : "your own cattle and
sheep are on it."

"I never had so many cattle and sheep," said he.

"I know that," said she ; "but so long as you keep me
you shall keep them. There is no good wife whose tocher
does not follow her."

He was now in good circumstances, indeed wealthy. He
had gold and silver, as well as cattle and sheep. He went
about with his gun and dogs hunting every day, and was a
great man. It occurred to him one day that he would go
to invite the King of Erin to dinner, but he did not tell
his wife that he was going. His first vow was now broken.
He sped away to the King of Erin, and invited him and
his great court to dinner. The King of Erin said to him,

" Do you intend to take away the cattle that I promised you ? "

"Oh ! no, King of Erin,' said O'Cronicert ; " I could give you as many to-day."

"Ah ! " said the king, " how well you have got on since I saw you last ! "

" I have indeed," said O'Cronicert ! " I have fallen in with a rich wife who has plenty of gold and silver, and of cattle and sheep."

" I am glad of that," said the King of Erin.

O'Cronicert said, " I shall feel much obliged if you will go with me to dinner, yourself and your great court."

" We will do so willingly," said the king.

They went with him on that same day. It did not occur to O'Cronicert how a dinner could be prepared for the king without his wife knowing that he was coming. When they were going on, and had reached the place where O'Cronicert had met the deer, he remembered that his vow was broken, and he said to the king, " Excuse me ; I am going on before to the house to tell that you are coming."

The king said, " We will send off one of the lads."

" You will not," said O'Cronicert ; " no lad will serve the purpose so well as myself."

He set off to the house ; and when he arrived his wife was diligently preparing dinner. He told her what he had done, and asked her pardon. " I pardon you this time," said she : " I know what you have done as well as you do yourself. The first of your vows is broken."

The king and his great court came to O'Cronicert's house ; and the wife had everything ready for them as befitted a king and great people ; every kind of drink and food.   They spent two or three days and nights at dinner, eating and drinking.   They were praising the dinner highly, and O'Cronicert himself was praising it ; but his wife was not.   O'Cronicert was angry that she was not praising it and he went and struck her in the mouth with his fist and knocked out two of her teeth.   " Why are you not praising the dinner like the others, you contemptible deer ? " said he.

" I am not," said she :   " I have seen my father's big dogs having a better dinner than you are giving to-night to the King of Erin and his court."

O'Cronicert got into such a rage that he went outside of the door.   He was not long standing there when a man came riding on a black horse, who in passing caught O'Cronicert by the collar of his coat, and took him up behind him : and they set off.   The rider did not say a word to O'Cronicert.   The horse was going so swiftly that O'Cronicert thought the wind would drive his head off.   They arrived at a big, big palace, and came off the black horse. A stableman came out, and caught the horse, and took it in. It was with wine that he was cleaning the horse's feet. The rider of the black horse said to O'Cronicert, " Taste the wine to see if it is better than the wine that you are giving to Brian Boru and his court to-night."

O'Cronicert tasted the wine, and said, " This is better wine."

The rider of the black horse said, " How unjust was the fist a little ago !   The wind from your fist carried the two teeth to me."

He then took him into that big, handsome, and noble house, and into a room that was full of gentlemen eating and drinking, and he seated him at the head of the table, and gave him wine to drink, and said to him, " Taste that wine to see if it is better than the wine that you are giving to the King of Erin and his court to-night."

" This is better wine," said O'Cronicert.

" How unjust was the fist a little ago ! " said the rider of the black horse.

When all was over the rider of the black horse said, " Are you willing to return home now ? "

" Yes," said O'Cronicert, " very willing."

They then rose, and went to the stable : and the black horse was taken out ; and they leaped on its back, and went away. The rider of the black horse said to O'Cronicert, after they had set off, " Do you know who I am ? "

" I do not," said O'Cronicert.

" I am a brother-in-law of yours," said the rider of the black horse ; and though my sister is married to you there is not a king or knight in Erin who is a match for her. Two of your vows are now broken ; and if you break the other vow you shall lose your wife and all that you possess."

They arrived at O'Cronicert's house ; and O'Cronicert said, " I am ashamed to go in, as they do not know where I have been since night came."

" Hoo ! " said the rider, " they have not missed you at all. There is so much conviviality among them, that they have not suspected that you have been anywhere. Here are the two teeth that you knocked out of the front of your wife's mouth. Put them in their place, and they will be as strong as ever."

" Come in with me," said O'Cronicert to the rider of the black horse.

"I will not : I disdain to go in," said the rider of the black horse.

The rider of the black horse bade O'Cronicert good-bye, and went away.

O'Cronicert went in ; and his wife met him as she was busy waiting on the gentlemen. He asked her pardon, and put the two teeth in the front of her mouth, and they were as strong as ever. She said, " Two of your vows are now broken." No one took notice of him when he went in, or said " Where have you been ? " They spent the night in eating and drinking, and the whole of the next day,

In the evening the king said, " I think that it is time for us to be going ; " and all said that it was. O'Cronicert said, " You will not go to-night. I am going to get up a dance. You will go to-morrow."

" Let them go," said his wife.

" I will not," said he.

The dance was set a-going that night. They were playing away at dancing and music till they became warm and hot with perspiration. They were going out one after another to cool themselves at the side of the house. They all went out except O'Cronicert and his wife, and a man called Kayn Mac Loy. O'Cronicert himself went out, and left his wife and Kayn Mac Loy in the house, and when she saw that he had broken his third vow she gave a spring through a room, and became a big filly, and gave Kayn Mac Loy a kick with her foot, and broke his thigh in two. She gave another spring, and smashed the door and went away, and was seen no more. She took with her the Tower of Castle Town as an armful on her shoulder and a light burden on her back, and she left Kayn Mac Loy in the old tumble-down black house in a pool of rain-drip on the floor.

At daybreak next day poor O'Cronicert could only see the old house that he had before. Neither cattle nor sheep, nor any of the fine things that he had was to be seen. One awoke in the morning beside a bush, another beside a dyke, and another beside a ditch. The king only had the honour of having O'Cronicert's little hut over his head. As they were leaving, Murdoch Mac Brian remembered that he had left his own foster-brother Kayn Mac Loy behind, and said there should be no separation in life between them and that he would go back for him. He found Kayn in the old tumble-down black house, in the middle of the floor, in a pool of rain-water, with his leg broken ; and he said the earth should make a nest in his sole and the sky a nest in his head if he did not find a man to cure Kayn's leg.

They told him that on the Isle of Innisturk was a herb that would heal him.

So Kayn Mac Loy was then borne away, and sent to the island, and he was supplied with as much food as would keep him for a month, and with two crutches on which he would be going out and in as he might desire. At last the food was spent, and he was destitute, and he had not found the herb. He was in the habit of going down to the shore, and gathering shell-fish, and eating it.

As he was one day on the shore, he saw a big, big man landing on the island, and he could see the earth and the sky between his legs. He set off with the crutches to try if he could get into the hut before the big man would come upon him. Despite his efforts, the big man was between him and the door, and said to him, "Unless you deceive me, you are Kayn Mac Loy."

Kayn Mac Loy said, "I have never deceived a man: I am he."

The big man said to him:

"Stretch out your leg, Kayn, till I put a salve of herbs and healing to it. Salve and binding herb and the poultice are cooling; the worm is channering. Pressure and haste hard bind me, for I must hear Mass in the great church at Rome, and be in Norway before I sleep.

Kayn Mac Loy said:

"May it be no foot to Kayn or a foot to any one after one, or I be Kayn son of Loy, if I stretch out my foot for you to put a salve of herbs and healing on it, till you tell me why you have no church of your own in Norway, so as, as now, to be going to the great church of Rome to Rome to-morrow.

Unless you deceive me you are Machkan-an-Athar, the son of the King of Lochlann."

The big man said, "I have never deceived any man: I am he. I am now going to tell you why we have not a church in Lochlann. Seven masons came to build a church, and they and my father were bargaining about the building of it. The agreement that the masons wanted was that my mother and sister would go to see the interior of the church when it would be finished. My father was glad to get the church built so cheaply. They agreed accordingly; and the masons went in the morning to the place where the church was to be built. My father pointed out the spot for the foundation. They began to build in the morning, and the church was finished before the evening. When it was

finished they requested my mother and sister to go to see
its interior. They had no sooner entered than the doors
were shut ; and the church went away into the skies in the
form of a tuft of mist.

"Stretch out your leg, Kayn, till I put a salve of herbs and
healing to it. Salve and binding herb and the poultice are
cooling; the worm is channering. Pressure and haste hard
bind me, for I must hear Mass in the great church at Rome,
and be in Norway before I sleep.

Kayn Mac Loy said :

"May it be no foot to Kayn or a foot to any one after one,
or I be Kayn son of Loy, if I stretch out my foot for you to
put a salve of herbs and healing on it, till you tell me if you
heard what befell your mother and sister."

"Ah!" said the big man, "the mischief is upon you ;
that tale is long to tell ; but I will tell you a short tale
about the matter.   On the day on which they were working
at the church I was away in the hill hunting game ; and
when I came home in the evening my brother told me what
had happened, namely, that my mother and sister had gone
away in the form of a tuft of mist.   I became so cross and
angry that I resolved to destroy the world till I should find
out where my mother and sister were.   My brother said to
me that I was a fool to think of such a thing.   ' I'll tell
you,' said he, 'what you'll do.   You will first go to try
to find out where they are.   When you find out where
they are you will demand them peaceably, and if you do not
get them peaceably you will fight for them.'

"I took my brother's advice, and prepared a ship to set
off with.   I set off alone, and embraced the ocean.   I was
overtaken by a great mist, and I came upon an island, and
there was a large number of ships at anchor near it ; I
went in amongst them, and went ashore.   I saw there a
big, big woman reaping rushes ; and when she would raise
her head she would throw her right breast over her shoulder
and when she would bend it would fall down between her
legs.   I came once behind her, and caught the breast
with my mouth, and said to her, 'You are yourself
witness, woman, that I am the foster-son of your right
breast.'   ' I perceive that, great hero,' said the old woman,
' but my advice to you is to leave this island as fast as you
can.'   ' Why ?' said I.   ' There is a big giant in the cave
up there,' said she, 'and every one of the ships that you
see he has taken in from the ocean with his breath, and he
has killed and eaten the men.   He is asleep at present, and

when he wakens he will have you in a similar manner. A large iron door and an oak door are on the cave. When the giant draws in his breath the doors open, and when he emits his breath the doors shut; and they are shut as fast as though seven small bars, and seven large bars, and seven locks were on them. So fast are they that seven crowbars could not force them open.' I said to the old woman, 'Is there any way of destroying him?' 'I'll tell you,' said she, 'how it can be done. He has a weapon above the door that is called the short spear: and if you succeed in taking off his head with the first blow it will be well; but if you do not, the case will be worse than it was at first.'

" I set off, and reached the cave, the two doors of which opened. The giant's breath drew me into the cave; and stools, chairs, and pots were by its action·dashing against each other, and like to break my legs. The door shut when I went in, and was shut as fast as though seven small bars, and seven large bars, and seven locks were on it; and seven crowbars could not force it open; and I was a prisoner in the cave. The giant drew in his breath again, and the doors opened. I gave a look upwards, and saw the short spear, and laid hold of it. I drew the short spear, and I warrant you that I dealt him such a blow with it as did not require to be repeated; I swept the head off him. I took the head down to the old woman, who was reaping the rushes, and said to her, ' There is the giant's head for you.' The old woman said, ' Brave man! I knew that you were a hero. This island had need of your coming to it to-day. Unless you deceive me, you are Mac Connachar son of the King of Lochlann.' 'I have never deceived a man. I am he,' said I. 'I am a soothsayer,' said she, ' and know the object of your journey. You are going in quest of your mother and sister.' 'Well,' said I, 'I am so far on the way if I only knew where to go for them.' 'I'll tell you where they are,' said she ; 'they are in the kingdom of the Red Shield, and the King of the Red Shield is resolved to marry your mother, and his son is resolved to marry your sister. I'll tell you how the town is situated. A canal of seven times seven paces breadth surrounds it. On the canal there is a drawbridge, which is guarded during the day by two creatures that no weapon can pierce, as they are covered all over with scales, except two spots below the neck in which their death-wounds lie. Their names are Roar and Rustle. When night comes the bridge is raised, and the monsters sleep. A very high and big wall surrounds the king's palace.'

"Stretch out your leg, Kayn, till I put a salve of herbs and healing to it. Salve and binding herb and the poultice are cooling ; the worm is channering. Pressure and haste hard bind me, for I must hear Mass in the great church at Rome, and be in Norway before I sleep.

Kayn Mac Loy said :

"May it be no foot to Kayn or a foot to any one after one, or I be Kayn son of Loy, if I stretch out my foot for you to put a salve of herbs and healing on it, till you tell me if you went farther in search of your mother and sister, or if you returned home, or what befell you."

"Ah !" said the big man, "the mischief is upon you ; that tale is long to tell ; but I will tell you another tale. I set off, and reached the big town of the Red Shield ; and it was surrounded by a canal, as the old woman told me ;

and there was a drawbridge on the canal. It was night when I arrived, and the bridge was raised, and the monsters were asleep. I measured two feet before me and a foot behind me of the ground on which I was standing, and I sprang on the end of my spear and on my tiptoes, and reached the place where the monsters were asleep; and I drew the short spear, and I warrant you that I dealt them such a blow below the neck as did not require to be repeated. I took up the heads and hung them on one of the posts of the bridge. I then went on to the wall that surrounded the king's palace. This wall was so high that it was not easy for me to spring over it; and I set to work with the short spear, and dug a hole through it, and got in. I went to the door of the palace and knocked; and the doorkeeper called out, 'Who is there?' 'It is I,' said I. My mother and sister recognised my speech; and my mother called, ' Oh! it is my son; let him in.' I then got in, and they rose to meet me with great joy. I was supplied with food, drink, and a good bed. In the morning breakfast was set before us; and after it I said to my mother and sister that they had better make ready, and go with me. The King of the Red Shield said, 'It shall not be so. I am resolved to marry your mother, and my son is resolved to marry your sister.' 'If you wish to marry my mother, and if your son wishes to marry my sister, let both of you accompany me to my home, and you shall get them there.' The King of the Red Shield said, ' So be it.'

" We then set off, and came to where my ship was, went on board of it, and sailed home. When we were passing a place where a great battle was going on, I asked the King of the Red Shield what battle it was, and the cause of it.

' Don't you know at all ? " said the King of the Red Shield.
' I do not,' said I.   The King of the Red Shield said,
' That is the battle for the daughter of the King of the Great
Universe, the most beautiful woman in the world ; and who-
ever wins her by his heroism shall get her in marriage.

Do you see yonder castle ? '   ' I do,' said I.   ' She is on
the top of that castle, and sees from it the hero that wins
her,' said the King of the Red Shield.   I requested to be
put on shore, that I might win her by my swiftness and
strength.   They put me on shore ; and I got a sight of

her on the top of the castle. Having measured two feet behind me and a foot before me, I sprang on the end of my spear and on my tiptoes, and reached the top of the castle ; and I caught the daughter of the King of the Universe in my arms and flung her over the castle. I was with her and intercepted her before she reached the ground, and I took her away on my shoulder, and set off to the shore as fast as I could, and delivered her to the King of the Red Shield to be put on board the ship. Am I not the best warrior that ever sought you ? said I. 'You can jump well' said she, 'but I have not seen any of your prowess. I turned back to meet the warriors, and attacked them with the short spear, and did not leave a head on a neck of any of them. I then returned, and called to the King of the Red Shield to come in to the shore for me. Pretending not to hear me, he set the sails in order to return home with the daughter of the King of the Great Universe, and marry her. I measured two feet behind me and a foot before me, and sprang on the end of my spear and on my tiptoes and got on board the ship. I then said to the King of the Red Shield, 'What were you going to do ? Why did you not wait for me ?' 'Oh !' said the king, 'I was only making the ship ready and setting the sails to her before going on shore for you. Do you know what I am thinking of ?' 'I do not,' said I. 'It is,' said the King, 'that I will return home with the daughter of the King of the Great Universe, and that you shall go home with your mother and sister.' 'That is not to be the way of it,' said I. 'She whom I have won by my prowess neither you nor any other shall get.'

"The king had a red shield, and if he should get it on,

no weapon could make an impression on him.   He began
to put on the red shield, and I struck him with the short
spear in the middle of his body, and cut him in two, and
threw him overboard.   I then struck the son, and swept his
head off, and threw him overboard.

"Stretch out your leg, Kayn, till I put a salve of herbs and
healing to it. Salve and binding herb and the poultice are
cooling; the worm is channering. Pressure and haste hard
bind me, for I must hear Mass in the great church at Rome,
and be in Norway before I sleep.

Kayn Mac Loy said :

"May it be no foot to Kayn or a foot to any one after one,
or I be Kayn son of Loy, if I stretch out my foot for you to
put a salve of herbs and healing on it, till you tell me
whether any search was made for the daughter of the King
of the Universe.

"Ah ! the mischief is upon you," said the big man ; " I
will tell you another short tale. I came home with my
mother and sister, and the daughter of the King of the
Universe, and I married the daughter of the King of the
Universe.   The first son I had I named Machkan-na-skaya-
jayrika (son of the red shield).   Not long after this a
hostile force came to enforce compensation for the King of
the Red Shield, and a hostile force came from the King
of the Universe to enforce compensation for the daughter
of the King of the Universe. I took the daughter of the
King of the Universe with me on the one shoulder and
Machkan-na-skaya-jayrika on the other, and I went on
board the ship and set the sails to her, and I placed the
ensign of the King of the Great Universe on the one

mast, and that of the King of the Red Shield on the other, and I blew a trumpet, and passed through the midst of them, and I said to them that here was the man, and that if they were going to enforce their claims, this was the time.   All the ships that were there chased me ; and we set out on the expanse of ocean.   My ship would be equalled in speed by but few.   One day a thick dark mist came on, and they lost sight of me.   It happened that I came to an island called The Wet Mantle.   I built a hut there ; and another son was born to me, and I called him Son of the Wet Mantle.

" I was a long time in that island ; but there was enough of fruit, fish, and birds in it.   My two sons had grown to be somewhat big.   As I was one day out killing birds, I saw a big, big man coming towards the island, and I ran to try if I could get into the house before him. He met me, and caught me, and put me into a bog up to the armpits, and he went into the house, and took out on his shoulder the daughter of the King of the Universe, and passed close to me in order to irritate me the more. The saddest look that I ever gave or ever shall give was that I gave when I saw the daughter of the King of the Universe on the shoulder of another, and could not take her from him.   The boys came out where I was ; and I bade them bring me the short spear from the house.   They dragged the short spear after them, and brought it to me ; and I cut the ground around me with it till I got out.

" I was a long time in the Wet Mantle, even till my two sons grew to be big lads.   They asked me one day if I had any thought of going to seek their mother.   I told them that I was waiting till they were stronger, and that they

should then go with me.   They said that they were ready
to go with me at any time.   I said to them that we had
better get the ship ready, and go.   They said, ' Let each of
us have a ship to himself.'   We arranged accordingly ; and
each went his own way.

" As I happened one day to be passing close to land I
saw a great battle going on.   Being under vows never to
pass a battle without helping the weaker side, I went on
shore, and set to work with the weaker side, and I knocked
the head off every one with the short spear.   Being tired,
I lay myself down among the bodies and fell asleep.

"Stretch out your leg, Kayn, till I put a salve of herbs and
healing to it.   Salve and binding herb and the poultice are
cooling; the worm is channering.   Pressure and haste hard
bind me, for I must hear Mass in the great church at Rome,
and be in Norway before I sleep."

Kayn Mac Loy said :

"May it be no foot to Kayn or a foot to any one after one,
or I be Kayn son of Loy, if I stretch out my foot for you to
put a salve of herbs and healing on it, till you tell me if you
found the daughter of the King of the Universe, or if you
went home, or what happened to you."

" The mischief is upon you," said the big man ; that tale
is long to tell, but I will tell another short tale.   When I
awoke out of sleep I saw a ship making for the place where
I was lying, and a big giant with only one eye dragging it
after him : and the ocean reached no higher than his knees.
He had a big fishing-rod with a big strong line hanging
from it on which was a very big hook.   He was throwing
the line ashore, and fixing the hook in a body, and lifting

it on board, and he continued this work till the ship was loaded with bodies. He fixed the hook once in my clothes; but I was so heavy that the rod could not carry me on board. He had to go on shore himself, and carry me on board in his arms. I was then in a worse plight than I ever was in. The giant set off with the ship, which he

dragged after him, and reached a big, precipitous rock, in the face of which he had a large cave: and a damsel as beautiful as I ever saw came out, and stood in the door of the cave. He was handing the bodies to her, and she was taking hold of them and putting them into the cave. As she took hold of each body she said, 'Are you alive?' At last the giant took hold of me, and handed me in to her, and said, 'Keep him apart; he is a large body, and I will have him to breakfast the first day that I go from home.'

My best time was not when I heard the giant's sentence upon me. When he had eaten enough of the bodies, his dinner and supper, he lay down to sleep. When he began to snore the damsel came to speak to me ; and she told me that she was a king's daughter the giant had stolen away and that she had no way of getting away from him. ' I am now,' she said, ' seven years except two days with him, and there is a drawn sword between us. He dared not come nearer me than that till the seven years should expire.' I said to her, ' Is there no way of killing him ? ' ' It is not easy to kill him, but we will devise an expedient for killing him,' said she. ' Look at that pointed bar that he uses for roasting the bodies. At dead of night gather the embers of the fire together, and put the bar in the fire till it be red. Go, then, and thrust it into his eye with all your strength, and take care that he does not get hold of you, for if he does he will mince you as small as midges.' I then went and gathered the embers together, and put the bar in the fire, and made it red, and thrust it into his eye ; and from the cry that he gave I thought that the rock had split. The giant sprang to his feet and chased me through the cave in order to catch me ; and I picked up a stone that lay cn the floor of the cave, and pitched it into the sea ; and it made a plumping noise. The bar was sticking in his eye all the time. Thinking it was I that had sprung into the sea, he rushed to the mouth of the cave, and the bar struck against the door-post of the cave, and knocked off his brain-cap. The giant fell down cold and dead, and the damsel and I were seven years and seven days throwing him into the sea in pieces.

KOISHA KAYN

" I wedded the damsel, and a boy was born to us.   After seven years I started forth again.

" I gave her a gold ring, with my name on it, for the boy, and when he was old enough he was sent out to seek me.

" I then set off to the place where I fought the battle, and found the short spear where I left it ; and I was very pleased that I found it, and that the ship was safe. I sailed a day's distance from that place, and entered a pretty bay that was there, hauled my ship up above the shore, and erected a hut there, in which I slept at night. When I rose next day I saw a ship making straight for the place where I was. When it struck the ground, a big, strong champion came out of it, and hauled it up ; and if it did not surpass my ship it was not a whit inferior to it ; and I said to him, 'What impertinent fellow are you that has dared to haul up your ship alongside of my ship ? ' ' I am Machkan-na-skaya-jayrika,' said the champion, ' going to seek the daughter of the King of the Universe for Mac Connachar, son of the King of Lochlann.' I saluted and welcomed him, and said to him, ' I am your father : it is well that you have come.' We passed the night cheerily in the hut.

" When I arose on the following day I saw another ship making straight for the place where I was ; and a big, strong hero came out of it, and hauled it up alongside of our ships ; and if it did not surpass them it was not a whit inferior to them. ' What impertinent fellow are you that has dared to haul up your ship alongside of our ships ? ' said I. ' I am,' said he, ' the Son of the Wet Mantle, going to seek the daughter of the King of the Universe for Mac Connachar, son of the King of Lochlann.' ' I am your

father, and this is your brother : it is well that you have
come,' said I.   We passed the night together in the hut,
my two sons and I.

"When I rose next day I saw another ship coming,
and making straight for the place where I was.   A big,
strong champion sprang out of it, and hauled it up alongside
of our ships ; and if it was not higher than they, it was not
lower.   I went down where he was, and said to him, 'What
impertinent fellow are you that has dared to haul up your
ship alongside of our ships ? '   'I am the Son of the Wet
Mantle,' said he, ' going to seek the daughter of the King of
the Universe for Mac Connachar, son of the King of Lochlann.
' Have you any token in proof of that ? ' said I.   'I have,'
said he : 'here is a ring that my mother gave me at my
father's request.'   I took hold of the ring, and saw my name
on it : and the matter was beyond doubt.   I said to him,
' I am your father, and here are two half-brothers of yours.
We are now stronger for going in quest of the daughter of
the King of the Universe.   Four piles are stronger than
three piles.'   We spent that night cheerily and comfortably
together in the hut.

"On the morrow we met a soothsayer, and he spoke to
us : ' You are going in quest of the daughter of the King of
the Universe.   I will tell you where she is : she is with
the Son of the Blackbird.

"Machkan-na-skaya-jayrika then went and called for
combat with a hundred fully trained heroes, or the sending
out to him of the daughter of the King of the Universe.
The hundred went out ; and he and they began on each
other, and he killed every one of them.   The Son of the
Wet Mantle called for combat with another hundred, or the

sending out of the daughter of the King of the Universe. He killed that hundred with the short spear. The Son of Secret called for combat with another hundred, or the daughter of the King of the Universe. He killed every one of these with the short spear. I then went out to the field, and sounded a challenge on the shield, and made the town tremble. The Son of the Blackbird had not a man to send out : he had to come out himself ; and he and I began on each other, and I drew the short spear, and swept his head off. I then went into the castle, and took out the daughter of the King of the Universe. It was thus that it fared with me.

"Stretch out your leg, Kayn, till I put a salve of herbs and healing to it. Salve and binding herb and the poultice are cooling ; the worm is channering. Pressure and haste hard bind me, for I must hear Mass in the great church at Rome, and be in Norway before I sleep."

Kayn Mac Loy stretched his leg ; and the big man applied to it leaves of herbs and healing ; and it was healed. The big man took him ashore from the island, and allowed him to go home to the king.

Thus did O'Cronicert win and lose a wife, and thus befell the Leeching of the leg of Kayn, son of Loy.

How Fin went to the Kingdom of the Big Men.

IN and his men were in the Harbour of the Hill of Howth on a hillock, behind the wind and in front of the sun, where they could see every person, and nobody could see them, when they saw a speck coming from the west. They thought at first it was the blackness of a shower; but when it came nearer, they saw it was a boat. It did not lower sail till it entered the harbour. There were three men in it; one for guide in the bow, one for steering in the stern, and one for the tackle in the centre. They came ashore, and drew it up seven times its own length in dry grey grass, where the scholars of the city could not make it stock for derision or ridicule.

They then went up to a lovely green spot, and the first lifted a handful of round pebbles or shingle, and commanded them to become a beautiful house, that no better could be found in Ireland; and this was done. The second one lifted a slab of slate, and commanded it to be slate on the top of the house, that there was not better in Ireland ; and this was done. The third one caught a bunch of shavings and commanded them to be pine-wood and timber in the house, that there was not in Ireland better ; and this was done.

This caused much wonder to Fin, who went down where the men were, and made inquiries of them, and they answered him. He asked whence they were, or whither they were going. They said, "We are three Heroes whom the King of the Big Men has sent to ask combat of the Fians." He then asked, "What was the reason for doing this ? " They said they did not know, but they heard that they were strong men, and they came to ask combat of Heroes from them. "Is Fin at Home ? " "He is not." (Great is a man's leaning towards his own life). Fin then put them under crosses and under enchantments, that they were not to move from the place where they were till they saw him again.

He went away and made ready his coracle, gave its stern to land and prow to sea, hoisted the spotted towering sails against the long, tough, lance-shaped mast, cleaving the billows in the embrace of the wind in whirls, with a soft gentle breeze from the height of the sea-coast, and from the rapid tide of the red rocks, that would take willom from the hill, foliage from the tree, and heather from its stock and roots. Fin was guide in her prow, helm in her stern, and tackle in her middle ; and stopping of head or foot he did not make till he reached the Kingdom of the Big Men. He went ashore and drew up his coracle in grey grass. He went up, and a Big Wayfarer met him. Fin asked who he was. "I am," he said, "the Red-haired Coward of the King of the Big Men ; and," said he to Fin, "you are the one I am in quest of. Great is my esteem and respect towards you ; you are the best maiden I have ever seen ; you will yourself make a dwarf for the King, and your dog (this was Bran) a lapdog. It is long since the King has been in want of a dwarf and a lapdog." He took with him Fin ; but another Big Man came, and was going to take Fin from him. The two fought ; but when they had torn each other's clothes, they left it to Fin to judge. He chose the first one. He took Fin with him to the palace of the King, whose worthies and high nobles assembled to see the little man. The king lifted him upon the palm of his hand, and went three times round the town with Fin upon one palm and Bran upon the other. He made a sleeping-place for him at the end of his own bed. Fin was waiting, watching, and observing everything that was going on about the house. He observed that the King, as soon as night came, rose and went out, and returned no more till morning. This caused him much wonder, and at last he asked the King why he went away every night and left the Queen by herself. " Why," said the King, " do you ask ? " " For satisfaction to myself," said Fin ; " for it is causing me much wonder." Now the King had a great liking for Fin ; he never saw anything that gave him more pleasure than he did ; and at last he told him. " There is," he said, " a great Monster who wants my daughter in marriage, and to have half my kingdom to himself ; and there is not another man in the kingdom who can meet him but myself ; and I must go every night to hold combat with him." " Is there," said Fin, " no man to combat with him but yourself ? " " There is not," said the King, " one who will war with him for a single night." " It is a pity,"

said Fin, "that this should be called the Kingdom of the
Big Men. Is he bigger than yourself?" "Never you
mind," said the King. "I will mind," said Fin; "take
your rest and sleep to-night, and I shall go to meet him."
"Is it you?" said the King; "you would not keep half a
stroke against him."

When night came, and all men went to rest, the King
was for going away as usual; but Fin at last prevailed
upon him to allow himself to go. "I shall combat him,"
said he, "or else he knows a trick." "I think much,"
said the King, "of allowing you to go, seeing he gives myself enough to do." "Sleep you soundly to-night," said
Fin, "and let me go; if he comes too violently upon me, I
shall hasten home."

Fin went and reached the place where the combat was
to be. He saw no one before him, and he began to pace
backwards and forwards. At last he saw the sea coming
in kilns of fire and as a darting serpent, till it came down
below where he was. A Huge Monster came up and looked
towards him, and from him. "What little speck do I see
there?" he said. "It is I," said Fin. "What are you
doing here?" "I am a messenger from the King of the
Big Men; he is under much sorrow and distress; the
Queen has just died, and I have come to ask if you
will be so good as to go home to-night without giving
trouble to the kingdom." "I shall do that," said he; and
he went away with the rough humming of a song in his
mouth.

Fin went home when the time came, and lay down in his
own bed, at the foot of the King's bed. When the King
awoke, he cried out in great anxiety, "My kingdom is lost,

and my dwarf and my lapdog are killed!" "They are not," said Fin; "I am here yet; and you have got your sleep, a thing you were saying it was rare for you to get." "How," said the King, "did you escape, when you are so little, while he is enough for myself, though I am so big."

"Though you," said Fin, "are so big and strong, I am quick and active."

Next night the King was for going; but Fin told him to take his sleep to-night again. "I shall stand myself in your place, or else a better hero than yonder one must come." "He will kill you," said the King, "I shall take my chance," said Fin.

He went, and as happened the night before, he saw no one; and he began to pace backwards and forwards. He saw the sea coming in fiery kilns and as a darting serpent; and that Huge Man came up. "Are you here to-night again?" said he. "I am, and this is my errand: when the Queen was being put in the coffin, and the King heard the coffin being nailed, and the joiner's stroke, he broke his heart with pain and grief; and the *Parliament* has sent me to ask you to go home to-night till they get the King buried." The Monster went this night also, roughly humming a song; and Fin went home when the time came.

In the morning the King awoke in great anxiety, and called out, "My kingdom is lost, and my dwarf and my lapdog are killed!" and he greatly rejoiced that Fin and Bran were alive, and that he himself got rest, after being so long without sleep.

Fin went the third night, and things happened as before. There was no one before him, and he took to pacing to and fro. He saw the sea coming till it came down below him: the Big Monster came up; he saw the little black speck, and asked who was there, and what he wanted. "I have come to combat you," said Fin.

Fin and Bran began the combat. Fin was going backwards, and the Huge Man was following. Fin called to Bran, "Are you going to let him kill me?" Bran had a venomous shoe; and he leaped and struck the Huge Man with the venomous shoe on the breast-bone, and took the heart and lungs out of him. Fin drew his sword, Mac-a-Luin, cut off his head, put it on a hempen rope, and went with it to the Palace of the King. He took it into the *Kitchen*, and put it behind the door. In the morning the servant could not turn it, nor open the door. The King went down ; he saw the Huge Mass, caught it by the top of the head, and lifted it, and knew it was the head of the Man who was for so long a time asking combat from him, and keeping him from sleep. " How at all," said he, "has this head come here ? Surely it is not my dwarf that has done it." " Why," said Fin, " should he not ? "

Next night the King wanted to go himself to the place of combat ; " because," said he, " a bigger one than the former will come to-night, and the kingdom will be destroyed, and you yourself killed ; and I shall lose the pleasure I take in having you with me." But Fin went, and that Big Man came, asking vengeance for his son, and to have the kingdom for himself, or equal combat. He and Fin fought ; and Fin was going backwards. He spoke to Bran, " Are you going to allow him to kill me ? " Bran whined, and went and sat down on the beach. Fin was ever being driven back, and he called out again to Bran. Then Bran jumped and struck the Big Man with the venomous shoe, and took the heart and the lungs out of him. Fin cut the head off, and took it with him, and left it in front of the house. The King awoke in great terror, and cried out, " My kingdom is lost, and my dwarf and my lapdog are killed ! " Fin raised himself up and said, " They are not ; " and the King's joy was not small when he went out and saw the head that was in front of the house.

The next night a Big Hag came ashore, and the tooth in the door of her mouth would make a distaff. She sounded a challenge on her shield : " You killed," she said, " my husband and my son." " I did kill them," said Fin. They

fought; and it was worse for Fin to guard himself from
the tooth than from the hand of the Big Hag. When
she had nearly done for him Bran struck her with the
venomous shoe, and killed her as he had done to the
rest. Fin took with him the head, and left it in front of
the house. The King awoke in great anxiety, and called
out, "My kingdom is lost, and my dwarf and my lapdog
are killed!" "They are not," said Fin, answering him;
and when they went out and saw the head, the King said,
"I and my kingdom will have peace ever after this. The
mother herself of the brood is killed; but tell me who you
are. It was foretold for me that it would be Fin-mac-Coul
that would give me relief, and he is only now eighteen
years of age. Who are you, then, or what is your name?"
"There never stood," said Fin, "on hide of cow or horse,
one to whom I would deny my name. I am Fin, the Son
of Coul, son of Looach, son of Trein, son of Fin, son
of Art, son of the young High King of Erin; and it is
time for me now to go home. It has been with much
wandering out of my way that I have come to your
kingdom; and this is the reason why I have come, that I
might find out what injury I have done to you, or the reason
why you sent the three heroes to ask combat from me, and
bring destruction on my Men." "You never did any injury
to me," said the King; "and I ask a thousand pardons.
I did not send the heroes to you. It is not the truth
they told. They were three men who were courting three
fairy women, and these gave them their shirts; and when
they have on their shirts, the combat of a hundred men is
upon the hand of every one of them. But they must
put off the shirts every night, and put them on the backs

of chairs ; and if the shirts were taken from them they would
be next day as weak as other people."

Fin got every honour, and all that the King could give
him, and when he went away, the King and the Queen
and the people went down to the shore to give him their
blessing.

Fin now went away in his coracle, and was sailing close
by the side of the shore, when he saw a young man
running and calling out to him.   Fin came in close to land
with his coracle, and asked what he wanted.   "I am,'
said the young man, "a good servant wanting a master."
"What work can you do?" said Fin.   "I am," said he,
"the best soothsayer that there is."   "Jump into the boat
then."   The soothsayer jumped in, and they went forward.

They did not go far when another youth came running.
"I am," he said, "a good servant wanting a master."
"What work can you do?" said Fin.   "I am as good a
thief as there is."   "Jump into the boat, then;" and Fin
took with him this one also.   They saw then a third young
man running and calling out.   They came close to land.
"What man are you?" said Fin.   "I am," said he, "the
best climber that there is.   I will take up a hundred pounds
on my back in a place where a fly could not stand on a calm
summer day."   "Jump in;" and this one came in also.
"I have my pick of servants now," said Fin; "it cannot
be but these will suffice."

They went; and stop of head or foot they did not make
till they reached the Harbour of the Hill of Howth.   He
asked the soothsayer what the three Big Men were doing.
"They are," he said, "after their supper, and making ready
for going to bed."

He asked a second time. " They are," he said, " after going to bed ; and their shirts are spread on the back of chairs."

After a while, Fin asked him again, " What are the Big Men doing now ? " " They are," said the soothsayer, " sound asleep." " It would be a good thing if there was now a thief to go and steal the shirts." " I would do that," said the thief, " but the doors are locked, and I cannot get in." " Come," said the climber, " on my back, and I shall put you in." He took him up upon his back to the top of the chimney, and let him down, and he stole the shirts.

Fin went where the Fian band was ; and in the morning they came to the house where the three Big Men were. They sounded a challenge upon their shields, and asked them to come out to combat.

They came out. " Many a day," said they, " have we been better for combat than we are to-day," and they confessed to Fin everything as it was. " You were," said Fin, " impertinent, but I will forgive you " ; and he made them swear that they would be faithful to himself ever after, and ready in every enterprise he would place before them.

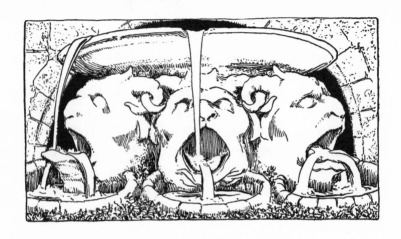

How Cormac Mac Art went to Faery.

CORMAC, son of Art, son of Conn of the Hundred Battles, was high King of Ireland, and held his Court at Tara. One day he saw a youth upon the green having in his hand a glittering fairy branch with nine apples of red. And whensoever the branch was shaken, wounded men and women enfeebled by illness would be lulled to sleep by the sound of the very sweet fairy music which those apples uttered, nor could any one upon earth bear in mind any want, woe, or weariness of soul when that branch was shaken for him.

"Is that branch thy own?" said Cormac.

"It is indeed mine."

"Wouldst thou sell it? and what wouldst thou require for it?"

" Will you give me what I ask ? " said the youth.

The king promised, and the youth then claimed his wife, his daughter, and his son. Sorrowful of heart was the king, heaviness of heart filled his wife and children when they learned that they must part from him. But Cormac shook the branch amongst them, and when they heard the soft sweet music of the branch they forgot all care and sorrow and went forth to meet the youth, and he and they took their departure and were seen no more. Loud cries of weeping and mourning were made throughout Erin when this was known : but Cormac shook the branch so that there was no longer any grief or heaviness of heart upon any one.

After a year Cormac said : " It is a year to-day since my wife, my son, and my daughter were taken from me. I will follow them by the same path that they took."

Cormac went off, and a dark magical mist rose about him, and he chanced to come upon a wonderful marvellous plain. Many horsemen were there, busy thatching a house with the feathers of foreign birds ; when one side was thatched they would go and seek more, and when they returned not a feather was on the roof. Cormac gazed at them for a while and then went forward.

Again, he saw a youth dragging up trees to make a fire ; but before he could find a second tree the first one would be burnt, and it seemed to Cormac that his labour would never end.

Cormac journeyed onwards until he saw three immense wells on the border of the plain, and on each well was a head. From out the mouth of the first head there flowed two streams, into it there flowed one ; the second head had a stream flowing out of and another stream into its mouth, whilst three streams were flowing from the mouth of the third head. Great wonder seized Cormac, and he said: "I will stay and gaze upon these wells, for I should find no man to tell me your story." With that he set onwards till he came to a house in the middle of a field. He entered and greeted the inmates. There sat within a tall couple clad in many-hued garments, and they greeted the king, and bade him welcome for the night.

Then the wife bade her husband seek food, and he arose and returned with a huge wild boar upon his back and a log in his hand. He cast down the swine and the log upon the floor, and said: "There is meat; cook it for yourselves."

"How can I do that?" said Cormac.

"I will teach you," said the youth. "Split this great log, make four pieces of it, and make four quarters of the hog; put a log under each quarter; tell a true story, and the meat will be cooked."

"Tell the first story yourself," said Cormac.

"Seven pigs I have of the same kind as the one I brought, and I could feed the world with them. For if a pig is killed I have but to put its bones into the stye again, and it will be found alive the next morning."

The story was true, and a quarter of the pig was cooked.

Then Cormac begged the woman of the house to tell a story.

"I have seven white cows, and they fill seven cauldrons with milk every day, and I give my word that they yield as much milk as would satisfy the men of the whole world if they were out on yonder plain drinking it."

That story was true, and a second quarter of the pig was cooked.

Cormac was bidden now to tell a story for his quarter, and he told how he was upon a search for his wife, his son and his daughter that had been borne away from him a year before by a youth with a fairy branch.

" If what thou sayest be true," said the man of the house, "thou art indeed Cormac, son of Art, son of Conn of the Hundred Battles."

" Truly I am," quoth Cormac.

That story was true, and a quarter of the pig was cooked.

" Eat thy meal now," said the man of the house.

"I never ate before," said Cormac, "having only two people in my company."

" Wouldst thou eat it with three others ? "

" If they were dear to me, I would," said Cormac.

Then the door opened, and there entered the wife and children of Cormac : great was his joy and his exultation.

Then Manannan mac Lir, lord of the fairy Cavalcade, appeared before him in his own true form, and said thus :

" I it was, Cormac, who bore away these three from thee. I it was who gave thee this branch, all that I might bring thee here. Eat now and drink."

" I would do so," said Cormac, " could I learn the meaning of the wonders I saw to-day."

" Thou shalt learn them," said Manannan. " The horsemen thatching the roof with feathers are a likeness of people who go forth into the world to seek riches and fortune ; when they return their houses are bare, and so they go on for ever. The young man dragging up the trees to make a fire is a likeness of those who labour for others : much trouble they have, but they never warm themselves at the fire. The three heads in the wells are three kinds of men. Some there are who give freely when they get freely ; some who give freely though they get little ; some who get much and give little, and they are the worst of the three, Cormac," said Manannan.

After that Cormac and his wife and his children sat down, and a table-cloth was spread before them.

"That is a very precious thing before thee," said Manannan, "there is no food however delicate that shall be asked of it but it shall be had without doubt."

"That is well," quoth Cormac.

After that Manannan thrust his hand into his girdle and brought out a goblet and set it upon his palm. "This cup has this virtue, said he, "that when a false story is told before it, it makes four pieces of it, and when a true story is related it is made whole again."

"Those are very precious things you have, Manannan," said the king.

"They shall all be thine," said Manannan, "the goblet, the branch and the tablecloth."

Then they ate their meal, and that meal was good, for they could not think of any meat but they got it upon the table-cloth, nor of any drink but they got it in the cup. Great thanks did they give to Manannan.

When they had eaten their meal a couch was prepared for them and they laid down to slumber and sweet sleep.

Where they rose on the morrow morn was in Tara of the kings, and by their side were tablecloth, cup, and branch.

Thus did Cormac fare at the Court of Manannan, and this is how he got the fairy branch.

The Ridere of Riddles.

HERE was a king once, and he married a great lady, and she departed on the birth of her first son. And a little after this the king married another wife, and she too had a son. The two lads grew up tall and strong. Then it struck the queen that it was not her son who would come into the kingdom ; and she set it before her that she would poison the eldest son. And so she sent advice to the cooks that they should put poison in the drink of the heir ; but as luck was in it, the youngest brother heard them, and he told his brother not to take the draught, nor to drink it at all ; and so he did. But the queen wondered that the lad was not dead ; and she thought that there was not enough of poison in the drink, and she asked the cook to put in more on the second night. It was thus they did : and when the cook made up the drink, she said that he would not be long alive after this draught. But his brother heard this also, and told him likewise. The eldest thought he would put the draught into a little bottle, and he said to his brother—" If I stay in

this house I have no doubt she will do for me some way or other, and the quicker I leave the house the better. I will take the world for my pillow, and there is no knowing what fortune will be on me." His brother said that he would go with him, and they took themselves off to the stable, and they put saddles on two horses and they took their soles out of that.

They had not gone very far from the house when the eldest one said—" There is no knowing if poison was in the drink at all, though we went away. Try it in the horse's ear and we shall see." The horse did not go far before he fell. " That was only a rattle-bones of a horse anyway," said the eldest one, and they got up together on the other horse, and so they went forwards. " But," said he, " I can scarce believe that there is any poison in the drink ; let's try it on this horse." That he did, and they went not far when the horse fell cold dead. They thought they'd take the hide off him, and that it would keep them warm at night which was close at hand. In the morning when they woke they saw twelve ravens come and light on the carcase of the horse, and they were not long there when they fell down dead.

They went and lifted the ravens, and they took them with them, and the first town they reached they gave the ravens to a baker, and they asked him to make a dozen pies of the ravens. They took the pies with them, and they went forward on their journey. About the mouth of night, and when they were in a great thick wood, there came four and twenty robbers who bade them to deliver up their purses ; but they said that they had no purse, but only a little food which they were carrying with them. " Good is

even meat !" said the robbers, and they began to eat it,
but had not eaten much when they fell hither and thither,
all stone dead. When they saw that the robbers were
dead they ransacked their pockets, and got much gold and
silver. They went forward till they reached the Knight of
Riddles.

The house of the Knight of Riddles was in the finest
place in that country, and if his house was pretty, his
daughter was prettier, and she had twelve maidens with her
only less fair than she. Her like was not on the surface of
the world, altogether so handsome was she ; and no one
would get her to marry but the man who could put a
question to her father that he could not solve. The brothers
thought that they would go and try to put a question to him ;
and the youngest was to stand in place of gillie to the
elder brother. They reached the house of the Knight of
Riddles and this was the question they put to him—"One
killed two, and two killed twelve, and twelve killed four and
twenty, and two got out of it ; " and they were to be kept
in great majesty and high honour till he should solve the
riddle.

They were thus a while with the Ridere, and try as he
might he could not guess the riddle. On a day of days
came one of the maidens who were with the knight's
daughter to the gillie, and asked him to tell her the
question. He took her plaid from her and let her go, but
he told her nothing. The same thing happened to the
twelve maidens, day after day, and the gillie said to the last
one that no creature had the answer to the riddle but his
master down below. One day after this came the knight's
daughter to the eldest brother, and looking her finest and

handsomest, and she asked him to tell her the question. And now there was no refusing her, and he told her, but he kept her plaid. The Knight of Riddles sent for him, and he gave him the answer of the riddle. And the knight said that he had two choices : to lose his head, or to be set adrift in a crazy boat without food or drink, without oar or scoop. The elder brother spoke, and he said—" I have another riddle to put to thee before all these things happen." " Say on," said the knight. " Myself and my gillie were one day in the forest shooting. My gillie fired at a hare, and she fell, and he took her skin off, and let her go ; and so he did to twelve, he took their skins off and let them go. And at last came a great fine hare, and I myself fired at her, and I took her skin off, and I let her go." " Indeed thy riddle is not hard to solve, my lad," said the knight, and he knew the lad knew he had not really guessed the riddle, but had been told the answer. So he gave him his daughter to wife, to make him hold his peace, and they made a great hearty wedding that lasted a day and a year. The youngest one went home now that his brother had got so well on his way, and the eldest brother gave him every right over the kingdom that was at home.

Now there were near the march of the kingdom of the Knight of Riddles three giants, and they were always murdering and slaying some of the knight's people, and taking spoil from them. On a day of days the Knight of Riddles said to his son-in-law, that if the spirit of a man were in him, he would go to kill the giants, as they were always bringing such losses on the country. Well, so it was, he went and he met the giants, and he came home with the three giants' heads, and he threw them at the knight's feet.

"Thou art an able lad doubtless, and thy name hereafter is
the Hero of the White Shield." The name of the Hero of
the White Shield went far and near.

Meanwhile the brother of the Hero of the White Shield

had wandered afar in many countries, and after long years
had come to the land of the giants where the Hero of the
White Shield was now dwelling, and the knight's daughter
with him. His brother came and he asked to make a

covrag or fight as a bull with him. The men began at each other, and they took to wrestling from morning till evening. At last and at length, when they were tired, weak, and spent, the Hero of the White Shield jumped over a great rampart, and he asked the stranger to meet him in the morning. This leap put the other to shame, and he said to him, " Well may it be that thou wilt not be so supple about this time to-morrow." The young brother now went to a poor little bothy that was near to the house of the Hero of the White Shield, tired and drowsy, and in the morning they dared the fight again. And the Hero of the White Shield began to go back, till he went backwards into a river. " There must be some of my blood in thee before that was done to me." "Of what blood art thou?" said the youngest. " 'Tis I am son of Ardan, great King of the Albann." " 'Tis I am thy brother." It was now they knew each other. They gave luck and welcome to each other, and the Hero of the White Shield now took him into the palace, and she it was that was pleased to see him—the knight's daughter. He stayed a while with them, and after that he thought that he would go home to his own kingdom ; and when he was going past a great palace that was there he saw twelve men playing at shinny over against the palace. He thought he would go for a while and play shinny with them ; but they were not long playing shinny when they fell out, and the weakest of them caught him and shook him as he would a child. He thought it was no use for him to lift a hand amongst these twelve worthies, and he asked them to whom they were sons. They said they were children of the one father, the brother of the Hero of the White Shield, who had not been heard of for

many years. " I am your father," said he ; and he asked
them if their mother was alive. They said that she
was.   He went with them till he found the mother, and
he took her home with him and the twelve sons ; and I
don't know but that his seed are kings on Alba till this
very day.

The Tail.

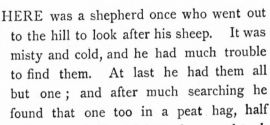HERE was a shepherd once who went out to the hill to look after his sheep. It was misty and cold, and he had much trouble to find them. At last he had them all but one; and after much searching he found that one too in a peat hag, half drowned; so he took off his plaid, and bent down and took hold of the sheep's tail, and he pulled! The sheep was heavy with water, and he could not lift her, so he took off his coat and he *pulled!!* but it was too much for him, so he spit on his hands, and took a good hold of the tail and he PULLED!! and the tail broke! and if it had not been for that this tale would have been a great deal longer.

MAN or WOMAN
BOY or GIRL
THAT READS WHAT
FOLLOWS
3 TIMES
SHALL FALL ASLEEP
AN HUNDRED YEARS

JOHN D. BATTEN DREW THIS: AUG 29ᵗʰ 1891   GOOD-NIGHT.

Notes and References.

I HAVE scarcely anything to add to the general account of the collection of Celtic Fairy Tales which I gave in the predecessor to this
volume, pages 237–42. Since the appearance of that volume in 1891,
the publication of such tales has gone on apace. Mr. Curtin has
published in the New York *Sun* no less than fifty more Irish fairy
tales, one of which he has been good enough to place at my disposal
for the present volume. Mr. Larminie has published with Mr. E. Stock
a volume of *West Irish Fairy Tales*, of which I have also the privilege
of presenting a specimen. A slight volume of Welsh Fairy Tales,
published by Mr. Nutt, and a few fairy anecdotes contained in the Prize
Essay on Welsh Folk-lore by the Rev. Mr. Evans, sum up Cambria's
contribution to our subject during the past three years. The fifth
volume of the *Waifs and Strays of Celtic Tradition*, just about to
appear at the moment of writing, is the sole addition to Celtic Fairy
Tales from the country of J. F. Campbell. Taken altogether, something like a hundred previously unpublished tales from Celtdom have
been rendered accessible to the world since I last wrote, a by no means
insignificant outcome in three years. It is at any rate clear, that the
only considerable addition to our folk-lore knowledge in these isles
must come from the Gaelic area. The time of harvest can be but
short ; may the workers be many, willing, and capable.

XXVII. THE FATE OF THE CHILDREN OF LIR.

Sources.—Abridged from the text and translation published by the
Society for the Preservation of the Irish Language in 1883. This
merely follows the text and version given by Professor O'Curry in
Atlantis, iv. He used three Dublin MSS., none of them, however, of

earlier date than the eighteenth century.   Dr. Joyce gives a free paraphrase in his *Old Celtic Romances*.

Parallels. — For " Jealous Stepmother," see the bibliographical references in the list of incidents at the end of my paper on the " Science of Folk-tales" in the *Transactions of the Folk-lore Congress*, *sub voce*. Add Miss Roalfe Cox in *Folk-lore Journal*, vii. app. 37 ; also the same list *sub voce* " Swan Maiden Transformation." In modern Irish literature Griffin has included the tale in his *Tales of the Jury-room*, and Tom Moore's " Song of Fiounala" beginning " Silent, O Moyle " is founded upon it.

Remarks.—The " Fate of the Children of Lir " is always referred to along with " The Story of Deirdre " (*cf.* the *Celtic Fairy Tales*, ix.), and the " Children of Tuireann " as one of the Three Sorrowful Tales of Erin.   But there is no evidence of equal antiquity to the other two stories, of which one is as old as the eleventh century. From the interspersed verse O'Curry concluded, however, that the story was at least of considerable antiquity, and the references to the unknown Saint Mochaomhog confirm his impression. The Hill of the White Field is near Newton Hannton, in the county of Armagh. The Lake of the Red Eye is Lough Derg, in the Shannon above Killaloe.

Fingula is Fair Shoulder.   The tradition that swans are inviolable is still extant in Ireland. A man named Connor Griffin killed eleven swans : he had previously been a prosperous man, and shortly afterwards his son was drowned in the Shannon, his goods were lost, and his wife died (*Children of Lir*, Dublin edit., note, p. 87).   In County Mayo it is believed that the souls of pure virgins are after death enshrined in the forms of swans ; if anybody injures them, it is thought he will die within a year (Walter's *Natural History of the Birds of Ireland*, pp. 94–5).   Mr. Gomme concludes from this that the swan was at one time a British totem (*Arch. Rev.*, iii. 226–7).

At first sight the tale seems little more than an argument against the Bill for Marriage with a Deceased Wife's Sister, but the plaintive lays of Fingula, the touching detail of the swans flying over the desolate hill and White Field, give a touch of Celtic glamour to the whole story.   There is probably also a deep religious significance implied in the fact that the wicked Aunt Stepmother's spell is broken when the transformed Children of Lir come across the first Christian they meet.

Mr. Nutt has kindly communicated the following remarks on this tale :—

The Fate of the Children of Lir belongs formally to the so-called mythological cycle, the personages of which are the Tuatha de Danann. The Irish annalists of the 10th–11th centuries described these as members of one of the races which possessed Ireland in pre-Christian times before the coming of the Milesians. But even in the most strongly euhemerised accounts the mythic nature of these beings is apparent, and most modern scholars are agreed that they are in fact the members of a Pagan Irish Pantheon. They live on to this very day in Irish folk-belief as chiefs and rulers of the fairies.

The MS. evidence for some of the stories concerning the Tuatha de Danann is as old as that for the oldest heroic cycle (the Ultonian of Conchobar and Cuchulainn). But the Tuatha de Danann legends have retained throughout Irish literature greater plasticity and vitality than those of the Ultonian cycle, and many stories are not older in their present state than the 14th and 15th centuries. This is probably the case with the present story. The oldest known MS. only goes back to 1718, but this and the MS. of 1721, used by O'Curry for his edition, are certainly copied from much older MSS.

The interesting question for storiologists is whether the themes of the story — the swan-metamorphosis consequent upon the step-mother's jealousy, and the protecting rôle assigned to the sister—are of old native or of recent imported nature. In support of the first hypo-thesis, it may be noted that the theme of stepmotherly jealousy was current in Ireland in the 10th century at the latest, as it is woven into the saga of the Destruction of Daderga's Fort (see my article "*Folk-lore*," ii.). The final episode of the sudden aging of the miraculously long-lived swans is also genuinely Irish, but its true significance is obscured in our story in a way that sufficiently demonstrates the late and secondary character of the text. The idea is that the dwellers in Faery, whether fairy-folk or mortals penetrating thither, enjoy perpetual life, forfeited by the latter the moment they return to this earth. As children of the Tuatha de Danann, Fionngula and her brothers are deathless, and the episode as it stands in our text results from a con-tamination of the original form of the story in which the swan-meta-morphosis was annulled under certain conditions (the removal of the chains), when the original shape was resumed, and the familiar story of the mortal returning from Faery after hundreds of years, which he deems to be but a short space of time, shrinking into dust the moment he touches earth.

There is a well-known Continental folk-tale—the " Seven Swans " (or Ravens)—of which we possess several mediæval (12th to 13th century)

versions, all connected with the romance of the "Swan Knight."
M. Gaston Paris has studied the whole story group (*Romania*, xix. 314,
&c.) with the following results : The folk-tale of the seven swans
had originally nothing to do with the saga of the swan-knight. The
connection apparent in the 12th century texts is artificial ; the swans
owe their shape-shifting capacity to the superhuman nature of their
mother ; this trait has been almost effaced even in the oldest versions.
The distinguishing mark of the swans in all the versions is the
possession of silver or gold chains, which are what may be called
metamorphosis tokens ; it follows from this that the contamination
of the two story-types (" Seven Swans " and " Swan Knight ") must be
older than the oldest version of the first story, as these chains can
only be derived from the one with which in the Swan Knight saga
the swan draws the knight back.

In *Romania* (xxi. 62, *seq.*) M. Ferd. Lot examines the question in the
light of our tale. He points out that it indicates clearly the superhuman nature of the mother, and that as the silver chains figure in
the story, they cannot be due in the Continental versions to con-
tamination with the Swan Knight saga, as M. Gaston Paris imagines.
M. Lot evidently inclines to look upon them as talismans, the aban-
donment of which was the original cause of the metamorphosis, and
the handling of which at the end brings about the change back to
human shape. He points out that these chains form an essential part
of the gear of beings appearing in bird guise (especially if they belong to
Faery); thus in the 10th-century 'Sickbed of Cuchulainn' the goddesses
Fand and Liban appear as two swans united by a golden chain ; in
the 8th to 9th century Conception of Cuchulainn, Dechtire, the mother
of the hero by the god Lug, appears with her companions in the
guise of many-hued birds linked together by chains of silver (or red
gold in one version). The MS. evidence for these tales reaches back
to the early 11th century.

Curiously enough, M. Lot has not cited the closest parallel to our
tale from old Irish literature, and one which is certainly connected
with it in some measure, the fine story called the " Dream of Angus." A
story of this title is cited in the epic catalogue of the Book of Leinster
(which dates back to the early 11th century) as one of the introductory
stories to the Tain bo Cuailgne. This assumed its present shape sub-
stantially between 650 and 750. The introductory stories had originally no connection with it, and were invented or re-shaped in the 8th to
10th centuries, after the Tain had taken undisputed place as the lead-

ing Irish epic. The tale may therefore be ascribed provisionally to the
9th century, if we can only be sure that the existing version, preserved
in a single MS. of the 15th century, is a faithful copy of the original.
There need be no doubt as to this. The text is due to a Christian
scribe, and, like nearly all portions of the mythological cycle, betrays
signs of Christian influence, though not of Christian remodelling.
Such influence is, however, far more likely to have exerted itself in
the first stage of the written existence of these tales, when the memory
of organised paganism was still tenacious, than later, when the tales
had become subject-matter for the play of free poetic fancy. The
story, printed and translated by Dr. E. Muller, *Rev. Celt.* iv. 342, &c.,
is as follows : Angus (the chief wizard of the Tuatha de Danann) is
visited in sleep by a maiden whose beauty throws him into love sickness. The whole of Ireland is scoured to find her ; the Dagda is
appealed to in vain. At length, Bodb, fairy king of Munster, finds
her at Loch bel Dracon (this is not the only trace of the impression
which the story of Bel and the Dragon made upon the Irish mind).
She lives there with 150 swans ; one year they are in swan shape
the next in human shape. They appear as white birds with silvery
chains and golden caps around their heads. Angus changes himself
into a swan to be with her, and it is recorded of the music they
made that " people fell asleep for three days and three nights." The
soporific power of music is that which is chiefly commended in old
Irish literature.

I think it is obvious that the writer of our story was familiar with
this and other legends in which swan-maids encircled with gold and
silver chains appear, and that we may fairly draw the following con-
clusions from the preceding facts : There existed an Irish folk-tale
of a king with two wives, one a water or sea fairy, whose children
derive from her the capacity of shape-shifting dependent upon certain
talismans ; jealousy impels the human wife to tamper with these talismans, and the children are condemned to remain in their animal form.
This folk-tale was, probably at some time in the 14th or 15th century,
arbitrarily fitted into the *cadre* of the Tuatha de Danann cycle, and
entirely re-fashioned in a spirit of pious edification by a man who was
in his way a great and admirable artist. The origin and nature of the
story, all the elements of which are genuinely national, assured for it
wide and lasting popularity. The evolution of the Irish folk-tale is in
no way dependent upon that of the Continental folk-tale of the Seven
Swans, but it is possible that the Celtic presentiment of the chain-

girdled swans may have influenced it as well as the Swan Knight
Romance.

XXVIII. JACK THE CUNNING THIEF.

Sources.—Kennedy, *Stories of Ireland,* pp. 38-46 ; Campbell, *West
Highland Tales,* i. 320 *seq.* ; " The Shifty Lad," Dasent, *Popular Tales
from the Norse,* pp. 232-51, " Master Thief." Köhler has a number
of variants in his notes on Campbell : *Orient und Occident,* Band ii.
Mr. Clouston has a monograph on the subject in his *Popular Tales,*
ii. 115-65. A separate treatise on the subject has been given by
S. Prato, 1882, *La Leggenda di Rhampsinite.* Both these writers
connect the modern folk-tales with Herodotus' story of King Ramp-
sinites. Mr. Knowles in his *Folk-tales of Kashmir,* has a number of
adventures of " Sharaf the Thief." The story of " Master Thief" has
been heard among the tramps in London workhouses (Mayhew,
London Labour and London Poor, iii. 119).

Remarks.—Thievery is universally human, and at first sight it might
seem that there was no connection between these various versions of
the " Master Thief." But the identity of the tricks by which the
popular hero-thief gains his ends renders it impossible that they should
have been independently invented wherever they are found.

XXIX. POWEL, PRINCE OF DYFED.

Source.—Lady Guest's *Mabinogion,* with the names slightly angli-
cised, and omitting the opening incident.

Parallels.—For the incident of tearing off the hands, *cf.* Morraha ;
the enchanted hill and maiden occur at the beginning of " Tuairisgeul
Mòr " in *Scottish Celtic Review,* i. 61, and are fully commented upon
by Mr. Nutt, *l.c.* 137.

XXX. PADDY O'KELLY AND THE WEASEL.

Sources.—Hyde, *Beside the Fire,* pp. 73-91.

Parallels.—On green hills as the homes of the fairies: see note on
" Childe Roland," *English Fairy Tales,* p. 241. The transformation
of witches into hares is a frequent *motif* in folk-lore.

XXXI. THE BLACK HORSE.

Sources.—From J. F. Campbell's manuscript collection now deposited
at the Advocates' Library in Edinburgh (MS. 53, vol. xi.). Collected

in Gaelic, February 14, 1862, by Hector MacLean, from Roderick MacNeill, in the island of Menglay : MacNeill learnt the story about 1840 from a Barra man. I have omitted one visit of the Black Horse to Greece, but otherwise left the tale untouched. Mr. Nutt gave a short abstract of the story in his report on the Campbell MSS. in *Folk-lore*, i. 370.

Parallels.—Campbell gives the following parallels in his notes on the tale, which I quote verbatim. On the throwing into the well he remarks : " So this incident of ' Lady Audley's Secret ' was in the mind of a Barra peasant about 1840. Part of a modern novel may be as old as Aryan mythology, which was one point to be proved." [The incident of throwing into the well almost invariably forms a part of the tales of the White Cat type.]

With regard to the Black Horse, Campbell notes that a Gaelic riddle makes a Black Horse identical with the West Wind, and adds : " It is for consideration whether this Horse throws light on the sacred Wheel in Indian Sculptures ; it is to be noted that a Black Horse is the sacrificial colour."

" The Cup is a well-known myth about winning a Fairy Cup which pervades Scandinavian England in many forms." " A silver ring, two quaint serpents' heads pointing opposite ways, is a common Scandinavian wedding-ring ; many were to be got in Barra and elsewhere in 1869, sold by emigrants bound for America."

" Those who can account for myths must settle the geography of the Snow Mountain. Avalanches and glaciers are in Iceland, in the Caucasus, and in Central Asia. There are none within sight of Menglay. Hindoo cosmogony, which makes the world consist of seven rings, separated by seas and by a wall of mountains, may account for this in some sort."

On the spikes driven into the Horse, Campbell compares the Norse story of " Dapple-grim " and the Horse sacrifice of the Mahabharata. On the building of the Magic Castle, Campbell remarks : " Twashtri was the Carpenter of the Vedic gods : can this be his work ? "

On the Horse's head being struck off Campbell comments : " This was the last act in the Aryan Horse's sacrifice, and the first step in the Horse apotheosis."

Remarks.—Campbell has the following note at the end of the tale, from which it would seem that in 1870 at least he was very nearly being an *Indiamaniac.*

" So ends this horse-riding story. Taking it as it is, with the test of language added, nothing short of an Asian origin will account for it. A Gaelic riddle makes 'a black horse' mean the invisible wind, and a theorist might suppose this horse to be the air personified. As Greece is mentioned, he might be Pegasus, who had to do with wells. But he had wings, and he was white, and there is nothing in classical fable like this Atlantic myth. 'The enchanted horse' of Arabian Nights was a flying machine, and his adventures are quite different. This is not the horse of Chaucer's Squire's Tale. He is more like 'Hrimfaxi,' the horse of the Edda, who drew the car of Nött in heaven, and was ridden round the earth in twelve hours, followed by Dagr and his glittering horse Skinfaxi. The black horse who always arrives at sunrise is like the horse of night, but there is no equivalent story in the Edda. 'Dapple-grim' in Norse tales is clad in a spiked bull's hide, and is mixed up with a blazing tar-barrel, but his adventures won't fit, and he was grey.

"The story is but an imperfect skeleton. The cup was to give strength; he had to open seven gates after he got the cup, but it does nothing. The hood is to hide with ; he went in and out of the palace unseen after he had got the hood, but it plays no part. The light shoes were the shoes of swiftness of course, but they never showed their paces. Baldr's horse was led to the funeral pile with all his gear ; and Odin laid the gold ring Draupnir on the pile. Such rites might account for the ring in the blazing lake. Hermothr's ride northwards and downwards to the abode of Hel to seek Baldr, his leap over the grate, and his return with the ring (Edda 25), might account for one adventure.

"The many-coloured horses of the sun in the Indian mythology and solar myths may account for all these horses, astronomically or meteorologically. The old Aryan Aswa Medha or sacrifice of a black horse, and the twelve adventures of Arjuna as told in the Mahabharata, are something like this story in some general vague way. But the simplest explanation of this Menglay myth, fished out of the Atlantic, is to admit that 'the black horse' and all this mythical breed came west with men who rode from the land where horses were tamed, which is unknown."

XXXII. THE VISION OF MACCONGLINNEY.

Source.—Kindly condensed by Mr. Alfred Nutt from Prof. Meyer's edition of *The Vision* published in book form in 1892. This contains two versions, a longer one from a fourteenth century MS., *Leabhar Breac or*

Speckled Book, and a shorter one from a sixteenth century MS. in the Library of Trinity College, Dublin. A translation of the former version was given by the late W. M. Hennessy in *Fraser's Magazine*, September, 1873. Prof. Wollner, who contributed to Prof. Meyer's edition an introduction dealing with the story from the standpoint of comparative literature, considers that the later version reproduces the original common source more nearly.

Parallels.—At first sight *The Vision* seems to picture the Land of Cockayne (on which see Poeschel, *Das Mährchen vom Schlaraffenlande*, Halle, 1878), but as Prof. Wollner remarks, the Irish form is much more simple and primitive, and represents rather an agricultural conception of a past *aurea aetas*. The conception of enormous appetite being due to the presence of a voracious animal or demon within the body is widespread among the folk. Prof. Wollner gives numerous parallels, *l.c.* XLVII.–LIII. The common expression "to wolf one's food" is said to be derived from this conception. On the personification of disease, see Tylor, *Primitive Culture*, ii. 148.

I can myself remember a tale somewhat similar to *The Vision* which I heard from my nurse in Australia, I fancy as a warning against gluttony. She told me of a man, who in swallowing large pieces of food had swallowed a little hairy monster, which grew and grew and grew and caused the man to be eating all day to satisfy his visitors He was cured by being made to fast, and then a bowl of brandy was brought in front of his mouth into which the hairy thing, attracted by the fumes, jumped and was drowned.

Remarks.—We have here an interesting example of the personification of disease in the form of a demon, of which some examples occui in the Gospels. The rollicking Rabelaisian tone in which the story is told prevents us, however, from attributing any serious belief in the conception by the Irish Monk the author of the tale, who was parodying, according to Prof. Wollner, the Visions of the Saints. Still he would be scarcely likely to use the conception, even for purposes of parody, unless it were current among the folk, and it occurs among them even at the present day. (See Hyde, *Beside the Fire*, p. 183.)

XXXIII. DREAM OF OWEN O'MULREADY.

Sources.—Kindly translated by Mr. Leland L. Duncan from *Gaelic Journal*, vol. iv. p. 57 *seq.*

Parallels.—Croker's *Daniel O'Rourke* may be compared in part.

Remarks.—At first sight a mere droll, the story has its roots in the most primitive philosophy. Owen's problem is to get in the Land of Dreams. Now Dreamland, so all our students of Mythology are agreed, is the source and origin of our belief in souls and spirits. Owen's problem therefore resolves itself into this: where was he to go in order to come into closest contact with the world of spirits. Mark what he does—he clears the hearth and has his bed made in it. Now it is round the hearth that the fullest associations with the spirit life are clustered. The late M. Fustel de Coulanges in his *Cité Antique* traces back most of the Greek and Roman religions and a large number of their institutions to the worship of the ancestors localised on the hearth. The late Professor Hearn extended his line of research to the whole of the Aryans in his *Aryan Household*. It will thus be seen from this course of reasoning, that Owen was acting on the most approved primitive principles in adopting this curious method of obtaining dreams. The story is not known elsewhere than in Ireland, and we are therefore at liberty to apply the method of survivals to this case.

XXXIV. MORRAHA.

Sources.—The second story in Mr. W. Larminie's *West Irish Folk-tales*, pp. 10-30. The framework was collected from P. McGrale of Achill Island, Co. Mayo. The story itself was from Terence Davis of Rendyle, Co. Galway. There is evidently confusion in the introductory portion between Niall's mother and wife.

Parallels.—Campbell's No. 1 has a very close parallel to the opening. Mr. Larminie refers to a similar tale collected by Kennedy. Another version from West Munster has been recently published in the *Gaelic Journal*, iv. 7, 26, 35. The evasion of the promise to give up the sword at the end seems a favourite incident in Achill folk-tales; it occurs in two others of Mr. Larminie's stories. On the framework, see note on "Conal Yellow claw" (*Celtic Folk-tales*, v.). I have there suggested that the plan comes from the East, ultimately from Buddha.

XXXV. THE STORY OF THE McANDREW FAMILY.

Sources.—Supplied by Mrs. Gale, now in the United States, from the recitation of her mother who left Ireland over fifty years ago.

Parallels.—"Noodle Tales" like this are found everywhere in

Europe, and have been discussed by Mr. Clouston in a special monograph in *The Book of Noodles*, 1889. The "sell" at the end is similar
to that in the "Wise Men of Gotham." Kennedy (*Fireside Stories
of Ireland*) gives a similar set of adventures, p. 119 *seq.*

Remarks.—Mrs. Gale remarks that it was a common superstition
in Ireland, that if a raven hovered over the head of cattle, a withering
blight had been set upon the animals. As birds of carrion they were
supposed to be waiting for the carcases.

XXXVI. THE FARMER OF LIDDESDALE

Sources.—MacDougal, *Waifs and Strays*, III. ix. pp. 216–21.

Parallels.—Campbell, *West Highland Tales*, "The Master and the
Man," iii. 288–92.

Remarks.—I need scarcely suggest the identification of the Ploughman with the ———. As usual in folk-tales, that personage does
not get the best of the bargain. The rustic Faust evades his contract
by a direct appeal to the higher powers. This is probably characteristic of Scotch piety.

XXXVII. THE GREEK PRINCESS AND THE YOUNG GARDENER.

Sources.—Kennedy, *Fireside Stories*, pp. 47–56.

Parallels.—Campbell, *West Highland Tales*, lvi.; *Mac Iain Direach*,
ii. 344–76. He gives other variants at the end. The story is clearly
that of the Grimms' "Golden Bird," No. 57. They give various
parallels in their notes. Mrs. Hunt refers to an Eskimo version in
Rae's *White Sea Peninsula*, called "Kuobba the Giant and the Devil."
But the most curious and instructive parallel is that afforded by the
Arthurian Romance of Walewein (*i.e.*, Gawain), now only extant in
Dutch, which, as Professor W. P. Ker has pointed out in *Folk-lore*,
v. 121, exactly corresponds to the popular tale, and thus carries it back
in Celtdom to the early twelfth century at the latest.

XXXVIII. THE RUSSET DOG.

Source.—I have made up this Celtic Reynard out of several fables
given by Campbell, *West Highland Tales*, under the title "Fables,"
vol. i. pp. 275 *seq.*; and "The Keg of Butter" and the "The Fox and
the little Bonnach," vol. iii. Nos. lxv. lxvi.

Parallels.—The Fox's ruse about a truce among the animals is a well-known Æsop's Fable ; see my edition of *Caxton's Æsop*, vol. ii. p. 307, and *Parallels*, vol. i. p. 267.   The trick by which the cock gets out of the fox's mouth is a part of the Reynard Cycle, and is given by Chaucer as his " Nonne Preste's Tale." How the wolf lost his tail is also part of the same cycle, the parallels of which are given by K. Krohn, *Bär (Wolf) und Fuchs* (Helsingfors, 1889), pp. 26-8. The same writer has studied the geographical distribution of the story in Finland, accompanied by a map, in *Fennia*, iv. No. 4.   I have given a mediæval Hebrew version in my *Jews of Angevin England*, pp. 170-2. See also Gerber, *Great Russian Animal Tales*, pp. 48-50.   The wolf was originally the bear, as we see from the conclusion of the incident, which professes to explain why the wolf is stumpy-tailed.   " The Keg of Butter" combines two of the Grimm stories, 2, 189.   " The Little Bonnach" occurs also in English and has been given in two variants in *English Fairy Tales*, No. xxviii. ; and *More English Fairy Tales*, No. lvii.

Remarks.—It would lead me too far afield to discuss here the sources of Reynard the Fox, with which I hope shortly to deal at length elsewhere.   But I would remark that in this case, as in several others we have observed, the stories, which are certainly reproductions, have received the characteristic Celtic dress.   It follows that we cannot conclude anything as to the origin of a tale from the fact that it is told idiomatically.   On the other hand, the stories of " The Fox and Wrens " and " The Fox and the Todhunter," and " How the Fox gets rid of his Fleas," have no parallels elsewhere, and show the possibility of a native beast tale or cycle of tales.

XXXIX. SMALLHEAD AND THE KING'S SON.

Source.—Mr. Curtin's " Hero Tales of Ireland," contributed to the *New York Sun*.

Parallels.—Campbell's No. xvii., " Maol a Chliobain," is the same story, which is also found among the Lowlanders, and is given in my *English Fairy Tales*, No. xxii., " Molly Whuppie," where see notes for other parallels of the Hop o' My Thumb type of story.   King Under the Waves occurs in Campbell, No. lxxxvi.

XL. THE LEGEND OF KNOCKGRAFTON.

Source.—Croker, *Fairy Legends of South of Ireland*.

Parallels.—Parnell's poem, *Edwin and Sir Topaz*, contains the same story.   As he was born in Dublin, 1679, this traces the tale back at least 200 years in Ireland. Practically the same story, however, has been found in Japan, and translated into English under the title, " Kobutori ; or, The Old Man and the Devils." In the story published by Kobunsha, Tokio, the Old Man has a lump on the side of his face. He sees the demons dancing, and getting exhilarated, joins in. Thereupon the devils are so delighted that they wish to see him again, and as a pledge of his return take away from him his lump. Another old man, who has a similar lump on the other side of his face, hearing of this, tries the same plan, but dances so badly that the devils, not wishing to see him again, and mistaking him for the other old man, give him back the lump, so that he has one on each side of his face.

I may add here that Mr. York Powell informs me that No. xvii. of the same series, entitled, " Shippietaro," contains a parallel to the " Hobyahs" of *More English Tales.*

Remarks.—Here we have a problem of diffusion presented in its widest form. There can be little doubt that " The Legend of Knockgrafton " and " Kobutori," one collected in Ireland and to be traced there for the last 200 years, and the other collected at the present day in Japan, are one and the same story, and it is impossible to imagine they were independently produced. Considering that Parnell could not have come across the Japanese version, we must conclude that " Kobutori " is a recent importation into Japan. On the other hand, as " the Hobyahs " cannot be traced in England, and was collected from a Scottish family settled in the United States, where Japanese influence has been considerable, it is possible that this tale was derived from Japan within the memory of men still living. It would be highly desirable to test these two cases, in which we seem to be able to observe the process of the diffusion of Folk Tales going on before our eyes.

XLI. ELIDORE.

Source.—Giraldus Cambrensis, *Itinerarium Cambriæ*, I. viii. I have followed the Latin text tolerably closely.

Parallels.—Mr. Hartland has a paper on " Robberies in Fairyland," in *Arch. Rev.*, iii. 39 *seq.* Davies, *Mythology of the British Druids*, p. 155, tells a story of a door in a rock near a cave in the mountains of Brecknock, which was left open for Mayday, and men used to enter, and so reach that fairy island in the middle of the lake. The visitors were treated very hospitably by their fairy hosts, but on the condition that they might eat all, but pocket none ; for once, a visitor took away with him a fairy flower, and as soon as he got outside the door the flower vanished, and the door was never more opened. "The Luck of Edenhall," still in existence, is supposed to be a trophy brought back from a similar visit.

Remarks.—Mr. Hartland suggests that these legends, and the relics connected with them, are in some way connected with the heathen rites prevalent in these islands before the introduction of Christianity, which may have lingered on into historic times. The absence of sunlight in this account of the House of the Fairies, as in "Childe Rowland" (on which see note in *English Fairy Tales*), may be regarded as a point in favour of Mr. MacRitchie's theories as to the identification of the fairies with the mound-dwellers. The object of the expectoration was to prevent Elidore's seeing his way back. Thus the fairies prevent the indiscretions of the human midwives they employ.

XLII. THE LEECHING OF KAYN'S LEG.

Source.—MacInnes, *Folk-Tales from Argyleshire*, vii., combined with Campbell of Tiree's version.

Parallels.—The earliest version, from an Egerton MS. of the fifteenth century, has been printed by Mr. S. H. O'Grady in his *Silva Gadelica*, No. 20, with an English version, pp. 332–42. Mr. Campbell of Tiree has given a short Gaelic version in the *Transactions of the Gaelic Society of Inverness*, 78–100. Campbell of Islay collected the fullest version of this celebrated story, which is to be found among his manuscript remains now in Edinburgh. Mr. Nutt has given his English abstract in *Folk-lore*, i. 373–7, in its original form. The story must have contained twenty-four tales or episodes of stories, nineteen of which are preserved in J. F. Campbell's version. For parallels to the various incidents, see Mr. Nutt's notes on MacInnes, pp. 470–3. The tale is referred to in MacNicol, *Remarks on Dr. Johnson's Journey to the Hebrides*, 1779.

Remarks.—Nothing could give a more vivid idea of what might be called the organisation of the art of story-telling among the Celts than this elaborate tale. Mr. Nutt is inclined to trace it, even in its present form, back to the twelfth or thirteenth century. It occurs in an MS. of the fifteenth century in an obviously unoriginal form which shows that the story-teller did not appreciate the significance of many features in the folk-tale he was retelling, and yet it was orally collected by the great Campbell in 1871, in a version which runs to 142 folio pages.

Formally, its interest consists in large measure in the curious framework in which the subsidiary stories are imbedded. This is not of the
elaborate kind introduced into Europe from the East by the Crusades,
but more *naive*, resembling rather, as Mr. Nutt points out to me, the
loosely-knit narratives of Charles Lever in his earlier manner.

XLIII. HOW FIN WENT TO THE KINGDOM OF THE BIG MEN.

Source.—J. G. Campbell, *The Fians* (*Waifs and Strays*, No. iv.), pp.
175–92.

Parallels.—*The Voyage to Brobdingnag* will occur to many readers,
and it is by no means impossible that, as Swift was once an Irish lad,
The Voyage may have been suggested by some such tale told him in
his infancy. It is not, however, a part of the earlier recorded Ossianic
cycle, though over-sea giants occur as opponents of the heroes in that
as well as in the earlier Ultonian cycle.

XLIV. HOW CORMAC MAC ART WENT TO FAERY.

Source.—Kindly condensed by Mr. Alfred Nutt from an English
version by Mr. S. H. O'Grady in *Ossianic Society's Publications*,
vol. iii. The oldest known version has been printed from fourteenth
century MSS., by Mr. Whitley Stokes, *Irische Texte*, iii. I. The story
existed in some form in the early eleventh century, as it is cited in the
epic catalogue contained in the Book of Leinster.

Parallels.—Mr. Nutt in his *Studies on the Legend of the Holy
Grail*, p. 193, connects this visit of Cormac to the Otherworld with
the bespelled Castle incident in the Grail Legend, and gives other
instances of visits to the Brug of Manannan. Manannan Mac Lir is
the Celtic sea-god.

XLV. RIDERE OF RIDDLES.

Source.—Campbell, *West Highland Tales*, No. xxii. vol. ii. p. 36,
seq. I have modified the end, which has a polygamous complexion.

Parallels.—Campbell points out that the story is in the main identical
with the Grimms' " Räthsel," No. xxii. There the riddle is: " One slew
none, and yet slew twelve." MacDougall has the same story in *Waifs
and Strays*, iii. pp. 76 *seq.*

Remarks.—There can be no doubt that the Celtic and German
Riddle Stories are related genealogically. Which is of the earlier

generation is, however, more difficult to determine. In favour of the Celtic is the polygamous framework ; while on the other hand, it is difficult to guess how the story could have got from the Highlands to Germany. The simpler form of the riddle in the German version might seem to argue greater antiquity.

XLVI. THE TAIL.

Source.—Campbell, No. lvii.

Parallels.—Most story-tellers have some formula of this kind to conclude their narrations. Prof. Crane gives some examples in his *Italian Popular Tales*, pp. 155–7. The English have : " I'll tell you a story of Jack a Nory," and " The Three Wise Men of Gotham" who went to Sea in a Bowl :

> " If the bowl had been stronger,
> My song would have been longer."

A CATALOGUE OF
SELECTED DOVER BOOKS
IN ALL FIELDS OF INTEREST

A CATALOGUE OF SELECTED DOVER BOOKS IN ALL FIELDS OF INTEREST

RACKHAM'S COLOR ILLUSTRATIONS FOR WAGNER'S RING. Rackham's finest mature work—all 64 full-color watercolors in a faithful and lush interpretation of the *Ring*. Full-sized plates on coated stock of the paintings used by opera companies for authentic staging of Wagner. Captions aid in following complete Ring cycle. Introduction. 64 illustrations plus vignettes. 72pp. 8⅝ x 11¼. **23779-6 Pa. $6.00**

CONTEMPORARY POLISH POSTERS IN FULL COLOR, edited by Joseph Czestochowski. 46 full-color examples of brilliant school of Polish graphic design, selected from world's first museum (near Warsaw) dedicated to poster art. Posters on circuses, films, plays, concerts all show cosmopolitan influences, free imagination. Introduction. 48pp. 9⅜ x 12¼. **23780-X Pa. $6.00**

GRAPHIC WORKS OF EDVARD MUNCH, Edvard Munch. 90 haunting, evocative prints by first major Expressionist artist and one of the greatest graphic artists of his time: *The Scream, Anxiety, Death Chamber, The Kiss, Madonna,* etc. Introduction by Alfred Werner. 90pp. 9 x 12. **23765-6 Pa. $5.00**

THE GOLDEN AGE OF THE POSTER, Hayward and Blanche Cirker. 70 extraordinary posters in full colors, from Maitres de l'Affiche, Mucha, Lautrec, Bradley, Cheret, Beardsley, many others. Total of 78pp. 9⅜ x 12¼. **22753-7 Pa. $5.95**

THE NOTEBOOKS OF LEONARDO DA VINCI, edited by J. P. Richter. Extracts from manuscripts reveal great genius; on painting, sculpture, anatomy, sciences, geography, etc. Both Italian and English. 186 ms. pages reproduced, plus 500 additional drawings, including studies for *Last Supper,* Sforza monument, etc. 860pp. 7⅞ x 10¾. (Available in U.S. only) **22572-0, 22573-9 Pa., Two-vol. set $15.90**

THE CODEX NUTTALL, as first edited by Zelia Nuttall. Only inexpensive edition, in full color, of a pre-Columbian Mexican (Mixtec) book. 88 color plates show kings, gods, heroes, temples, sacrifices. New explanatory, historical introduction by Arthur G. Miller. 96pp. 11⅜ x 8½. (Available in U.S. only) **23168-2 Pa. $7.95**

UNE SEMAINE DE BONTÉ, A SURREALISTIC NOVEL IN COLLAGE, Max Ernst. Masterpiece created out of 19th-century periodical illustrations, explores worlds of terror and surprise. Some consider this Ernst's greatest work. 208pp. 8⅛ x 11. **23252-2 Pa. $6.00**

DRAWINGS OF WILLIAM BLAKE, William Blake. 92 plates from Book of Job, *Divine Comedy, Paradise Lost*, visionary heads, mythological figures, Laocoon, etc. Selection, introduction, commentary by Sir Geoffrey Keynes. 178pp. 8⅛ x 11.   22303-5 Pa. $4.00

ENGRAVINGS OF HOGARTH, William Hogarth. 101 of Hogarth's greatest works: *Rake's Progress, Harlot's Progress, Illustrations for Hudibras, Before and After, Beer Street and Gin Lane*, many more. Full commentary. 256pp. 11 x 13¾.   22479-1 Pa. $12.95

DAUMIER: 120 GREAT LITHOGRAPHS, Honore Daumier. Wide-ranging collection of lithographs by the greatest caricaturist of the 19th century. Concentrates on eternally popular series on lawyers, on married life, on liberated women, etc. Selection, introduction, and notes on plates by Charles F. Ramus. Total of 158pp. 9⅜ x 12¼.   23512-2 Pa. $6.00

DRAWINGS OF MUCHA, Alphonse Maria Mucha. Work reveals draftsman of highest caliber: studies for famous posters and paintings, renderings for book illustrations and ads, etc. 70 works, 9 in color; including 6 items not drawings. Introduction. List of illustrations. 72pp. 9⅜ x 12¼. (Available in U.S. only)   23672-2 Pa. $4.00

GIOVANNI BATTISTA PIRANESI: DRAWINGS IN THE PIERPONT MORGAN LIBRARY, Giovanni Battista Piranesi. For first time ever all of Morgan Library's collection, world's largest. 167 illustrations of rare Piranesi drawings—archeological, architectural, decorative and visionary. Essay, detailed list of drawings, chronology, captions. Edited by Felice Stampfle. 144pp. 9⅜ x 12¼.   23714-1 Pa. $7.50

NEW YORK ETCHINGS (1905-1949), John Sloan. All of important American artist's N.Y. life etchings. 67 works include some of his best art; also lively historical record—Greenwich Village, tenement scenes. Edited by Sloan's widow. Introduction and captions. 79pp. 8⅜ x 11¼.   23651-X Pa. $4.00

CHINESE PAINTING AND CALLIGRAPHY: A PICTORIAL SURVEY, Wan-go Weng. 69 fine examples from John M. Crawford's matchless private collection: landscapes, birds, flowers, human figures, etc., plus calligraphy. Every basic form included: hanging scrolls, handscrolls, album leaves, fans, etc. 109 illustrations. Introduction. Captions. 192pp. 8⅞ x 11¾.   23707-9 Pa. $7.95

DRAWINGS OF REMBRANDT, edited by Seymour Slive. Updated Lippmann, Hofstede de Groot edition, with definitive scholarly apparatus. All portraits, biblical sketches, landscapes, nudes, Oriental figures, classical studies, together with selection of work by followers. 550 illustrations. Total of 630pp. 9⅛ x 12¼.   21485-0, 21486-9 Pa., Two-vol. set $15.00

THE DISASTERS OF WAR, Francisco Goya. 83 etchings record horrors of Napoleonic wars in Spain and war in general. Reprint of 1st edition, plus 3 additional plates. Introduction by Philip Hofer. 97pp. 9⅜ x 8¼.   21872-4 Pa. $4.00

THE EARLY WORK OF AUBREY BEARDSLEY, Aubrey Beardsley. 157 plates, 2 in color: *Manon Lescaut, Madame Bovary, Morte Darthur, Salome,* other. Introduction by H. Marillier. 182pp. 8⅛ x 11. 21816-3 Pa. $4.50

THE LATER WORK OF AUBREY BEARDSLEY, Aubrey Beardsley. Exotic masterpieces of full maturity: *Venus and Tannhauser, Lysistrata, Rape of the Lock, Volpone,* Savoy material, etc. 174 plates, 2 in color. 186pp. 8⅛ x 11. 21817-1 Pa. $5.95

THOMAS NAST'S CHRISTMAS DRAWINGS, Thomas Nast. Almost all Christmas drawings by creator of image of Santa Claus as we know it, and one of America's foremost illustrators and political cartoonists. 66 illustrations. 3 illustrations in color on covers. 96pp. 8⅜ x 11¼. 23660-9 Pa. $3.50

THE DORÉ ILLUSTRATIONS FOR DANTE'S DIVINE COMEDY, Gustave Doré. All 135 plates from Inferno, Purgatory, Paradise; fantastic tortures, infernal landscapes, celestial wonders. Each plate with appropriate (translated) verses. 141pp. 9 x 12. 23231-X Pa. $4.50

DORÉ'S ILLUSTRATIONS FOR RABELAIS, Gustave Doré. 252 striking illustrations of *Gargantua and Pantagruel* books by foremost 19th-century illustrator. Including 60 plates, 192 delightful smaller illustrations. 153pp. 9 x 12. 23656-0 Pa. $5.00

LONDON: A PILGRIMAGE, Gustave Doré, Blanchard Jerrold. Squalor, riches, misery, beauty of mid-Victorian metropolis; 55 wonderful plates, 125 other illustrations, full social, cultural text by Jerrold. 191pp. of text. 9⅜ x 12¼. 22306-X Pa. $7.00

THE RIME OF THE ANCIENT MARINER, Gustave Doré, S. T. Coleridge. Dore's finest work, 34 plates capture moods, subtleties of poem. Full text. Introduction by Millicent Rose. 77pp. 9¼ x 12. 22305-1 Pa. $3.50

THE DORE BIBLE ILLUSTRATIONS, Gustave Doré. All wonderful, detailed plates: Adam and Eve, Flood, Babylon, Life of Jesus, etc. Brief King James text with each plate. Introduction by Millicent Rose. 241 plates. 241pp. 9 x 12. 23004-X Pa. $6.00

THE COMPLETE ENGRAVINGS, ETCHINGS AND DRYPOINTS OF ALBRECHT DURER. "Knight, Death and Devil"; "Melencolia," and more—all Dürer's known works in all three media, including 6 works formerly attributed to him. 120 plates. 235pp. 8⅜ x 11¼. 22851-7 Pa. $6.50

MECHANICK EXERCISES ON THE WHOLE ART OF PRINTING, Joseph Moxon. First complete book (1683-4) ever written about typography, a compendium of everything known about printing at the latter part of 17th century. Reprint of 2nd (1962) Oxford Univ. Press edition. 74 illustrations. Total of 550pp. 6⅛ x 9¼. 23617-X Pa. $7.95

THE COMPLETE WOODCUTS OF ALBRECHT DURER, edited by Dr. W. Kurth. 346 in all: "Old Testament," "St. Jerome," "Passion," "Life of Virgin," Apocalypse," many others. Introduction by Campbell Dodgson. 285pp. 8½ x 12¼. 21097-9 Pa. $7.50

DRAWINGS OF ALBRECHT DURER, edited by Heinrich Wolfflin. 81 plates show development from youth to full style. Many favorites; many new. Introduction by Alfred Werner. 96pp. 8⅛ x 11. 22352-3 Pa. $5.00

THE HUMAN FIGURE, Albrecht Dürer. Experiments in various techniques—stereometric, progressive proportional, and others. Also life studies that rank among finest ever done. Complete reprinting of Dresden Sketchbook. 170 plates. 355pp. 8⅜ x 11¼. 21042-1 Pa. $7.95

OF THE JUST SHAPING OF LETTERS, Albrecht Dürer. Renaissance artist explains design of Roman majuscules by geometry, also Gothic lower and capitals. Grolier Club edition. 43pp. 7⅞ x 10¾ 21306-4 Pa. $3.00

TEN BOOKS ON ARCHITECTURE, Vitruvius. The most important book ever written on architecture. Early Roman aesthetics, technology, classical orders, site selection, all other aspects. Stands behind everything since. Morgan translation. 331pp. 5⅜ x 8½. 20645-9 Pa. $4.50

THE FOUR BOOKS OF ARCHITECTURE, Andrea Palladio. 16th-century classic responsible for Palladian movement and style. Covers classical architectural remains, Renaissance revivals, classical orders, etc. 1738 Ware English edition. Introduction by A. Placzek. 216 plates. 110pp. of text. 9½ x 12¾. 21308-0 Pa. $10.00

HORIZONS, Norman Bel Geddes. Great industrialist stage designer, "father of streamlining," on application of aesthetics to transportation, amusement, architecture, etc. 1932 prophetic account; function, theory, specific projects. 222 illustrations. 312pp. 7⅞ x 10¾. 23514-9 Pa. $6.95

FRANK LLOYD WRIGHT'S FALLINGWATER, Donald Hoffmann. Full, illustrated story of conception and building of Wright's masterwork at Bear Run, Pa. 100 photographs of site, construction, and details of completed structure. 112pp. 9¼ x 10. 23671-4 Pa. $5.50

THE ELEMENTS OF DRAWING, John Ruskin. Timeless classic by great Viltorian; starts with basic ideas, works through more difficult. Many practical exercises. 48 illustrations. Introduction by Lawrence Campbell. 228pp. 5⅜ x 8½. 22730-8 Pa. $3.75

GIST OF ART, John Sloan. Greatest modern American teacher, Art Students League, offers innumerable hints, instructions, guided comments to help you in painting. Not a formal course. 46 illustrations. Introduction by Helen Sloan. 200pp. 5⅜ x 8½. 23435-5 Pa. $4.00

THE ANATOMY OF THE HORSE, George Stubbs. Often considered the great masterpiece of animal anatomy. Full reproduction of 1766 edition, plus prospectus; original text and modernized text. 36 plates. Introduction by Eleanor Garvey. 121pp. 11 x 14¾.   23402-9 Pa. $6.00

BRIDGMAN'S LIFE DRAWING, George B. Bridgman. More than 500 illustrative drawings and text teach you to abstract the body into its major masses, use light and shade, proportion; as well as specific areas of anatomy, of which Bridgman is master. 192pp. 6½ x 9¼. (Available in U.S. only)
22710-3 Pa. $3.50

ART NOUVEAU DESIGNS IN COLOR, Alphonse Mucha, Maurice Verneuil, Georges Auriol. Full-color reproduction of *Combinaisons ornementales* (c. 1900) by Art Nouveau masters. Floral, animal, geometric, interlacings, swashes—borders, frames, spots—all incredibly beautiful. 60 plates, hundreds of designs. 9⅝ x 8-1/16.   22885-1 Pa. $4.00

FULL-COLOR FLORAL DESIGNS IN THE ART NOUVEAU STYLE, E. A. Seguy. 166 motifs, on 40 plates, from *Les fleurs et leurs applications decoratives* (1902): borders, circular designs, repeats, allovers, "spots." All in authentic Art Nouveau colors. 48pp. 9⅝ x 12¼.
23439-8 Pa. $5.00

A DIDEROT PICTORIAL ENCYCLOPEDIA OF TRADES AND IN-DUSTRY, edited by Charles C. Gillispie. 485 most interesting plates from the great French Encyclopedia of the 18th century show hundreds of working figures, artifacts, process, land and cityscapes; glassmaking, paper-making, metal extraction, construction, weaving, making furniture, clothing, wigs, dozens of other activities. Plates fully explained. 920pp. 9 x 12.
22284-5, 22285-3 Clothbd., Two-vol. set $40.00

HANDBOOK OF EARLY ADVERTISING ART, Clarence P. Hornung. Largest collection of copyright-free early and antique advertising art ever compiled. Over 6,000 illustrations, from Franklin's time to the 1890's for special effects, novelty. Valuable source, almost inexhaustible.
Pictorial Volume. Agriculture, the zodiac, animals, autos, birds, Christmas, fire engines, flowers, trees, musical instruments, ships, games and sports, much more. Arranged by subject matter and use. 237 plates. 288pp. 9 x 12.
20122-8 Clothbd. $14.50

Typographical Volume. Roman and Gothic faces ranging from 10 point to 300 point, "Barnum," German and Old English faces, script, logotypes, scrolls and flourishes, 1115 ornamental initials, 67 complete alphabets, more. 310 plates. 320pp. 9 x 12.   20123-6 Clothbd. $15.00

CALLIGRAPHY (CALLIGRAPHIA LATINA), J. G. Schwandner. High point of 18th-century ornamental calligraphy. Very ornate initials, scrolls, borders, cherubs, birds, lettered examples. 172pp. 9 x 13.
20475-8 Pa. $7.00

ART FORMS IN NATURE, Ernst Haeckel. Multitude of strangely beautiful natural forms: Radiolaria, Foraminifera, jellyfishes, fungi, turtles, bats, etc. All 100 plates of the 19th-century evolutionist's *Kunstformen der Natur* (1904). 100pp. 9⅜ x 12¼.   22987-4 Pa. $5.00

CHILDREN: A PICTORIAL ARCHIVE FROM NINETEENTH-CENTURY SOURCES, edited by Carol Belanger Grafton. 242 rare, copyright-free wood engravings for artists and designers. Widest such selection available. All illustrations in line. 119pp. 8⅜ x 11¼.
23694-3 Pa. $4.00

WOMEN: A PICTORIAL ARCHIVE FROM NINETEENTH-CENTURY SOURCES, edited by Jim Harter. 391 copyright-free wood engravings for artists and designers selected from rare periodicals. Most extensive such collection available. All illustrations in line. 128pp. 9 x 12.
23703-6 Pa. $4.50

ARABIC ART IN COLOR, Prisse d'Avennes. From the greatest ornamentalists of all time—50 plates in color, rarely seen outside the Near East, rich in suggestion and stimulus. Includes 4 plates on covers. 46pp. 9⅜ x 12¼.   23658-7 Pa. $6.00

AUTHENTIC ALGERIAN CARPET DESIGNS AND MOTIFS, edited by June Beveridge. Algerian carpets are world famous. Dozens of geometrical motifs are charted on grids, color-coded, for weavers, needleworkers, craftsmen, designers. 53 illustrations plus 4 in color. 48pp. 8¼ x 11. (Available in U.S. only)   23650-1 Pa. $1.75

DICTIONARY OF AMERICAN PORTRAITS, edited by Hayward and Blanche Cirker. 4000 important Americans, earliest times to 1905, mostly in clear line. Politicians, writers, soldiers, scientists, inventors, industrialists, Indians, Blacks, women, outlaws, etc. Identificatory information. 756pp. 9¼ x 12¾.   21823-6 Clothbd. $40.00

HOW THE OTHER HALF LIVES, Jacob A. Riis. Journalistic record of filth, degradation, upward drive in New York immigrant slums, shops, around 1900. New edition includes 100 original Riis photos, monuments of early photography. 233pp. 10 x 7⅞.   22012-5 Pa. $7.00

NEW YORK IN THE THIRTIES, Berenice Abbott. Noted photographer's fascinating study of city shows new buildings that have become famous and old sights that have disappeared forever. Insightful commentary. 97 photographs. 97pp. 11⅜ x 10.   22967-X Pa. $5.00

MEN AT WORK, Lewis W. Hine. Famous photographic studies of construction workers, railroad men, factory workers and coal miners. New supplement of 18 photos on Empire State building construction. New introduction by Jonathan L. Doherty. Total of 69 photos. 63pp. 8 x 10¾.
23475-4 Pa. $3.00

THE DEPRESSION YEARS AS PHOTOGRAPHED BY ARTHUR ROTH-STEIN, Arthur Rothstein. First collection devoted entirely to the work of outstanding 1930s photographer: famous dust storm photo, ragged children, unemployed, etc. 120 photographs. Captions. 119pp. 9¼ x 10¾.
23590-4 Pa. $5.00

CAMERA WORK: A PICTORIAL GUIDE, Alfred Stieglitz. All 559 illustrations and plates from the most important periodical in the history of art photography, Camera Work (1903-17). Presented four to a page, reduced in size but still clear, in strict chronological order, with complete captions. Three indexes. Glossary. Bibliography. 176pp. 8⅜ x 11¼.
23591-2 Pa. $6.95

ALVIN LANGDON COBURN, PHOTOGRAPHER, Alvin L. Coburn. Revealing autobiography by one of greatest photographers of 20th century gives insider's version of Photo-Secession, plus comments on his own work. 77 photographs by Coburn. Edited by Helmut and Alison Gernsheim. 160pp. 8⅛ x 11.
23685-4 Pa. $6.00

NEW YORK IN THE FORTIES, Andreas Feininger. 162 brilliant photographs by the well-known photographer, formerly with Life magazine, show commuters, shoppers, Times Square at night, Harlem nightclub, Lower East Side, etc. Introduction and full captions by John von Hartz. 181pp. 9¼ x 10¾.
23585-8 Pa. $6.95

GREAT NEWS PHOTOS AND THE STORIES BEHIND THEM, John Faber. Dramatic volume of 140 great news photos, 1855 through 1976, and revealing stories behind them, with both historical and technical information. Hindenburg disaster, shooting of Oswald, nomination of Jimmy Carter, etc. 160pp. 8¼ x 11.
23667-6 Pa. $5.00

THE ART OF THE CINEMATOGRAPHER, Leonard Maltin. Survey of American cinematography history and anecdotal interviews with 5 masters—Arthur Miller, Hal Mohr, Hal Rosson, Lucien Ballard, and Conrad Hall. Very large selection of behind-the-scenes production photos. 105 photographs. Filmographies. Index. Originally Behind the Camera. 144pp. 8¼ x 11.
23686-2 Pa. $5.00

DESIGNS FOR THE THREE-CORNERED HAT (LE TRICORNE), Pablo Picasso. 32 fabulously rare drawings—including 31 color illustrations of costumes and accessories—for 1919 production of famous ballet. Edited by Parmenia Migel, who has written new introduction. 48pp. 9⅜ x 12¼. (Available in U.S. only)
23709-5 Pa. $5.00

NOTES OF A FILM DIRECTOR, Sergei Eisenstein. Greatest Russian filmmaker explains montage, making of Alexander Nevsky, aesthetics; comments on self, associates, great rivals (Chaplin), similar material. 78 illustrations. 240pp. 5⅜ x 8½.
22392-2 Pa. $4.50

HOLLYWOOD GLAMOUR PORTRAITS, edited by John Kobal. 145 photos capture the stars from 1926-49, the high point in portrait photography. Gable, Harlow, Bogart, Bacall, Hedy Lamarr, Marlene Dietrich, Robert Montgomery, Marlon Brando, Veronica Lake; 94 stars in all. Full background on photographers, technical aspects, much more. Total of 160pp. 8⅜ x 11¼.   23352-9 Pa. $6.00

THE NEW YORK STAGE: FAMOUS PRODUCTIONS IN PHOTO-GRAPHS, edited by Stanley Appelbaum. 148 photographs from Museum of City of New York show 142 plays, 1883-1939. *Peter Pan, The Front Page, Dead End, Our Town,* O'Neill, hundreds of actors and actresses, etc. Full indexes. 154pp. 9½ x 10.   23241-7 Pa. $6.00

DIALOGUES CONCERNING TWO NEW SCIENCES, Galileo Galilei. Encompassing 30 years of experiment and thought, these dialogues deal with geometric demonstrations of fracture of solid bodies, cohesion, leverage, speed of light and sound, pendulums, falling bodies, accelerated motion, etc. 300pp. 5⅜ x 8½.   60099-8 Pa. $4.00

THE GREAT OPERA STARS IN HISTORIC PHOTOGRAPHS, edited by James Camner. 343 portraits from the 1850s to the 1940s: Tamburini, Mario, Caliapin, Jeritza, Melchior, Melba, Patti, Pinza, Schipa, Caruso, Farrar, Steber, Gobbi, and many more—270 performers in all. Index. 199pp. 8⅜ x 11¼.   23575-0 Pa. $7.50

J. S. BACH, Albert Schweitzer. Great full-length study of Bach, life, background to music, music, by foremost modern scholar. Ernest Newman translation. 650 musical examples. Total of 928pp. 5⅜ x 8½. (Available in U.S. only)   21631-4, 21632-2 Pa., Two-vol. set $11.00

COMPLETE PIANO SONATAS, Ludwig van Beethoven. All sonatas in the fine Schenker edition, with fingering, analytical material. One of best modern editions. Total of 615pp. 9 x 12. (Available in U.S. only)
                            23134-8, 23135-6 Pa., Two-vol. set $15.50

KEYBOARD MUSIC, J. S. Bach. Bach-Gesellschaft edition. For harpsichord, piano, other keyboard instruments. English Suites, French Suites, Six Partitas, Goldberg Variations, Two-Part Inventions, Three-Part Sinfonias. 312pp. 8⅛ x 11. (Available in U.S. only)   22360-4 Pa. $6.95

FOUR SYMPHONIES IN FULL SCORE, Franz Schubert. Schubert's four most popular symphonies: No. 4 in C Minor ("Tragic"); No. 5 in B-flat Major; No. 8 in B Minor ("Unfinished"); No. 9 in C Major ("Great"). Breitkopf & Hartel edition. Study score. 261pp. 9⅜ x 12¼.
                                                  23681-1 Pa. $6.50

THE AUTHENTIC GILBERT & SULLIVAN SONGBOOK, W. S. Gilbert, A. S. Sullivan. Largest selection available; 92 songs, uncut, original keys, in piano rendering approved by Sullivan. Favorites and lesser-known fine numbers. Edited with plot synopses by James Spero. 3 illustrations. 399pp. 9 x 12.   23482-7 Pa. $9.95

CATALOGUE OF DOVER BOOKS

PRINCIPLES OF ORCHESTRATION, Nikolay Rimsky-Korsakov. Great classical orchestrator provides fundamentals of tonal resonance, progression of parts, voice and orchestra, tutti effects, much else in major document. 330pp. of musical excerpts. 489pp. 6½ x 9¼. 21266-1 Pa. $7.50

TRISTAN UND ISOLDE, Richard Wagner. Full orchestral score with complete instrumentation. Do not confuse with piano reduction. Commentary by Felix Mottl, great Wagnerian conductor and scholar. Study score. 655pp. 8⅛ x 11. 22915-7 Pa. $13.95

REQUIEM IN FULL SCORE, Giuseppe Verdi. Immensely popular with choral groups and music lovers. Republication of edition published by C. F. Peters, Leipzig, n. d. German frontmaker in English translation. Glossary. Text in Latin. Study score. 204pp. 9⅜ x 12¼. 23682-X Pa. $6.00

COMPLETE CHAMBER MUSIC FOR STRINGS, Felix Mendelssohn. All of Mendelssohn's chamber music: Octet, 2 Quintets, 6 Quartets, and Four Pieces for String Quartet. (Nothing with piano is included). Complete works edition (1874-7). Study score. 283 pp. 9⅜ x 12¼. 23679-X Pa. $7.50

POPULAR SONGS OF NINETEENTH-CENTURY AMERICA, edited by Richard Jackson. 64 most important songs: "Old Oaken Bucket," "Arkansas Traveler," "Yellow Rose of Texas," etc. Authentic original sheet music, full introduction and commentaries. 290pp. 9 x 12. 23270-0 Pa. $7.95

COLLECTED PIANO WORKS, Scott Joplin. Edited by Vera Brodsky Lawrence. Practically all of Joplin's piano works—rags, two-steps, marches, waltzes, etc., 51 works in all. Extensive introduction by Rudi Blesh. Total of 345pp. 9 x 12. 23106-2 Pa. $14.95

BASIC PRINCIPLES OF CLASSICAL BALLET, Agrippina Vaganova. Great Russian theoretician, teacher explains methods for teaching classical ballet; incorporates best from French, Italian, Russian schools. 118 illustrations. 175pp. 5⅜ x 8½. 22036-2 Pa. $2.50

CHINESE CHARACTERS, L. Wieger. Rich analysis of 2300 characters according to traditional systems into primitives. Historical-semantic analysis to phonetics (Classical Mandarin) and radicals. 820pp. 6⅛ x 9¼. 21321-8 Pa. $10.00

EGYPTIAN LANGUAGE: EASY LESSONS IN EGYPTIAN HIERO-GLYPHICS, E. A. Wallis Budge. Foremost Egyptologist offers Egyptian grammar, explanation of hieroglyphics, many reading texts, dictionary of symbols. 246pp. 5 x 7½. (Available in U.S. only) 21394-3 Clothbd. $7.50

AN ETYMOLOGICAL DICTIONARY OF MODERN ENGLISH, Ernest Weekley. Richest, fullest work, by foremost British lexicographer. Detailed word histories. Inexhaustible. Do not confuse this with Concise Etymological Dictionary, which is abridged. Total of 856pp. 6½ x 9¼. 21873-2, 21874-0 Pa., Two-vol. set $12.00

A MAYA GRAMMAR, Alfred M. Tozzer. Practical, useful English-language grammar by the Harvard anthropologist who was one of the three greatest American scholars in the area of Maya culture. Phonetics, grammatical processes, syntax, more. 301pp. 5⅜ x 8½.   23465-7 Pa. $4.00

THE JOURNAL OF HENRY D. THOREAU, edited by Bradford Torrey, F. H. Allen. Complete reprinting of 14 volumes, 1837-61, over two million words; the sourcebooks for *Walden*, etc. Definitive. All original sketches, plus 75 photographs. Introduction by Walter Harding. Total of 1804pp. 8½ x 12¼.   20312-3, 20313-1 Clothbd., Two-vol. set $70.00

CLASSIC GHOST STORIES, Charles Dickens and others. 18 wonderful stories you've wanted to reread: "The Monkey's Paw," "The House and the Brain," "The Upper Berth," "The Signalman," "Dracula's Guest," "The Tapestried Chamber," etc. Dickens, Scott, Mary Shelley, Stoker, etc. 330pp. 5⅜ x 8½.   20735-8 Pa. $4.50

SEVEN SCIENCE FICTION NOVELS, H. G. Wells. Full novels. *First Men in the Moon, Island of Dr. Moreau, War of the Worlds, Food of the Gods, Invisible Man, Time Machine, In the Days of the Comet.* A basic science-fiction library. 1015pp. 5⅜ x 8½. (Available in U.S. only)   20264-X Clothbd. $8.95

ARMADALE, Wilkie Collins. Third great mystery novel by the author of *The Woman in White* and *The Moonstone.* Ingeniously plotted narrative shows an exceptional command of character, incident and mood. Original magazine version with 40 illustrations. 597pp. 5⅜ x 8½.   23429-0 Pa. $6.00

MASTERS OF MYSTERY, H. Douglas Thomson. The first book in English (1931) devoted to history and aesthetics of detective story. Poe, Doyle, LeFanu, Dickens, many others, up to 1930. New introduction and notes by E. F. Bleiler. 288pp. 5⅜ x 8½. (Available in U.S. only)   23606-4 Pa. $4.00

FLATLAND, E. A. Abbott. Science-fiction classic explores life of 2-D being in 3-D world. Read also as introduction to thought about hyperspace. Introduction by Banesh Hoffmann. 16 illustrations. 103pp. 5⅜ x 8½.   20001-9 Pa. $2.00

THREE SUPERNATURAL NOVELS OF THE VICTORIAN PERIOD, edited, with an introduction, by E. F. Bleiler. Reprinted complete and unabridged, three great classics of the supernatural: *The Haunted Hotel* by Wilkie Collins, *The Haunted House at Latchford* by Mrs. J. H. Riddell, and *The Lost Stradivarius* by J. Meade Falkner. 325pp. 5⅜ x 8½.   22571-2 Pa. $4.00

AYESHA: THE RETURN OF "SHE," H. Rider Haggard. Virtuoso sequel featuring the great mythic creation, Ayesha, in an adventure that is fully as good as the first book, *She.* Original magazine version, with 47 original illustrations by Maurice Greiffenhagen. 189pp. 6½ x 9¼.   23649-8 Pa. $3.50

UNCLE SILAS, J. Sheridan LeFanu. Victorian Gothic mystery novel, considered by many best of period, even better than Collins or Dickens. Wonderful psychological terror. Introduction by Frederick Shroyer. 436pp. 5⅜ x 8½. 21715-9 Pa. $6.00

JURGEN, James Branch Cabell. The great erotic fantasy of the 1920's that delighted thousands, shocked thousands more. Full final text, Lane edition with 13 plates by Frank Pape. 346pp. 5⅜ x 8½. 23507-6 Pa. $4.50

THE CLAVERINGS, Anthony Trollope. Major novel, chronicling aspects of British Victorian society, personalities. Reprint of Cornhill serialization, 16 plates by M. Edwards; first reprint of full text. Introduction by Norman Donaldson. 412pp. 5⅜ x 8½. 23464-9 Pa. $5.00

KEPT IN THE DARK, Anthony Trollope. Unusual short novel about Victorian morality and abnormal psychology by the great English author. Probably the first American publication. Frontispiece by Sir John Millais. 92pp. 6½ x 9¼. 23609-9 Pa. $2.50

RALPH THE HEIR, Anthony Trollope. Forgotten tale of illegitimacy, inheritance. Master novel of Trollope's later years. Victorian country estates, clubs, Parliament, fox hunting, world of fully realized characters. Reprint of 1871 edition. 12 illustrations by F. A. Faser. 434pp. of text. 5⅜ x 8½. 23642-0 Pa. $5.00

YEKL and THE IMPORTED BRIDEGROOM AND OTHER STORIES OF THE NEW YORK GHETTO, Abraham Cahan. Film *Hester Street* based on *Yekl* (1896). Novel, other stories among first about Jewish immigrants of N.Y.'s East Side. Highly praised by W. D. Howells—Cahan "a new star of realism." New introduction by Bernard G. Richards. 240pp. 5⅜ x 8½. 22427-9 Pa. $3.50

THE HIGH PLACE, James Branch Cabell. Great fantasy writer's enchanting comedy of disenchantment set in 18th-century France. Considered by some critics to be even better than his famous *Jurgen*. 10 illustrations and numerous vignettes by noted fantasy artist Frank C. Pape. 320pp. 5⅜ x 8½. 23670-6 Pa. $4.00

ALICE'S ADVENTURES UNDER GROUND, Lewis Carroll. Facsimile of ms. Carroll gave Alice Liddell in 1864. Different in many ways from final Alice. Handlettered, illustrated by Carroll. Introduction by Martin Gardner. 128pp. 5⅜ x 8½. 21482-6 Pa. $2.50

FAVORITE ANDREW LANG FAIRY TALE BOOKS IN MANY COLORS, Andrew Lang. The four Lang favorites in a boxed set—the complete *Red, Green, Yellow* and *Blue* Fairy Books. 164 stories; 439 illustrations by Lancelot Speed, Henry Ford and G. P. Jacomb Hood. Total of about 1500pp. 5⅜ x 8½. 23407-X Boxed set, Pa. $15.95

CATALOGUE OF DOVER BOOKS

HOUSEHOLD STORIES BY THE BROTHERS GRIMM. All the great Grimm stories: "Rumpelstiltskin," "Snow White," "Hansel and Gretel," etc., with 114 illustrations by Walter Crane. 269pp. 5⅜ x 8½.
21080-4 Pa. $3.50

SLEEPING BEAUTY, illustrated by Arthur Rackham. Perhaps the fullest, most delightful version ever, told by C. S. Evans. Rackham's best work. 49 illustrations. 110pp. 7⅞ x 10¾.
22756-1 Pa. $2.50

AMERICAN FAIRY TALES, L. Frank Baum. Young cowboy lassoes Father Time; dummy in Mr. Floman's department store window comes to life; and 10 other fairy tales. 41 illustrations by N. P. Hall, Harry Kennedy, Ike Morgan, and Ralph Gardner. 209pp. 5⅜ x 8½.
23643-9 Pa. $3.00

THE WONDERFUL WIZARD OF OZ, L. Frank Baum. Facsimile in full color of America's finest children's classic. Introduction by Martin Gardner. 143 illustrations by W. W. Denslow. 267pp. 5⅜ x 8½.
20691-2 Pa. $3.50

THE TALE OF PETER RABBIT, Beatrix Potter. The inimitable Peter's terrifying adventure in Mr. McGregor's garden, with all 27 wonderful, full-color Potter illustrations. 55pp. 4¼ x 5½. (Available in U.S. only)
22827-4 Pa. $1.25

THE STORY OF KING ARTHUR AND HIS KNIGHTS, Howard Pyle. Finest children's version of life of King Arthur. 48 illustrations by Pyle. 131pp. 6⅛ x 9¼.
21445-1 Pa. $4.95

CARUSO'S CARICATURES, Enrico Caruso. Great tenor's remarkable caricatures of self, fellow musicians, composers, others. Toscanini, Puccini, Farrar, etc. Impish, cutting, insightful. 473 illustrations. Preface by M. Sisca. 217pp. 8⅜ x 11¼.
23528-9 Pa. $6.95

PERSONAL NARRATIVE OF A PILGRIMAGE TO ALMADINAH AND MECCAH, Richard Burton. Great travel classic by remarkably colorful personality. Burton, disguised as a Moroccan, visited sacred shrines of Islam, narrowly escaping death. Wonderful observations of Islamic life, customs, personalities. 47 illustrations. Total of 959pp. 5⅜ x 8½.
21217-3, 21218-1 Pa., Two-vol. set $12.00

INCIDENTS OF TRAVEL IN YUCATAN, John L. Stephens. Classic (1843) exploration of jungles of Yucatan, looking for evidences of Maya civilization. Travel adventures, Mexican and Indian culture, etc. Total of 669pp. 5⅜ x 8½.
20926-1, 20927-X Pa., Two-vol. set $7.90

AMERICAN LITERARY AUTOGRAPHS FROM WASHINGTON IRVING TO HENRY JAMES, Herbert Cahoon, et al. Letters, poems, manuscripts of Hawthorne, Thoreau, Twain, Alcott, Whitman, 67 other prominent American authors. Reproductions, full transcripts and commentary. Plus checklist of all American Literary Autographs in The Pierpont Morgan Library. Printed on exceptionally high-quality paper. 136 illustrations. 212pp. 9⅛ x 12¼.
23548-3 Pa. $12.50

AN AUTOBIOGRAPHY, Margaret Sanger. Exciting personal account of hard-fought battle for woman's right to birth control, against prejudice, church, law. Foremost feminist document. 504pp. 5⅜ x 8½.
20470-7 Pa. $5.50

MY BONDAGE AND MY FREEDOM, Frederick Douglass. Born as a slave, Douglass became outspoken force in antislavery movement. The best of Douglass's autobiographies. Graphic description of slave life. Introduction by P. Foner. 464pp. 5⅜ x 8½. 22457-0 Pa. $5.50

LIVING MY LIFE, Emma Goldman. Candid, no holds barred account by foremost American anarchist: her own life, anarchist movement, famous contemporaries, ideas and their impact. Struggles and confrontations in America, plus deportation to U.S.S.R. Shocking inside account of persecution of anarchists under Lenin. 13 plates. Total of 944pp. 5⅜ x 8½.
22543-7, 22544-5 Pa., Two-vol. set $12.00

LETTERS AND NOTES ON THE MANNERS, CUSTOMS AND CONDITIONS OF THE NORTH AMERICAN INDIANS, George Catlin. Classic account of life among Plains Indians: ceremonies, hunt, warfare, etc. Dover edition reproduces for first time all original paintings. 312 plates. 572pp. of text. 6⅛ x 9¼. 22118-0, 22119-9 Pa.. Two-vol. set $12.00

THE MAYA AND THEIR NEIGHBORS, edited by Clarence L. Hay, others. Synoptic view of Maya civilization in broadest sense, together with Northern, Southern neighbors. Integrates much background, valuable detail not elsewhere. Prepared by greatest scholars: Kroeber, Morley, Thompson, Spinden, Vaillant, many others. Sometimes called Tozzer Memorial Volume. 60 illustrations, linguistic map. 634pp. 5⅜ x 8½.
23510-6 Pa. $10.00

HANDBOOK OF THE INDIANS OF CALIFORNIA, A. L. Kroeber. Foremost American anthropologist offers complete ethnographic study of each group. Monumental classic. 459 illustrations, maps. 995pp. 5⅜ x 8½.
23368-5 Pa. $13.00

SHAKTI AND SHAKTA, Arthur Avalon. First book to give clear, cohesive analysis of Shakta doctrine, Shakta ritual and Kundalini Shakti (yoga). Important work by one of world's foremost students of Shaktic and Tantric thought. 732pp. 5⅜ x 8½. (Available in U.S. only)
23645-5 Pa. $7.95

AN INTRODUCTION TO THE STUDY OF THE MAYA HIEROGLYPHS, Syvanus Griswold Morley. Classic study by one of the truly great figures in hieroglyph research. Still the best introduction for the student for reading Maya hieroglyphs. New introduction by J. Eric S. Thompson. 117 illustrations. 284pp. 5⅜ x 8½. 23108-9 Pa. $4.00

A STUDY OF MAYA ART, Herbert J. Spinden. Landmark classic interprets Maya symbolism, estimates styles, covers ceramics, architecture, murals, stone carvings as artforms. Still a basic book in area. New introduction by J. Eric Thompson. Over 750 illustrations. 341pp. 8⅜ x 11¼.
21235-1 Pa. $6.95

GEOMETRY, RELATIVITY AND THE FOURTH DIMENSION, Rudolf Rucker. Exposition of fourth dimension, means of visualization, concepts of relativity as Flatland characters continue adventures. Popular, easily followed yet accurate, profound. 141 illustrations. 133pp. 5⅜ x 8½.
23400-2 Pa. $2.75

THE ORIGIN OF LIFE, A. I. Oparin. Modern classic in biochemistry, the first rigorous examination of possible evolution of life from nitrocarbon compounds. Non-technical, easily followed. Total of 295pp. 5⅜ x 8½.
60213-3 Pa. $4.00

PLANETS, STARS AND GALAXIES, A. E. Fanning. Comprehensive introductory survey: the sun, solar system, stars, galaxies, universe, cosmology; quasars, radio stars, etc. 24pp. of photographs. 189pp. 5⅜ x 8½. (Available in U.S. only)
21680-2 Pa. $3.75

THE THIRTEEN BOOKS OF EUCLID'S ELEMENTS, translated with introduction and commentary by Sir Thomas L. Heath. Definitive edition. Textual and linguistic notes, mathematical analysis, 2500 years of critical commentary. Do not confuse with abridged school editions. Total of 1414pp. 5⅜ x 8½.   60088-2, 60089-0, 60090-4 Pa., Three-vol. set $18.50

Prices subject to change without notice.

Available at your book dealer or write for free catalogue to Dept. GI, Dover Publications, Inc., 180 Varick St., N.Y., N.Y. 10014. Dover publishes more than 175 books each year on science, elementary and advanced mathematics, biology, music, art, literary history, social sciences and other areas.